The Devil's Angels MC
Book 1 – Gunner

Lola Wright

Contents

Contents i
Acknowledgements vii
Preface ix
Chapter 1 1
Chapter 2 19
Chapter 3 31
Chapter 4 57
Chapter 5 69
Chapter 6 79
Chapter 7 89
Chapter 8 95
Chapter 9 119
Chapter 10 127
Chapter 11 145
Chapter 12 167
Chapter 13 175
Chapter 14 185
Chapter 15 195
Chapter 16 211
Chapter 17 225

Chapter 18 243
Chapter 19 259
Chapter 20 279
Chapter 21 295
Chapter 22 311
Chapter 23 333
Chapter 24 345
Chapter 25 353
Chapter 26 371
Chapter 27 385
Chapter 28 411
Chapter 29 431
Chapter 30 443
Chapter 31 447
Epilogue 465
About the Author 473
Also by Lola Wright 475

First published by Lola Wright 2019

Copyright ©2019 by Lola Wright

All rights reserved. No part of this publication may be reproduced, stored or transmitted in any form or by any means: electronic, mechanical, photocopying, recording, scanning, or otherwise without written permission from the publisher. It is illegal to copy this book, post it to a website, or distribute it by any other means without permission.

This novel is entirely a work of fiction. The names, characters and incidents portrayed in it are the work of the author's imagination. Any resemblance to actual persons, living or dead, events or localities is entirely coincidental.

Lola Wright asserts the moral right to be identified as the author of this work.

Lola Wright has no responsibility for the persistence or accuracy of URLs for external or third-party Internet Websites referred to in this publication and does not guarantee that any content on such Websites is, or will remain, accurate or appropriate.

Designations used by companies to distinguish their products are often claimed as trademarks. All brand names and product names used in this book and on its cover are trade names, service marks, trademarks and registered trademarks of their respective owners. The publishers and the book are not associated with any product or vendor mentioned in this book. None of the companies referenced within the book have endorsed the book.

Adult Content Warning: This book is intended for readers 18 years of age and older. It contains adult language, violence, explicit sex and may contain triggers for some people.

First edition

Editing by Pam Clinton

This book was professional typeset on Reedsy

Find out more at reedsy.com

Acknowledgements

Cover Design: Cal5086
@ Fiverr.com

Editor: Pam Clinton
@ pccProofreading.com

Preface

Ava

Left to die as an infant, Ava Beaumont has not had an easy life. Being raised by the system has taught her to be independent, hardworking, and cautious. When Ava becomes a victim, she uses her inner strength to put it behind her and move forward. Now she lives a good life with the family she's created through adopting pets that were also throwaways, including a smart-mouthed parrot and a skateboarding pig. When Ava meets Gunner, she realizes what her life is lacking but does she have the courage to trust a big, rough biker enough to let him into her safe little life?

Gunner

Being the President of the Devil's Angels MC was not something Gunner asked to become, but through the loss of his dad, the job was thrust upon him. While he loves his club and club brothers wholeheartedly, Gunner wants his club to move in a better direction. And when Gunner spots bakery owner, Ava, he realizes that's not the only change he wants to make in his life.

Nothing worth having is easy to acquire.

This is an MC story with a heart. Come meet the crazy pets and even crazier club members of the Devil's Angels MC.

Chapter 1

Ava

Ughhh! I'm so tired of this neighbor of mine. He whines about everything. My music is too loud, my cat stares at his house from the back of my couch, and the dog looked at him in a funny way. He complained last week that my dog gave him an "I'm going to kill and bury you in the backyard" look, and he said it with a straight face. And he called the cops, telling them the same thing. Don't even get me started on what he thinks of my Macaw and pig. You'd think we lived in downtown New York instead of living on the outskirts of Denver. It doesn't matter that I've been extremely nice and have tried befriending him. He's still a class-A jerk.

"Loki, come. Out the back door for you, big guy," I say to my beautiful Native American dog as I stand holding the sliding glass door open. He walks by with that sad dog look he has perfected and goes through the door into my fenced backyard. We were in the front yard planting flowers along my sidewalk. It's not fenced, but Loki never left my side. He seldom does due to being very overprotective. Apparently, that doesn't register with my neighbor. All he noticed was Loki off-leash, looking in his direction, and that was enough to scream that he was calling the police. Then he ran for his house. He's such a dramatic little bitch.

So, now I'm back to planting my flowers, waiting for the police to show up again. Not something I'm looking forward to either. I'm not a cop-hater, but I'm not a fan. Growing up in the foster care system doesn't make you fond of the government, caseworkers, or cops. There are good ones out there, but they are outnumbered by the bad ones, it seems. I have other reasons for distrusting cops, but I work hard at keeping those memories buried deep.

While crouched down, patting the dirt around the base of the plant, I hear the unmistakable sound of a Harley. Actually, I hear a few of them. The house next to my annoying neighbor belongs to an older, big, tattooed biker which puts his house across the street and at an angle to mine. He's seldom around and keeps to himself, but I get a shiver every time I hear his Harley coming down the street. Not from fear but excitement. I love that sound. Throaty, deep rumbling with a side of attitude. Once again, I think maybe I should buy one for myself. But I know nothing about them or how to ride one, just that I love the sound.

I look toward the road and see four bikes being followed by a truck. They drive past and pull into my biker neighbor's driveway. The lead bike was a black matte and chrome beast ridden by a huge man with longish black hair, tanned, muscular, tattooed arms, and a face the angels must have created themselves. He has shades on, so I didn't get to see his whole face, but what I saw was spectacular. I am close enough to the road to see the small smirk and chin lift aimed in my direction as he rode past.

Crap! I think I just came a little. It's been too long, way too long since anyone has caught my attention in that way. In fact, I'm pretty sure it's never happened before. But watching him dismount the bike is like watching biker porn. I can't seem to pull my eyes away from those huge thighs and tight ass. This man is pure muscle, and did I mention huge? Two minutes of watching him, and I have rub club material for the next month.

"I don't need a man. I don't need a man. I don't want a man. I don't want a man," I whisper to myself repeatedly as nefarious thoughts enter my head. But even as I'm saying this, I'm still staring at the big biker dude. Then I notice he has taken off his sunglasses and is staring back at me. Wowzer! I didn't think he could get any hotter, but I was so wrong. No idea what color his eyes are, but he is simply gorgeous. I think I'm drooling a bit. But I know it's all fantasy. I'm not a one-night-stand kind of girl, and he's definitely a hit-it and quit-it kind of guy. I'm judging, but it's just in my head, so let it be, please.

"Ma'am? Excuse me, ma'am?"

I look up and see a cop standing above me, looking like he may have been there a while. It kind of startles me a bit because I'm so careful about staying alert of my surroundings. And he is standing way too close and is obviously looking down my tank top. Gah! What an ass.

I immediately stand up and step back two steps to get him out of my personal space. His eyes start roving, and I'm aware of what he is seeing. Tank top, denim shorts, bare feet, hair in a very messy bun, and probably dirt smears everywhere. A normal Saturday for me.

"Can I help you, Officer?" I ask.

I note that his name tag says Officer Stanaway, and he's of medium build with reddish hair and the ever-present cop mustache. He also takes a step forward and is once again in my personal space.

I resist stepping back this time. Don't ever want to let them think you're intimidated. By them, I mean cops, men, bullies, people in general. A trick I learned in foster care. I make, and keep, eye contact as I ask, "Can I help you, Officer?"

"We got a call about a dog threatening your neighbor. Are you the owner of the dog?" he questions.

"I have a dog, but he didn't threaten anyone. He was lying in the grass next to me while I planted flowers. My neighbor freaks every time he sees Loki, but he's a great dog and has never even crossed the road. I'm not sure how that's threatening. Have you spoken with Ralph, my neighbor?" I answer.

"No, I haven't yet. He gave this address when he called in the complaint. I saw you were outside and stopped here first. Where's this dog? And has he ever bit anyone before?" he asks.

"No, he hasn't, and he's in the backyard. I put him there when Ralph started screaming that he was calling the cops. Look, I don't need or want a problem with the neighbor or you guys, but Ralph is nuts. Talk to him, and you'll see I'm not lying. He's straight-up looney toons."

Just then, I see Ralph coming across the road waving his arms like the lunatic he is. He's panting and sweating like he's just run a marathon as he approaches me and the officer.

As he gets to us, he starts pointing his finger in my face and screaming, "Her dog is going to kill someone! You have to do something about this, Officer! I can't live in fear every day!"

I push his hand away from my face and keep careful watch. Ralph has never laid a hand on me before, but he does seem to be losing it worse today than before. And I don't know him that well since I only moved here a few months ago.

Officer Stanaway steps between us and backs Ralph up five or six steps while telling him to calm down.

Unfortunately, I notice we have an audience with the bikers all standing around watching along with another neighbor from directly next door to me, Mrs. Conner.

Just great! I love the dose of embarrassment that goes along with the irritation of having to deal with Ralph's craziness again.

I tune back into the situation just in time to hear Ralph lose his shit. Screaming, he says, "She's got the dog from hell. Big and evil! Her cat is the size of a small pony and gives me the demon eyes all day from her couch. The pig's a farm animal and shouldn't be allowed to motherfucking skateboard on the same sidewalk humans use, and the bird uses foul language every time it sees me! I can't walk down the sidewalk in front of her place without the bird telling me to fuck off! That's just wrong!" Arms waving, head bobbing, Ralph looks like the wild animal here.

"Sir, you have to calm down and shut up for a moment here," demands Officer Stanaway.

Ralph's arms quit waving, but his bottom lip pops out like a two-year-old. Not a good look on a sixty-ish, chubby, pasty-white face. The man is no looker.

"Ma'am, I will need to see the dog and get your personal information for the complaint," the officer says to me.

Then he turns to Ralph and asks if the dog had crossed the road or came onto his property. Ralph replies, "No, he didn't, but he was looking at me like he was going to come over and hurt me. I felt threatened because she didn't have a leash on the dog."

At this point, the officer starts explaining to Ralph that there isn't anything he can do since the dog hadn't actually done anything and that I haven't broken any laws, but he will discuss the matter further with me to find a resolution. He then strongly suggested Ralph return home and shut his curtains if the cat was that intimidating.

Ralph leaves grumbling and complaining.

Officer Stanaway then turns to face me and asks to see Loki. He starts walking towards my front door when I say, "He's in the backyard. You can see him from the fence on the side of the house."

"I need to get your personal information, and a cold drink would be nice while I'm getting that," he smiles.

I continue walking towards the side of the house and toward the fence where Loki is standing, ignoring his comment. He sighs and follows me.

When he arrives, I watch in amusement as his eyes get big at the sight of Loki. My beautiful boy is just standing there staring up at the officer, but I know that he looks intimidating. He's colored similar to a German Shepherd with some gray shades mixed in. He's tall enough that his back's level with my waist, and he weighs in the neighborhood of 190 pounds. Very broad and boxy head. Black eyes and a bushy coat. And the personality of a teddy bear, if you're not a threat to me.

"Are you sure he hasn't bit anyone before?" the officer asks while taking a step back from the fence.

"Nobody I haven't asked him to bite," I say, smiling a little.

"Let's head back up front and get that information now. Did your neighbor say you also have a bird and a pig?" he asks as we walk back to the front of the house.

"Yes, I do. I have a dog, cat, a Macaw, and a miniature pig that are all licensed and have all their shots," I answer. "And none of them have ever been aggressive toward anyone either. The bird wouldn't say anything to Ralph if he wasn't standing on the sidewalk in front of my house, screaming at the cat all the time. Mac is just repeating what he hears."

I answer the rest of his questions and give the information he needs for his report. Same as I did for the last cop that came here because of Ralph.

"So, this phone number you gave me is the best one to reach you at?" he asks. I nod my head yes.

"So, if I call this number and ask to buy you a coffee, you'll answer?" he says, smiling a little.

I cringe a little inside but answer, "I'll answer the phone, but the coffee is a no-go. Sorry, but I don't date right now. Too busy."

"You know Ralph is going to continue calling in about your pets and having coffee with a cop just might make the complaints swing in your favor," he replies with a creepy-ass look on his face.

Now I'm getting pissed and wanting to unload verbally, but I feel someone coming up behind me at the same time I see Officer Stanaway's eyes go above my head. I don't turn around because I don't care at this point who hears what I'm about to say.

"So, what you're saying, Officer Stanaway, is that if I date—"

"What he's saying is illegal and unethical, isn't it Officer Stanaway?" says a very deep and rumbling voice from right behind me.

Officer Stanaway continues to look above my head as he backs slowly toward his car. With a sneer on his face, he says, "I didn't realize she was one of yours. She's got the looks but not the plastic, so I obviously assumed she wasn't one of your strippers or club whores."

He turns, walks to his patrol car and, while getting in it, says, "Offer still stands, Ava. You decide to aim a little higher, give me a call." Then he starts the car and slowly pulls away.

I turn around and see the biker I was drooling over earlier standing directly behind me. I look up into that gorgeous face and see a devastating smile. I notice he's taller than I originally thought, at least six foot six inches, maybe more. And broader. Eyes so dark they're almost black. Strong jawline with a day or two of scruff. I would guess early to mid-thirties. And even more stunning, especially with that smile. And yes, you guessed it. I am pretty sure I just came a little again.

I suddenly realize I'm staring, most likely with my mouth open, when he speaks.

"Hey. Sounds like you're having as bad a day as Big Petey is having. None of my business, but when I saw which cop was here, thought I'd step over and keep an eye. I'm Gunner, by the way," he rumbles.

"Ava. And thank you. He was starting to creep me out," I say, holding my hand out to him.

He takes my hand in his huge paw and shakes it gently. I still can't seem to stop staring, but his concern is very nice. I've not had many show concern for me.

When I realize I'm still staring and holding onto his hand, I remove mine and ask, "Big Petey?"

Shaking his head and smiling again, he says, "Yeah. Big Petey's your neighbor and my club brother. He took a minor fall today off his bike and broke his leg. Nothing too serious, but it'll ground him for a while. You don't know Petey?"

"Oh wow. Sorry for him. And no, I don't know him. I see him around, but I haven't been here real long. And frankly, he's kind of scary, so I haven't ventured over to his house yet," I say, smiling back. I'm not really scared of him, but he is a big guy. Better to use caution than be sorry later is my belief.

Gunner throws his head back and barks out a laugh, tanned throat moving with the sound. Eyes return to mine, and they are full of laughter.

"He's not that big, and he's really a pussycat in disguise. You just have to be around him for a while, and you'll see he's one of the nicer ones in the club. He plays at being a grumpy old man, but it's not real," he replies.

"Not many people are going to seem 'that big' to you, though," I blurt out.

Another bark of laughter and more of those nearly black eyes smiling at me. Suddenly, he reaches a hand toward my face, and I jerk back. His hand stops but stays in the air between us, and his eyes lose the humor.

"You don't have to be afraid because of my size or my being a biker. I haven't ever hit a woman, and you're not going to be the one to change that fact," he says quietly.

Then he goes on to say, "You have a smudge of dirt on your cheek, and I was going to brush it away. I should have told you. But now that you know, I'm going to brush it off."

He gently sweeps his fingers against my cheek and slowly removes his hand. He's looking at me intently like he has questions to ask.

I avert my eyes. I am embarrassed to have had that reaction in front of him, but I'm ashamed that he thinks it's because of his size and being a biker. And I'm surprised that a hand that big can be so gentle.

I look up to meet his eyes and say, "I'm sorry. That wasn't because of you in any way. You just caught me off-guard is all."

He stares back down at me for a moment, and I'm not sure if he believes me or not. The look on his face tells me he's thinking about it, but then he says, "Want to meet your neighbor now? I was hoping maybe you could keep an eye out for him when one of the club members can't be here. Maybe give him your number to call if he falls or something. You don't have to entertain or babysit him. I'd just feel better if someone this close could just check on him occasionally. He's stubborn and won't want a nurse, though. I know it's a lot to ask. You don't know us at all, but it would be much appreciated."

I think about it for a moment, and I know I can't say no to him. His request is reasonable, and he did have my back with the cop. And it wouldn't hurt to have another neighbor on my side when Ralph goes off again.

"Sure. I can do that. I should have introduced myself to him before this anyway. Let me just run in the house and get rid of the dirty hands, and I'll come over there. That okay?"

"Perfect and thank you. Don't let Big Petey run you off if he goes into bear mode. Just stand your ground," he says.

"Um, okay. That's encouraging. See you in a few minutes," I say with a small laugh.

He winks and turns to walk back to Big Petey's. I'm somewhat ashamed to admit I stand watching that very fine backside amble away and even more ashamed when he turns around, walking backward, and catches me. Damn!

He grins and says, "Do you really have a motherfucking skateboarding pig and a foul-mouthed bird?"

"Well, the pig prefers roller blades, and the bird's more of a smartass than foul-mouthed," I answer.

He laughs and, shaking his head, turns away and continues to Petey's.

I turn and head indoors to get cleaned up. As I enter the door, I hear Mac. "Mom, you going to be a jailbird? Jailbird! Jaillllllbirrrrrrrrrddd!" His voice gets louder with each word.

I laugh as I approach him sitting on his perch near the window. He's a beautiful bright green, red, and blue Macaw who's very intelligent and is an attention whore. I stroke his head, and he purrs like cats do. He's notorious for mimicking sounds and picking up words and phrases alarmingly fast.

"No, Mac, I'm not going to be a jailbird. It was just Ralph being Ralph again."

Mac cocks his head to the side and replies, "Ralph sucks."

I laugh and have to agree with him.

On my way to the bathroom, I open the slider and call to Loki. He comes in and flops down on the rug. I head into the bathroom and screech when I see my face in the mirror. O – M – G! I have more than one smudge still left on my face. Also on my neck, arms, and shirt. Jeez! What a way to make an impression on the hot biker. Ugh!

I wash up and comb out my hair before pulling it back up and then change into a new t-shirt and jean shorts. I peek into the second bedroom and see Gee and Duffy sleeping. I head to the front door and slip on a pair of flip flops. I start to open the door and then decide I should bring a sweet treat to Petey. Never hurts to show up with cupcakes. I put twelve of them in a bakery box and head back to the front door.

On my way out the door, I say, "Loki's in charge. Behave, Mac. I don't need the cops back here again today."

I hear a ruff from Loki and a "No way! Mac's in charge!" as I close the door behind me.

Lola Wright

Chapter 2

Gunner

I keep glancing over at Ava's house, waiting to see her headed this way. I hope she hasn't changed her mind. It would be great to have someone this close to Petey to kind of keep an eye on him, but I know it was a lot to ask of a stranger. Especially one who seems to keep her eyes open, head up, and watches her environment. There's got to be a reason why she's so careful when most women don't have a clue where they are or what's happening around them until it's too late. She's cautious but doesn't appear fearful. I like that. A lot. And it doesn't hurt that she's stunning. Natural blond hair, big green eyes, lightly tanned with perfect boobs. Never hurts to have perfect boobs, especially when combined with legs that go on forever and an ass that makes me drool. Damn!

This isn't the first time I've spotted Ava. This is the first time I had a reason to approach her and, thanks to Officer FuckFace, I looked like the good guy. She's right, though. He is a creep, and our club has had run-ins before with him. But he did give me an in with Ava, so for that reason, I'll cut him some slack today.

The guys are talking about something or another, but I'm not really listening. I'm standing here wondering how I'm going to get a shot at Ava. I don't want an Ol' Lady or a girlfriend. I'm not that guy.

But I want Ava, and I heard her answer to the cop. She doesn't date. Does that mean she's taken, though I didn't see a ring, or does it mean she's not the kind to need a relationship to go along with sex? I'm hoping for the latter.

But now I'm wondering if I should've asked her to come over with Vex here. He's the pretty boy in our club, The Devil's Angels. I might be the Prez and have no trouble finding women to get dirty with me, but he's a legend in our club for never getting turned down. But, as I look up, I realize it's too late to send Vex on an errand because Ava is headed our way.

"Holy shit! Fuck me sideways. She is hot," says Fang.

All eyes go in the direction of Ava.

"Shut it, Fang," I bark at him.

All eyes turn in my direction. Eyebrows raise with faint smiles on a couple of their mugs.

Ava arrives and is carrying what looks like a bakery box. She doesn't look nervous to be facing five bikers and one prospect. She's just looking at each person for a few seconds each and then moving to the next. I notice her gaze lands on Vex and stays there a bit longer, and she smiles slightly before moving on to Petey. I step forward and do the introductions.

"Ava, these ugly men are Chubs, Fang, Petey, Vex and Prospect. This is Ava, Petey's neighbor."

"Hi, guys. I brought cupcakes. Not sure if anyone likes them but…"

Her voice stops abruptly, and she stiffens as Chubs dives towards her and snatches the box out of her hands. Just as quickly, Vex is on his feet and moves in close to her. He holds out his hand as if to shake hers, and when she grips his, he grins and places a kiss on the back of her hand. Like some fucking Romeo or some shit. He's instantly turning on the charm, and I'm getting annoyed.

She smiles, firmly removes her hand, and turns to Petey. She also takes one step sideways, closer to me. Boom, Vex! I realize instantly that she's unsure of everyone but is keeping a good poker face. Also, she may not know any of us, but she has already met me, so I'm the safer bet if things are unsafe.

"Hi, Petey. I'm sorry to hear about your accident. It must suck not being able to ride for a while. I'm also sorry it's taken until now to come over and meet you," Ava says while smiling. Damn, her voice is pure silk.

Petey's sitting in a lawn chair with his casted leg propped up, looking irritated. As soon as he realizes she's speaking to him, he sits a little straighter and looks up at her. His face smooths out, and I release the breath I didn't realize I was holding. He can be grumpy and being injured hasn't improved his disposition. But having a beautiful woman standing in front of him and ignoring the rest of us to give him her attention has helped his attitude.

"That's fine, darlin'. Just glad to finally meet someone who annoys Ralph more than I do," he says, chuckling. He chuckled! Amazing what a little feminine attention can do to an old sourpuss.

Ava laughs, and I reach down and drag the prospect out of his chair and gestured toward it for Ava to have a seat. She sits down and turns slightly toward Big Petey.

"I can't believe he'd give you a hard time. You're twice his size. He must be suicidal, along with being certifiably nuts. Can I ask what he complains about with you?" Ava asks Petey.

"He makes noise complaints about my bike. But he's never said a word directly to me," Petey replies.

"So, what you're saying is that I need to double in size or grow a dick to get him to back off?" Ava says.

Petey barks out a laugh and shakes his head. "No way, darlin'. You stay like you are, and if he gives you any more grief, let me know. I'll have a chat."

Ava gifts Petey with the sweetest smile. Lucky dickhead.

Just then, a commotion in the side yard gets everyone's attention. It's nothing serious. Just Chubs running with a cupcake in one hand, the box in the other, his jeans slowly sliding down his ass with Fang and the prospect right behind him. Fang grabs the box just as the jeans win, and Chubs face-plants. Whooping and hollering commence as Fang jogs toward us.

"I didn't drop a single crumb," shouts Chubs while he lies on his back finishing his cupcake.

"Give me that box, Fang," demands Petey.

Fang grabs a cupcake and hands over the box. Chubs walks over, licking pink frosting off his fingers while his other hand is hiking his jeans back up above the equator.

No shame with that man when it comes to food. And I guess I'm right about that when he walks right up to Ava, drops to his knee, and says, "Please, Ava. My beautiful Angel. Will you marry me and make me cupcakes until death do us part?"

"You idiot," says Fang. "Those came from Sweet Angel Treats Bakery. You just proposed to a woman, no offense, Ava, that knows how and where to shop for cupcakes but may not be able to boil water."

We all laugh, as does Ava. But Chubs is determined and replies to Fang. "Don't care. She's smart enough to shop there, and that's good enough for me."

Ava is sitting there laughing at their antics, but it really makes Chubs' day when she says, "No, I won't marry you, and you shouldn't use that dirty word to someone you just met. But I did bake them myself, and I would be happy to have a taste tester if you're volunteering, when I try new recipes. I own Sweet Angel Treats and do most of the baking there."

Chubs suddenly stands up, leans down to Ava's chair and throws both arms around her, pinning her arms to her sides, picks her up, and rocks her back and forth playfully.

She lets out a startled laugh as Chubs says, "Chubs loves Ava. Chubs loves Ava."

Ava's giggling when she looks down into Chubs face and states, "You are really into food, huh?"

Chubs set her down gently and steps back grinning and points to himself with both thumbs saying, "I didn't get all this awesome stuff eating carrots, honey."

Chubs isn't a bad-looking guy. Not real tall, very stocky, verging on chubby. Curly mop of brown hair, a few days scruff, the personality of a large golden retriever and is very well-liked by the club members, family and with the women and hangarounds. He's a goof and wears it well. He's also a great brother to have in a bad spot because he's loyal as fuck.

Petey snort laughs at Chubs but looks up at Ava and points to her chair and says to her, "Ava, please have a seat, and we'll keep that moron off of you. Prospect, get Ava a drink. Beer or a Coke, darlin'?"

Taking her seat again, Ava asks for a diet Coke instead.

I'm hoping she's not into dieting because her curves are heaven-made!

The prospect hands Ava a diet Coke, and she leans back into the chair and takes a sip.

Even that is a sexy look on her. Damn, this kind of reaction never happens to me, but I am intrigued with Ava.

"So, Fang, how did you know where those cupcakes came from?" asks Ava, directing her eyes to Fang.

Suddenly, Fang doesn't look so comfortable having the attention on him. Feet shuffling, eyes looking everywhere but at Ava, he mumbles, "I... uh... I've... um, well, I've had some from there before."

Ava squints her eyes at him a bit and replies, "Odd. I don't remember seeing you in there before, and you would've stood out being a biker in a pink and black girlie-type store."

Vex looks at Fang and says, "That chick you were fucking a while back worked at a bakery. That it?"

Fang looks like he is hoping the ground will swallow him up at that moment, but he shoots Vex a nasty look promising retribution before saying, "Yeah. She worked there."

Everyone is suddenly looking at Ava as she has eyes only for Fang now. I can literally see the wheels turning in that beautiful head.

Ava slowly questions, "Marybelle?"

Fang nods his head once.

"You're the rat bastard that screwed over Marybelle!?" Ava states, not really asking.

Fang nods his head once again.

Suddenly, Ava leans over and snatches the forgotten cupcake out of Fang's hand and gives it to Chubs.

Squinty, scary-ass-looking eyes pointed to Fang, she hisses, "No cupcakes for you. No pie, cake, doughnuts. Nothing! You are on Sweet Angel Treats restriction. You cost me my best cake artist. She went home a sobbing mess to her parents, and I haven't seen her since! She quit and moved. No notice. Nothing. Left me in a huge bind. Hope that threesome she found you in was worth it. She was a great person!"

"Can I have his share since he's on restriction now?" asks Chubs through a mouthful of cake and frosting. Honestly, that man has no shame.

Ava stands up and sets down her bottle on the cooler lid. She turns to Petey and says, "If you don't mind, I'd like to stop over sometimes and check on you. I know you don't want or need someone hovering over you, but I'll worry otherwise. And I'd be happy to bring dinner and hang out if you're up for it. I've enjoyed getting to meet you and the others, well, most of the others, and I don't know many in this 'hood yet. But feel free to say no. I don't want to overstep."

Petey smiles and says, "Darlin', I would love the company and the home-cooked meal. Got nobody that cooks me dinner, and that would be great. Bring that dog over, though. Would love to meet the beast up close. You're always welcome here." He pulls his phone out of his shirt pocket and hands it to Ava. "Put your number in there, honey, and call yourself. I need something, or if you do, we'll have each other's digits."

Ava does as he asks and hands back his phone with a sweet smile. I quickly hand her my phone as well, and after a moment of hesitation, she adds her numbers to mine. Whew! She hands my phone back, looks up at me and says, "Thank you for the help earlier. Much appreciated. And the Coke."

She turns to the others and tells Chubs, "Door to the bakery is always open to you. Come by anytime, and we'll have a treat and a cup of coffee together. If you have a woman, bring her too. Would love to meet her."

My big, burly biker brother grins at Ava like she just hung the moon and replies, "You'll be seeing me, honey."

She gives a low wave, says goodnight, and heads back across the street. We all watch her until she enters her house, and then I turn to Fang.

"So, tell us. Who were the other two in the threesome that just got you banned from a bakery?

Fuck, brother, I thought she was going to bitch slap you. That was some funny shit!" I can't hold in the laughter any longer.

The look on his face was priceless. Not many bikers get an ass chewing from a woman and just take it without saying anything back. He'll never admit it, but I think he was a little scared of her. She was fearless, and that in itself is another plus in her favor. I'm pretty sure she's going to be a star in my head for a long while to come.

Chapter 3

Ava

After a hectic Sunday due to an oven malfunction, it's now 5am Monday morning, and I'm bent over a workstation in the bakery, currently frosting cake donuts. Up next are the cinnamon rolls that we can't make enough of because they're that good. I'm not bragging—it's fact. We sell around fifteen hundred to two thousand of them a week. My crew and I are hard at work at our various stations, and a lot of sweets are being completed.

I look up and around the kitchen and feel a sense of pride at how smooth everything is going. I have a great crew of seven full-time employees and four part-time workers. We're not a huge bakery, but we're all about quality and flavor. The bakery is open six days a week, so our shifts are varied, and I get to work with each employee at some point during the week. I like that I get to spend time with each one, and while they are employees, not technically friends, I have a good relationship with each of them.

Trudy comes into the kitchen to load up her tray to continue stocking the glass cases in the front. I'm not sure I've ever seen her when she didn't have a smile on her round face, and her brown curls weren't bouncing. She makes me smile just because. She loads up her tray with various items and disappears through the swinging saloon-style doors that separate the bakery from the kitchen. Trudy isn't a baker. She works the front counter and is perfect for that job with her great people skills.

After several hours, I take a break and walk up front to check on things. I take a moment to just look around the front and fall in love again with the visual. Light pink, black and white checkered tile floors. The walls are a very light pink with white and black trim. Along the walls, just above reach, are clear boxes and beautiful cake stands displaying some of our cake creations. But the best display sits off to the right of the front door, along a wall next to an old-fashioned jukebox. In a large

4x4 clear case sits a pink and chrome Harley Sportster cake. It's very authentic and detailed. I spent several days making that cake and making sure it was correct in every way except the size. It's on a smaller scale than a real bike, but that's the only difference. I think it's the coolest cake I've ever done. What the customers don't get to see is that it has a tiny motor mounted to the back that makes the perfect Harley sound.

After admiring the bike again, I look toward the counters and see the glass cases are being restocked again, and the storefront is busy. Several women sit at some of the small tables and booths, sipping coffee and eating sweets. A few college-age boys and girls are scattered about enjoying their morning cups of java and taking advantage of the free wi-fi. A couple of men are scattered down the diner-style counter with stools sipping coffee, reading newspapers, and eating donuts. There is a line at the counter, and Trudy is moving fast. I walk behind the counter, turn to the next customer and get busy.

I have a serious coffee addiction, so I spent quite some time picking out the perfect coffees to be sold here. We have many male customers that brave the pink shop just for the coffee. I have strict rules about how the coffee is made and sold. We don't make most of those fancy yuppie coffees, though. I believe that good coffee doesn't need a ton of flavorings added. Good coffee should be tasted and not covered up with all that other stuff. And the men come for that and then find the sweets. If you want a fancy coffee, go find a barista. If you want just good strong coffee, come see me.

After helping Trudy catch up the line of customers, I head to the very back of the building where my small office is located. I busy myself doing paperwork and placing some ingredient orders when my phone vibrates on the desktop. Glancing down, I see a text. I swipe my finger across the screen and see it's from Petey.

Big Petey: Hey darlin. This old man is getting bored sitting around. Want to meet your fur family.

Me: Can do that tonight if you're up for dinner.

Big Petey: Hell yeah. Come over whenever you want.

Me: See you around 5-ish!

I have to smile to myself. Gunner was worried Petey would be more than I could handle, and I've found him to be a sweet bear-sized man. I look forward to seeing him tonight, and I love the idea of cooking dinner for someone. I used to cook in some of the foster homes I was in, but feeding the smaller kids was where my heart melted. There were a few good homes that encouraged my love of cooking and baking, but most didn't. Most were not good in any way.

Me: Anything you won't eat?

Big Petey: Snake

I have to laugh at the lovable biker. This isn't our first time texting, and he always makes me smile.

Me: Snake is off the menu. See you around 5.

I finish up my paperwork for the day and head to the kitchen to find some dessert for tonight. I decide to take two pies—a coconut cream and a caramel apple pie with a crumb top crust. They're both luscious and whatever leftovers there are, I'm sure the club members that stop by will help him finish them. On my way home, I stop at Whole Foods and pick up the ingredients for Chicken Marsala and a salad.

Coming down my street, I see Ralph standing outside of my house on the walk. I pull into my driveway and park outside of the garage, not wanting to open the garage door with Ralph standing close enough he could enter. I know, overly cautious but better safe than… well, you know.

I swing out of the car while watching Ralph as he continues to be animated and hollering at my front window. I grab the groceries, pies and my purse, shut my car door, and turn to Ralph.

"You know, Ralph, if you didn't stand directly in front of the window and holler at Mac, he wouldn't swear at you. It's not hard to figure out. You just need to be smarter than the bird," I snap at him.

He turns his head my direction and bellows, "Your bird has a filthy fucking mouth! You shut him up or I will!"

Of course, Mac responds with a loud, "Ralph sucks. Ralph sucks donkey dick!"

Next to the big picture window are two narrow windows that slide up and have screens in them. My mistake, and Mac has discovered it. I won't forget to shut the front side windows again.

Ralph suddenly picks up a rock and heaves it at the window. The rock was small and bounces off the glass without leaving any damage, but I'm so done with his crap at this point.

I unload my arms by putting everything onto the hood of my car and rush towards Ralph, who's searching for another rock.

"Stop, Ralph! This is ridiculous! Go to your side of the road, and you won't be able to hear Mac anyway. Grow the hell up, you old bastard! If you break that window, I'll be the one calling the cops, and you'll be paying for it," I holler at him.

Ralph whirls my direction and moves in tight to my front. He's no taller than me and not much heavier, even though he has a bit of a beer gut. I'm not backing down from this moron.

He starts screaming in my face, spit flying everywhere, "They have to go! I won't be intimidated in my own house! Get rid of them or I will!"

Wiping the spit off my cheek, I bellow back, "You're not being intimidated in your own house! You're not even on your own land! And your language is worse than Mac's! Get off my sidewalk, you lunatic, and stay the hell on your own side of the street! And don't ever threaten my pets again!"

"Or what?" he screams back.

"Or you will live to regret it," I hiss at him.

He steps back a half a step, winds up, and tries to hit me. I duck and slide to the side of his poorly thrown punch and instantly twist his arm behind his back, hard. I grab his shirt collar with my other hand and start marching him across the street toward his house. Every time he tries to wiggle loose, I lift his arm up higher on his back until he's half crouched over.

He starts screaming, "Assault! Assault! I'm being assaulted! Call 911! Call 911!"

We continue forward until we reach his lawn, where I shove him away from me and release him at the same time. He stumbles forward a few steps and then whirls toward me but doesn't step my direction. I position my feet so I'm ready for whatever he decides to do.

"I can't believe you just assaulted me, you bitch! You're in so much trouble now!" he bellows.

"And I can't believe a grown-ass man would waste his days arguing with a bird! Get a better hobby than that or, better yet, get a job, you dumbass!"

"I'm disabled, you cunt!"

"No! You're mentally unstable, cockface!"

He lunges toward me and I sidestep him again. When he spins around to face me, I warn him, "You try to put your hands on me again, and I'm going to throat punch you and put you down like a dog!"

"I'd listen to the lady and take this as a good time to head into your house, Ralph. Try to lay another hand on her and, when she's done kicking your ass, you'll be dealing with me. And I'm not as nice as her."

I look over and see Big Petey leaning on his crutches on his porch. Even with a cast to his knee, he's intimidating.

"This is between me and her, Pete," says Ralph, suddenly very calm.

"Not anymore, Ralph," returns Pete. "I've taken a liking to her, and she has my protection now. Mess with that and you'll have much more serious issues to deal with than a bird."

After a moment of hesitation, Ralph walks to his house and goes inside, slamming the front door behind him.

"God, Pete, I'm so sorry about this. I never wanted an issue with a neighbor," I say.

"Not your fault, darlin'. He's always been a pain in everyone's ass. Go do what you have to, and I'll see you and that dog in a while," Pete says, smiling. "And you can entertain me with the story of how you came to have those moves. You did good, girl. Real good."

I head toward my house with a warm feeling inside. I've not had anyone that stood up for me before until I met these bikers. Ironic that it's them that's made me feel safer and cared for when the people that were supposed to never did.

I grab up everything from the hood of my car and go inside the house. Setting everything down on the kitchen counter, I go immediately to the back slider and open it to allow whoever wants to go outside to go through.

First comes Loki, stopping by my side, with a head rub to my waist. I crouch down and give him a good body rub. He's such a good boy. During the altercation with Ralph, I heard Loki barking and snarling, and I was very happy he didn't dive through the window to get to me. Maybe because I wasn't getting hurt, or wasn't in any real danger, is what kept him in check. He heads outside, and then here comes Gee sliding around the corner. His little red and black body is jiggling a little as he tries to stop but instead crashes into me full force. He comes up on his hind feet for his hug and a quick rub. He's so lovable. And then he goes out the door heading directly toward his sandbox. I shut the door and turn to the living room. Duffy is sprawled out on his back on the couch. This is normal for him. Not much gets him very excited. I walk over and give him his belly rub that he expects at all times. Looking around the room, I don't spot Mac.

I walk into the pet bedroom and finally see him on the floor, standing in the corner. His beak is actually touching the wall.

"What'cha doing, Mac?" I ask.

He says nothing. I repeat myself, "What'cha doing, Mac?"

Still, no reply. Not that I'm surprised. Mac has it in his head that if he can't see you, you can't see him. So, I go over to him, pick him up, and set him on his perch facing me.

"Mac?"

"Hi, Mom," he says.

"Hi, Mac. Why were you in the corner?"

"Am I in trouble?" he squawks.

"No, you're not. Ralph is nuts and that's not your fault," I answer him.

"He started it, Mom."

"I know. Let's not worry about Ralph anymore tonight. I have to cook dinner because I'm going over to Big Petey's later. Want to hang with me in the kitchen?"

"Yes. Ride, please."

He climbs onto my shoulder, and we head to the kitchen. Mac is incredibly intelligent, and we're very bonded, but even knowing that he always amazes me with his antics. He's humor in bird form. I adopted Mac after he'd been rescued from a bad situation, and I firmly believe he knows how important he is to me now. He barely said a few words when he came to live with me, and now he is very vocal. It took time, though. Time, patience, and love. He's interactive and loves attention. If he's not getting it, he'll do something to make sure he's noticed. But I wouldn't have it any other way. He's my best buddy.

He jumps off onto the edge of the counter and starts humming Toby Keith's "Should Have Been A Cowboy" while bobbing his head to the beat. And I get to work preparing dinner.

"What did you say this is called again?" asks Pete.

"Chicken Marsala," I answer.

"I've had that before and it didn't taste like this. This is the shit!" he states.

"Thank you. I love to cook, and it's so nice having someone to cook for and eat it with. I'm so glad you like it, Pete. I made a lot, so you would have leftovers for tomorrow," I say.

"Not sure there will be any left by tomorrow," he laughs.

We continue eating in comfortable silence with Loki lying on the floor near the wall in the dining room. Pete and Loki hit it off immediately when we arrived. Big Petey was wowed by Loki's size, and Loki seemed happy to have made another friend.

As Pete is reaching for another helping, we hear a Harley coming down the street. I notice a small smile on his face, but he doesn't make any moves toward the door. When the bike turns off, I start to rise to answer the door.

"Keep your seat, darlin'. Door isn't locked and he has a key if it was."

"Should I get another plate?" I ask.

"Nah, he knows where they are if he's hungry."

Loki's head rises as the door opens and in walks Gunner. Tight, worn jeans, black t-shirt straining to fit the width of his shoulders, black leather cut with numerous patches, and scuffed boots. He shuts the door behind him and looks up toward the dining room. Pete's house is an open floor plan, so the kitchen, dining room area, and living room are all one large room separated by a long counter. Very similar to mine.

Our eyes meet, and he gives a half-smile, the left side of his face rising part way. It's a good look on him. There isn't much that wouldn't be a good look on him, though. He's absolutely gorgeous. I'm not sure what's going on in his mind, but I know mine is so far in the gutter. It's pathetic. The temperature has suddenly risen enough to be noticeable. I don't get why he makes me react this way when I've never gotten these feelings from anyone else before. He's not the first gorgeous guy I've spoken with or seen, but he has taken control of way too many of my thoughts.

He walks into the kitchen, grabs a plate and silverware, snatches a beer from the fridge and sits down at the table on my left side. He glances over at Loki and then does a double-take. Loki thumps his tail once on the floor and puts his head back down on his front paws.

"Fuck me! He's a beast," says Gunner, speaking for the first time.

Big Petey chuckles and says, "That he is."

Gunner starts filling up his plate and catches my eye and grins. I realize I'm still staring at him and quickly turn back to my food. For the next several minutes, the only sound in the room is the clinking of silverware on plates and Loki lightly snoring and snuffling in the background.

"Holy shit! What is this?" asks Gunner, looking directly at me.

"Chicken Marsala with homemade fresh pasta, broccoli salad, and hot cross buns," I answer as Petey chuckles.

"You like?" I ask, grinning at Gunner.

"Uh, yeah, dollface, this is unbelievable. Knew you could bake, didn't know you could cook like this too," Gunner says while loading up his fork again.

"I'm thinking of asking the doc to leave my cast on for a long time just to get her to cook for me out of sympathy," laughs Petey.

"Petey, you don't need a cast for me to cook for you. I am the one that's thrilled with having someone to cook for now. You'll get tired of seeing my face when I'm showing up regularly with things for you to eat and taste and critique. I'll drive you nuts if you let me," I declare. "I do a little catering on the side and am always trying out new recipes or tweaking things. I think I may have scared off Mrs. Connor with my constant knocks on her door with a tray of things to try."

"You cater?" both men ask at the same time, eyebrows raised and looking at each other.

"Well, yeah, a little bit. I love doing it, though. I'm just getting started at the catering, so I haven't had a lot of business yet. But it's building, and I've been thinking of expanding the bakery to include the catering end of the business."

The men are eyeing each other, and I suddenly feel left out. They're having a conversation without a word being spoken. This goes on for a moment, and then Gunner nods his head slightly, and turns to me.

"What types of food do you make when you are catering an event?" Gunner questions.

"I can make most anything the client wants, but I try to fit the food to the occasion and the people that will be attending. And of course, how many people I'll be feeding. That matters a lot since it's usually just me doing the cooking and serving. I have a part-time girl that helps a bit, but it's usually on me," I answer.

"Okay, say you're feeding a bunch of bikers outdoors, and it's buffet style where they serve themselves. Dinner and desserts would be expected. Probably about seventy-five people total. What would you make?" asks Gunner.

"Um, well, I'd have to sit down and plan that out, but off the top of my head, I would go with things like some easy finger foods as appetizers. Jalapeno poppers or stuffed cherry tomatoes, BBQ ribs and chicken, some salads, baked or scalloped potatoes, beans. Desserts would be different pies, a few cakes, and some cookies."

The guys continue eating as we're having this conversation. When they both push their plates back, I rise and grab the two pies. I love the look on both their faces when I place them on the table and start cutting them into sixths. I point to the pies while looking at Petey and then Gunner and ask, "Coconut cream or caramel apple?"

"Both," they answer in unison.

I laugh out loud at them as I place a piece of each flavor of pie onto their plates. I grab a thermos I brought and pour myself a cup of coffee. I hold it out toward the guys, but neither stops eating pie long enough to answer, just shaking their heads no. I sit back down and enjoy their sounds of appreciation while sipping my cup of coffee.

We can hear another bike coming down the street and Petey groans.

"That better not be Chubs because he'll wipe us out of pie," grumbles Petey.

"Can't be him. I sent him on a run today, and he won't be back until the day after tomorrow," says Gunner, smiling.

"Good thinking, Prez," Petey answers back, grinning like a kid.

The front door opens, and in walks the second most beautiful man I've ever seen, second only to Gunner. Very tall, 6'4", shaved head, tattooed arms, beautiful bright blue eyes and a day or two's worth of light-colored scruff on his face. Very muscular. Like his muscles have muscles. More so than even Gunner, who is built solid but not a muscle-bound gym rat type. This guy is huge and scary-looking but oh so beautiful. He has a slight frown on his face as he approaches the dining room staring me down. He stops next to the table, directly across from where I'm sitting, and continues staring as he crosses those impressive arms over his chest and says in a very deep rumble, "So, you're the chick Chubs wants to marry over a damn cupcake?"

"I make awesome cupcakes. So yes, I would be *that chick*," I retort.

He continues staring until Big Petey says, "Take a seat, Axel. Eat some dinner or pie and quit trying to stare her down. Darlin', this miscreant with the bad manners is Axel, VP of the club. And my son. Axel, meet Ava, my neighbor."

"Nice to meet you, Axel. If you're hungry, I can nuke some dinner for you. Or get you a plate of pie," I say.

"No, you won't. He can nuke his own damn dinner if he's hungry," states Gunner while looking a bit ticked off.

Axel's eyebrows raise, and a small smirk appears as he looks at Gunner and asks, "It's like that, is it?"

"Yup," replies Gunner.

"Actually, Axel, I'm going to make her MY Ol' Lady and have a child that is born with brains, looks, AND manners. You know, since I didn't get that the first time around," laughs Petey.

"Fuck you, Pops," Axel replies, lightly punching his dad in the shoulder on his way to the cupboard.

He comes back, fills up his plate with the leftovers and heads to the microwave. He stops suddenly when he notices Loki next to the wall. He slowly swings his head back toward his dad and asks, "Why the fuck do you have a horse in your house, Pops?"

"That's Loki, Ava's dog. The dog that annoys the fuck out of Ralph. Have to like him just for that," snickers Petey while tossing a small piece of chicken to Loki. Loki catches it and swallows without chewing.

"Christ, you'd think even Ralph would be smart enough not to antagonize a dog that size," says Axel as he brings his plate to the table, sits and starts eating.

"It's Chicken Marsala before you ask," says Petey, grinning at Axel as he stops eating and looks up at me.

"Huh. Not sure I've had that before. Not really biker food but still great," says Axel.

"Bikers don't like good food, Axel?" I question. "Or do you have just a few foods you'll eat that are manly enough for you and the rest are ignored?"

"Snarky. I like it," he replies, grinning at me.

"Quit fucking with her, you jackass. You just cleaned up all the leftovers, so you must like it," grumbles Gunner. "We were just talking with her about her catering business she's starting up. I'm thinking she'd make the club look good serving great food at the poker run next week. We're not known for having great food, or even edible food, at our cookouts. And I, for one, don't want to end up in the E.R. again over the Ol' Ladies' lack of cooking skills."

Axel and Petey both wince at the same time. Petey says, "Yeah, that wasn't a lot of fun. I couldn't leave my house for a week. Not sure I've ever been that sick before. And it was damn embarrassing that the support clubs and their members were sick too. I'm all for letting Ava save our dignity this time."

All eyes turn to me.

"Are you serious about this?" I ask.

Gunner replies, "Yes, I am. It's a damn shame when bikers are known for their cookouts and parties, and ours suck. The partying part we have no issues with, but the cookouts and food are really bad. What would we be looking at for a cost?"

I am getting my hopes up, and I'm hoping they won't crush them. I would love to do that kind of an event. It could really help get my name out there as a caterer instead of just as a baker. But if I blow it, it could stop the business before it really even gets going. I won't blow this. I know I won't because I'll make sure I don't.

"I'll make you a deal," I say while looking at Gunner. "If you'll let me do this, I'll do the shopping, cooking, serving and cleanup for free. The club only has to pay for the food costs. It'll be a test run for me doing larger events than I've done, and if you all are happy with the food, then I would appreciate some free advertising through word of mouth. I can plan out the menu and give you an estimate on food costs by tomorrow afternoon."

Gunner looks at the other men, and they quickly nod their heads. He turns to me and smiles. His smile is unbelievably hot. I'm kind of losing track of what we were talking about because my brain is heading south. With some effort, I refocus on the conversation.

"The club women will help with the serving and do the cleanup since they don't have to do the cooking. We put in a new industrial kitchen in the clubhouse last year, and you can use that to prepare the food, so you don't have to transport it once it's done. Does that work for you?"

"That's perfect for me. But I need to see the kitchen first, so I can plan things out accordingly. Is that a problem?"

"Nope, it's not. Come by tomorrow anytime, and I'll show you around. I'll text you the directions," Gunner replies.

The conversation flows after that with me asking about food likes, dislikes, expectations, quantities, and so forth. Before I know it, it was getting late, and I needed to get home.

I got up and put the pies in the fridge and started stacking up the dirty dishes when Gunner came to the sink and started rinsing them. I was more than a little shocked to have him standing that close and doing something so domestic. He grinned down at me and gave me a bump with his shoulder.

"What? You've never seen a man with dishpan hands before?" he questions.

"Yeah, I have, but not someone who looks like you!" I blurt.

"Looks like me?" he questions with another shoulder bump.

"Hot, huge, badass biker guy types don't do dishes. They ride Harleys and maim people and give the finger to the world. And they don't have that kind of smile. You know, the 'smile that's dropped a thousand panties' smile. They… Oh, God, stop talking, Ava!" I exclaim, horribly embarrassed that I'd said any of that.

I can feel my face turning eight shades of red as Gunner, Axel, and Petey all bust out laughing at me. I can't even make eye contact at this point. I turn slightly away and start placing the rinsed dishes in the dishwasher. I have such a runaway mouth sometimes. Gah!

"Can I just leave now, go home, and hide in the closet for the next five years? Please!" I shout through the laughter.

"Not until you tell me what kind of smile I have," says Axel, barely able to get the words out through his laughter.

"Oh God, kill me now," I beg.

I turn, grab my purse, and call Loki. Before getting another step toward freedom, Petey gently grabs my arm and pulls me towards him. I struggle to look at him, but I finally make eye contact, and he's smiling huge.

"Darlin', you're a breath of fresh air. And your food is stellar. Thank you for taking the time to cook an old man dinner and sharing that time with him. Looking forward to doing that again soon."

He melts my heart. He's so sweet, and you'd never think he was based on his appearance. I lean toward him and give him a kiss on the temple.

"Thank you, Petey. I enjoyed it also. We'll do it again soon."

As I start toward the door, I hear Gunner say, "Don't forget about tomorrow." I can actually hear the smile in his voice. Ugh!

I simply wave over my shoulder and make it almost to the door when Axel speaks up. "What? No kiss for me too?"

My wave turns into a one-fingered salute as I exit. The laughter roars behind me.

Lola Wright

Chapter 4

Gunner

Placing my elbows on my desk, I clasp my hands, and rest my chin on them. I'm not getting much done today. My desk's covered in things that need to be completed, and yet I'm sitting here thinking about a curvy, blond baker. At thirty-three years old, you'd think I'd be mature enough to keep my mind on my work, but I can't. All I can seem to think about is how cute her face looked when she realized that she had just called me hot. And badass. She was so horrified, but yeah, I liked that she noticed and thought that. I have no trouble getting women being the Prez of a large MC. They flock to the club and are a dime a dozen. And yet this gorgeous neighbor of Big Petey's is different.

She's real. Like Officer Stanaway said, there's no plastic. Not in the body or the soul. And that caught my attention in a big way. I'm still not sure if she has a man in her life, but Big Petey doesn't think so, and I'm not sure that would matter to me at this point.

I'm very surprised at myself for these thoughts. I've never been one of those men that wanted a permanent woman in my life. I'm not one to turn down a free ride, so to speak, and dirty sex is a favorite pastime of mine. I like variety. In women and in bed. But I've never found myself thinking about one for more than the time it took to get her into bed and then out of it soon afterward. For the last few days, only one woman has been in my thoughts. I wasn't even interested in the offers last night when I returned to the clubhouse with Axel. Instead, I went home, took a shower and stroked myself off to visions of Ava doing it for me. God, it was good.

My office door opens and in strolls Axel and Pooh. They flop down in chairs across from my desk and instantly prop their heels on my desk. I raise an eyebrow at their boots and then to them. Both grin but do not remove their boots. I sigh.

"What do you two jackasses want?" I ask.

"Nothing really," answers Axel with a wide grin.

"Just thought we'd hang out with you to help kill time until your little lady baker shows up," snorts Pooh.

"Aren't you supposed to be covering the towing today, Pooh?" I question.

"I'm on call and, lucky me, no calls yet," he states. Then, unfortunately, he goes on to say, "I've heard so much about this little ripe piece of pu—"

"Say it and die," I growl.

They both laugh, but lucky for Pooh, he doesn't finish his sentence.

"See? I told you!" laughs Axel, looking at Pooh.

"So, tell me, Prez, are we going to see a knockdown between you and Chubs? You know, since he's already proposed to her and all," chuckles Pooh.

I study him for a minute and decide to get this chat out of the way regardless of whatever shit I get from them.

"Ava will be here sometime today and will probably be in the kitchen for a few days next week and then again for the Poker Run and cookout. Spread the word among the members and hang-arounds that she is to be treated with respect at all times. She's not to be touched. Period. If she is, that person will answer to me in the basement. She's doing this club a huge favor, and she'll not be treated like a club whore or hang-around while she's doing it, understood?" I declare.

The smiles slowly leave their faces, and they both look me in the eye seeing how serious I am about this.

"Absolutely," answers Axel.

"I'll get the word out and make sure it's understood, Prez," says Pooh.

"I think she can handle herself just fine, Gunner," says Big Petey as he hobbles on his crutches into the room. "But I second what the Prez said, and anyone giving her shit will answer to me after Gunner is done with them."

"What are you doing here, Pops?" asks Axel.

Petey sits down, lays his crutches on the floor next to him and answers, "Came to make sure that message was made. Glad to see you're already on that, Prez."

I nod at Petey and then ask, "She can take care of herself?"

Big Petey smiles huge and says, "She frog-marched Ralph across the road to his yard yesterday when he tried punching her. I think she has some skills we haven't seen yet, but Ralph was put on notice that she's not some helpless female he can scare."

I swear I see a look of pride on Petey's face. He's really taken to Ava, and I'm happy to see that considering he's been alone for a long time. But I hope he's not too taken with her because I like Pete, he's like a father to me and has been for years, but Ava is going to be mine. Crap! I can't believe I just thought that. What the hell! I've never thought that about another woman in my life. I've never had one on the back of my bike either, but that thought has my cock getting hard. Ava, pressed up against my back, thighs spread tight on the outside of mine, her hands touching me. Yeah, that's got my favorite part of me making wood. Holy shit!

I snap back to the conversation and interrupt to ask, "He tried punching her?"

Petey looks my way and nods his head. He says, "Ralph was on her side of the road shouting at her bird when she pulled in the drive. They got into it verbally, and she told him he needs to be smarter than the bird. He swung, she ducked and put his arm behind his back. Hard. Marched him to his side of the street and shoved him toward his house. I got outside by then. It was great! The look on his face was worth the pain of trying to get out of my chair and get outside. I added my two cents to the argument, and Ralph decided he didn't want his ass kicked by a chick and then by me, so he went inside. You think she's hot, you ought to see her when she's pissed off and standing up for herself. Now that was bone-making stuff. She's a little spitfire."

I'm not shocked that she stood up for herself. She was set to tell Officer Stanaway what she thought, and she didn't bat an eye at having dinner with three rough-looking bikers. She has guts to go along with the looks. This knowledge is not making my cock settle down in the least. I'm glad I'm sitting behind a desk, or I'd never hear the end of it from my brothers.

"Fuck me! I can't wait to meet this little baker," exclaims Pooh.

I look at Axel and notice he has something working behind his eyes. Not sure what, but I'm pretty sure I don't like it much. My phone starts vibrating on my desk before I can question Axel about his thoughts.

Ava: Address?

I text Ava the address of the clubhouse and then text the prospect at the front gate and tell him to let her through when she arrives.

Me: I'll meet you out front. Give the prospect at the gate your name and he'll wave you through. Follow the road and you'll find me.

Ava: Be there in 10

I sit the phone back down and find three sets of eyes looking my direction.

"She's on her way," I sigh.

Three faces light up, and I realize I might actually have to kill some of my brothers to get what I want. Or rather, who I want.

———

I am watching a glossy black 1969 Chevy Camaro Z28 with two wide white stripes on the hood coming up the driveway to the clubhouse. It's got a beautiful sound to it, the engine rumbling and purring at the same time. Hot fucking car! I'm not a cage man, but if I was, that'd be the car I'd drive. It comes to a stop, shuts off, and out steps Ava.

"I'm making wood here, brother, and I'm not sure if it's because of the car or the woman standing next to it," breathes Axel.

I shoulder slam him as I walk past and head toward Ava. She rounds the hood with a huge-ass purse over her shoulder, jeans, knee-high fuck-me black leather boots, and a dark green blouse that's just barely able to contain that perfect rack. I know I'm staring, and I'm hoping I'm not drooling.

She reaches me, stops, puts her hands on her hips, and states, "Last night did not happen. I didn't say anything embarrassing, and we will not be discussing it if you remember things differently than I do. That clear?"

"Yup. Crystal clear. We won't mention that you think I'm a hot, badass biker with a panty-dropping smile. I would never be the kind of man to remind you of those words," I smile down at her.

"Ugh, I should have known better," she moans.

I laugh and put my hand on her lower back and start guiding her to the clubhouse door. Upon entering, my first thought's "what the fuck" when I see the number of brothers has increased dramatically, and my next is "oh fuck" they're not going to play fair.

Vex is leaning up against the bar that Petey is sitting at. Pooh is standing near Axel in the center of the room. Fang's on a couch with a beer in his hand. Two prospects are pretending to be playing pool, and a few more brothers are scattered around the tables and seats in the main room. All eyes are on Ava.

Ava stops, looks around, and spots Axel. Looking up at me, she asks, "Will it do me any good to state the rules to Axel?"

"Not in the least," I answer.

"Fuck me sideways," she mumbles.

"Is that an order or a request?" I say, smiling big when I overhear her.

She smacks the back of her hand into the middle of my chest and makes a beeline toward Petey. I chuckle and follow her over to the full-length bar that takes up the whole wall on the left side of the door. Petey opens his arms, she leans in and kisses him on the cheek. Wolf whistles and catcalls commence. Pete says something in her ear, and she pulls back with the biggest smile I've seen yet. It lights up her whole face. Vex slides a little closer, and she turns to him.

"Hey, Vex. Nice to see you again," Ava says.

"Ah, you remember my name. That's a good start," he answers as he slides a bit closer again. He gives her his best smile and, using his pickup voice, says, "Nice to see you again too, Ava. No treats today?"

"Well, yes, I brought some cookies, but sorry, they're for Petey. It's up to him if he wants to share," she replies while digging around in that huge-ass purse. She pulls out a large ziplock bag packed full of cookies. She hands them to Petey, and his whole face lights up.

"But first, you need to get your leg elevated, Petey. Sitting on a bar stool is not helping your leg. If you park yourself over there in that recliner, I'll bring your cookies and a cup of coffee over to you," she smiles sweetly at Petey.

Petey instantly grabs his crutches and heads over to the chair she indicated. She pulls a small thermos out of her purse, turns to the prospect behind the bar and asks for a cup. She takes it and heads over to Petey. She opens the bag of cookies, pours him a cup of coffee, and places both on the small end table next to him within reach. Everyone watches this in awe because anytime we tell him to sit or elevate his leg, we all get our heads bit off.

"If you need a ride home, I'm heading that direction when I leave here. Be happy to share the ride," she tells Petey.

"Sounds good, darlin'. Holler when you're ready," he answers back, cookie and coffee in hand.

She turns around, ignores all the attention she is receiving, looks at me and says, "Where's the kitchen?"

Lola Wright

Chapter 5

Ava

I'm ignoring all the stares and keeping my eyes directly on Gunner. I know Axel is just itching to say something, and I'm trying to escape to the kitchen before that happens. I know that plan is doomed when Axel and another guy move in my direction. I brace.

"First, Pops gets a kiss, then a hug, and now cookies. Do you not see this big, badass biker man-meat in front of you?" he states loudly.

I hear some chuckles, and I stop when I'm next to Axel. I stare him down for a moment and notice there is nothing but pure mischief in his eyes. I lean in, wrap my arms around his waist and snuggle up to his chest. Very impressive chest, I might add.

"You need some attention today, Axel?" I ask, smirking.

He wraps his arms around me and answers with a shouted, "Yes!"

I hear a growl from somewhere but ignore it and wait for Axel to relax. When he does, I pull back from him, smiling big, while I reach up and twist his nipple. Hard. He howls and jerks back rubbing the abused nub.

"You good now, Axel, or do you still need some more attention?" I purr.

"No, you evil witch, I'm good. Thanks!" he says sarcastically.

The guy standing next to him immediately takes one step back and places both his palms over his nipples when I look in his direction. I can hear the laughter howling around the room.

Looking back and forth between the two troublemakers, I say, "You be nice; I'll be nice. Cookies and pies and all sorts of sweets appear for those who are nice. Not so much for those who aren't."

A little respect and a lot of humor are shining in his eyes when I wink at Axel and walk toward a scowling Gunner.

The kitchen is spectacular. It's huge with several long worktables and counters to spread trays out on, a professional floor mixer, a six-burner stove with large double ovens built into the wall. Two industrial size fridges with an equally sized freezer standing against one wall. It's much nicer and laid out better than I expected. Especially after hearing about the cooking skills of the club women. I can easily feed a crew of seventy-five using this kitchen. Bring along a few of my specialty tools, and I'll be set to churn out some delicious food.

I walk around peeking in cupboards to see what dishes and pans they have and what I'll need to bring. Gunner is sitting on a stool by one of the counters, quietly watching me. I love this kitchen. It has a couple of big windows, one over the sink that overlooks the area the cookout will be, and one behind a counter that looks out into the main room. I spotted the grill out back, and I could grill a full pig on it because of its size.

I turn to Gunner and state, "This is perfect. I can easily get everything done here. But I'll need at least one or two days before the cookout to clean the kitchen and prep. Is that okay?"

He looks around the kitchen for a moment and replies, "The kitchen will be spotless the next time you see it, so you won't have to clean first. As for the prep, you can use it however many days you need."

I'm relieved because coming in for a few hours on Thursday and then all day on Friday will make things much easier on Saturday for me.

"Thanks, Gunner," I say. "That helps a lot."

I explain what my schedule will look like while I'm cooking for them, and he has no objections.

"Do you want to talk food costs and the budget now?" I ask.

"Sure. At every cookout we've had, or I've been to, it's been basically the same food. Burgers, hot dogs, and potato salad. Frankly, I'm bored with that and am looking forward to a little change. We aren't any different than other people—we want good food to go along with beer and hang out with our brothers. Any ideas?" he asks.

"Got a budget in mind?" I toss back at him.

"Last party, not counting alcohol, cost $800, and six people went to the E.R. with food poisoning and several others were sick enough they couldn't ride. And there were only about forty of us that were dumb enough to eat that day. Can you do better than that?" he chuckles.

I laugh at the look on his face and nod my head.

"Yes, I can. For a little more than that, I can feed seventy-five biker-type people some awesome-ass food that will not injure anyone, I promise. I'll buy the food and supplies I need and give you the bill after dinner Saturday if that works for you."

"It does. So, are you going to give me an idea of what we'll be eating?"

"I'm leaning towards ribs and BBQ chicken, maybe some beer brats. Mostly, I want to have lots of bite-size food to snack on while everyone is arriving and waiting for dinner to be served. They seem to keep the natives calm," I answer.

He chuckles, nods, and gives me that panty-dropping smile. The man is drop-dead gorgeous. His hair is just a smidge past needing a cut, silky with a tiny bit of curl at the tips, carelessly brushed back out of his face, and black as night. His eyes are very dark, nearly as dark as his hair. Add to all that his size, and he's definitely fantasy material.

But you can sense that beneath that easy smile, he's not a man to be crossed. There's an aura of danger that seems to follow him, and I keep in mind that he is the President of a 1% MC, and he must've earned that title one way or another. But I have never felt even a bit scared or threatened in his presence. In fact, it's been just the opposite. He has this protective quality about him that is reassuring for someone like me. I like it. I like it a lot. And I have to remind myself that he's so far out of my league, it's not even computable. But I can enjoy the view while I have it and go home to BOB. Sad, but that's my life.

"Uh, dollface, where did you just go?"

He's looking at me, eyes lit with humor, and I snap back to attention. Crap! He was talking to me, and I was spaced out thinking about all the ways he's going to be a star tonight in my thoughts. My very dirty thoughts.

"Oh, I was just thinking about the food," I say lamely while my face heats up.

He smirks at me, and I know he knows I am lying out my ass. Damn! I seem to always embarrass myself around him.

To change the subject before he asks for details, I ask, "So, this is my first MC party, and I'm not very familiar with the ins and outs of one. Anything I should know? Look out for? Avoid? Rules I need to remember?"

His face turns thoughtful. He thinks for a moment and says, "Yeah, there are a few things you should know. There'll be several different clubs here. Some we are close with and have great working relationships. Others, not so much. Because this is a poker run for charity, and we're hosting it, all of the riders will be invited back to the clubhouse for the cookout. Do your thing but keep your eyes open and pay attention to what's going on around you. If anything, anything or anyone at all, makes you feel uncomfortable, find me and stick close. We'll deal with it. It's not unheard of for a few fights to break out, and it's usually not a big deal, but things can get out of hand sometimes when you add booze. Petey, Axel, basically anyone that's a Devil's Angel will look out for you. I've already put the word out that you're to be treated with respect, but I can't say how other clubs will behave. But I can promise you'll be safe as hell with me, Petey or Axel. Hell, Chubs too. He probably won't let you too far from his side anyway," he smiles at that.

"Something else to keep in mind is that the women can be worse than the men. Don't let them get to you. Just be you and handle things however you need to handle them. I'm not worried about you on that front. You can hold your own with those bitches. Just don't believe much of whatever they'll say. They can get pretty territorial and catty when a new face appears," he says wryly.

"And don't get on the back of anyone's bike. That means something in this world, and you don't want to get into that type of situation," he says sternly.

I've listened intently, and I do understand most of what he is saying, though, I'm a bit confused on the "getting on the back of a bike" thing, but I trust that he knows more about this than I do, so I just make a mental note.

"Okay, thanks for the tips. At least with your height, you should be easy to spot if needed," I say.

He looks at me with an odd look on his face and questions, "None of that scares you, does it?"

"Not really. I've been alone most of my life, so I've always relied on myself to stay safe. I'm pretty good at figuring out when to stand and fight and when to get the fuck out of Dodge. I'll be careful, but if you see me coming at you at a dead run, prepare for shit to go down," I tell him.

He throws his head back and barks out a laugh. Eyes smiling, he tilts his head back down and states, "I'll be prepared."

Lola Wright

Chapter 6

Gunner

I'm in trouble. I know it, and I'm not sure what to do about it. I'm once again sitting in my office with my head on my hands, thinking about Ava instead of getting my paperwork done. I don't want to be tied down to one woman, but I can't stand the thought of one of the brothers making a move. Being tied down doesn't sound as bad now as it has in the past, though.

The more I'm around her, the more I realize what a great Ol' Lady she'd make. Especially for the club president. She's not scared of much; she'll speak her mind, and she's not afraid to put someone in their place. She's obviously a hard worker, and it seems like she's been an outcast for a lot of her life. Many members here were outcasts, and that's how they found their way to the club. A family they didn't have or weren't born with.

I want to know her backstory. Who she is and why she's alone. Someone like her must get all sorts of offers from men all the time, and yet she seems happy to not have one in her life. Why is that? She was checking me out way too much to be into women, so I know that's not why. Some man has made her prefer being alone. I feel it in my gut. I have to wonder if it's because she's still in love with him or because he hurt her so badly, she doesn't want to risk her heart again. Okay, so now I know I must be growing a vagina to be having these thoughts.

I pick up my phone and call Rex, our computer geek. Great brother, just loves technology more than Harleys, I sometimes think. But he's very talented with computers, and he'll be able to find out more than I can on my own. I'm not sure Ava would be open to telling me why she is alone when it makes no sense. I know that I should just wait and let her tell me in her own time instead of digging up her dirt, but I'm impatient.

"Prez," answers Rex.

"Hey, brother, I need some intel on…" I start to say.

"Little blond bombshell baker Ava." Rex states.

I'm a little dumbfounded that he knows that's who I'm calling about, but I shouldn't be, considering several of the brothers have been giving me shit about her.

"Uh, yeah. Since she's catering and will be on the compound, I wanted a background check done on her," I answer.

"Yeah, right. Okay, boss, whatever you say," he chuckles. "I'll get started on that right away. Get back to you in a day or so, that okay?"

"Yeah, asshole, that's fine," I say before hanging up on him.

Before I set my phone down, it rings.

"Yeah," I bark into the phone.

"Hello to you too, you little ray of sunshine," laughs Petey. "Sexual frustration is a horrible thing, isn't it, brother?"

"Fuck you, Petey. You call for some reason or just to bust my balls?"

"Both, but mostly to bust your balls since it's common knowledge you're not busting a nut lately." The asswipe is giggling. Actually giggling.

Nothing is sacred in an MC clubhouse. The fact that lately, I've steered clear of the club whores and strippers that hang around here has garnered me several comments already. Bunch of gossiping old women aren't as bad as most of these guys.

"You concerned about my sex life, Old Man?" I ask.

"I'm concerned with your lack of a sex life, kid. You get mean as a bear when you're not getting it on the regular. Just a little worried about the guys' safety," he says through his laughter.

Fuck me. I can't catch a break from these morons. If it's not Petey giving me shit, it's Axel. Or it's Chubs bugging me about when Ava will be here again. He's still upset he missed out on her visit here, and of course, the cookies she brought.

"So, guess who's cooked me dinner the last three nights?" he asks. "I've ate better this week than I have in my entire life. So, seriously Gunner, one of us needs to make her a permanent fixture in the club. I'm thinking I might have a shot. She doesn't seem to mind my age at all."

"Fuck off, Petey! She'd give you a heart attack just by shedding her clothes. And she probably sees you as a father figure, old-timer!" I grumble.

He continues laughing in my ear. He's been in a better mood than we all expected with his broken leg. Of course, having Ava catering to his every need would keep anyone's spirits up.

"I'm having leftovers tonight, though, because she has a class. Her leftovers are still pretty spectacular if you want to stop by and have dinner. She even carried them home for me last night because of the crutches," he says.

"Wait. You had dinner at her house?"

"Yeah, she asked me over for dinner and a movie night. I've been there a few times now. I like it there. It's worth the pain of hobbling over there. Her pets are a hoot. That bird is a character. Smart as hell. We watched Heartbreak Ridge," he answers.

"A class? What kind of class? Like a baking kind of thing?" I question, realizing I'm starting to sound a little nosy and not caring in the least.

"No, brother. She takes martial arts training classes two nights a week. I don't remember what kind, though. She said she's been taking various ones for several years now. She mentioned that she never had anyone to stand up for her, so she decided she needed to learn how to protect herself. She takes the classes very seriously too. She also takes her security serious because she put all new locks in her house and has a security system. And, of course, she has Loki to back her up if needed. Did you know she did all the training herself with that dog, and he is extremely well trained in attack and protection?" he asks.

"No, I didn't," I reply, sorting through the information I've just learned about Ava. I should have just asked Petey instead of having Rex do a background on her. He seems to know a lot about her.

"So, what kind of leftovers do you have that would be worth driving over there for?" I ask, changing the subject but having full intentions of revisiting the subject of Ava over dinner.

"The best pot roast I've ever eaten before," says Petey.

"Be there around five then," I say, hanging up.

Dinner was spectacular.

Ava: Got a minute for a few questions?

Me: Yep

Ava: Where the tables are going to be set up, are there a few outlets within reach?

Me: 2 or 3 and we have extension cords if needed

Ava: A hose or a source of water?

Me: Yep to that too (smiley face)

Ava: Ice?

Me: Ice machine behind the bar.

Ava: Thx!

We've texted a few times over the last week, and I get hard every time I see her name light up my phone. Pathetic, I know. But she has that effect on me. I'm lying in my bed, smiling like hell that she texted.

Me: Anything else I can help with?

I see the little dots indicating she's typing, but then they disappear. Then reappear. Then disappear. Now I'm curious about what she is deleting, especially after that loaded question I asked.

Me: Are you deleting out dirty thoughts (eggplant emoji)

Ava: OMG I can't believe you sent that!

Me: So you know what that is (wink emoji)

Ava: I'm not a nun

Me: How un-nun like do you get (huge smiley face)

Ava: It would scare you to know that

My eyebrows shoot up! Damn! I expected another OMG or something along those lines, but this is getting good. I reach down and rub my hand over my hardening cock. My jeans are getting uncomfortable.

Me: I don't scare easy. Tell me

Ava: What took so long to answer? Were you shaking in your boots?

Me: I had to readjust a few things. Now tell me!

Me: No wait! Tell me what you're wearing first. Then details

Ava: You can't handle the truth

Me: R U quoting A Few Good Men at me? Details woman!

Ava: Where is your hand right now?

Me: On my very hard cock! Quit stalling!

Ava: Sorry, Champ, but I need to hit the shower and then bed. Early morning tomorrow! Sweet dreams biker boy!

Me: Don't you dare!

Me: Ava!

Me: That's just mean

She is evil. But I do have a great imagination, so I set my phone down, undo my jeans, and pull my cock out. It's hard and weeping. I get a good grip, close my eyes, and picture Ava showering while I slowly stroke myself.

I imagine her naked, all those curves wet and on display, as she twists and turns, soaping every inch of that luscious body. I pick up the pace as I get more into the visual in my head. Perfect tits, plump, not too big, not small with rosy-colored nipples. Hard nipples that are calling for my mouth. Long, toned legs. An ass I want to bite. Round, tight and sweet!

Yes! And we have blastoff, ladies and gentlemen. I should be embarrassed as to how quick that was, but she is killing me, and it's been a while since

I've been with anyone. Since I've met Ava, I haven't had any interest in getting naked with anyone else. And that fact alone is concerning. But I seem to be okay with that as long as there is hope that Ava will be naked and under me soon.

Chapter 7

Ava

I'm at the bakery and busy trying to finish up a wedding cake, so Tony can deliver it later tonight. I have a few more minor details to add, and then it's a wrap for this order. This is the last thing for me to accomplish before I need to start loading up the SUV with the food and supplies I need to take to the clubhouse. It's Thursday, and I'm going to start prepping for the cookout on Saturday.

It's been a busy week trying to get ahead on things, so I can be missing from the bakery all day Friday and Saturday. Trudy is taking an extra shift on Friday to help cover for me. I have the best staff ever!

I've actually spent a lot of time with Big Petey this week. I find I like having a male friend. He's easy to be around, and he likes my pets. He's been teaching Mac biker slang, so yeah, that's been interesting. Mac can now make a sound that is very similar to a Harley. That, I like. Some of the slang, not so much.

I suspect that Big Petey is a bit of a matchmaker too. When we're talking, he casually mentions things Gunner and I have in common. He brings Gunner's name up a lot, and he does seem like he's very fond of him. But he's not the most subtle person. Like, last night over dinner, he said, "Rumor has it that Gunner has not touched a single whore since meeting you."

Like, seriously, how do you respond to that?

"Um, well, wow. Not sure how to respond to that, Petey," I reply.

"No need to. Just wanted to mention that little tidbit," he says.

My thoughts are interrupted when I hear Trudy whisper shout, "Ava! There's a guy here, he says he wants to speak with you, and he says he's your fiancé!"

I raise my eyes to her and see hers are wide open. Trudy is usually pretty calm, cool, and collected but she looks a little freaked out at the moment.

Everyone in the kitchen stops what they're doing and looks in my direction. I straighten up from where I was bent over decorating the cake, set my icing bag down, and look at Trudy.

"He said he's who?" I question.

"Your fiancé," she yells at me, loudly this time.

"You're engaged?" questions Carrie.

"No! This has to be a mistake," I laugh.

I walk through the saloon doors, and I don't see any males in the shop. Then I see just a head pop-up from the other side of one of the glass display cases, and I see a mop of curly hair and brown eyes. Chubs.

"Hi, Chubs," I laugh, walking around the case.

He stands up fully and smiles huge at me.

"How's my future Ol' Lady?"

"She's currently needing a break and a cup of coffee. Do you have time to join me?" I ask.

"Abso-fucking-lutley!"

I step behind the display cases and ask, "What's your pleasure today, Chubs? I'll grab it and some coffee and meet you over there," I say, pointing to a small table next to the bike cake display.

"Surprise me. I'm not fussy," he replies.

I put a selection of bite-size treats, two cookies and a cupcake on a plate, grab two large coffees and head over to the table where Chubs is currently standing while admiring the bike cake.

"Where did you get this?" he asks, pointing to the bike.

"I made it. It's made out of mostly cake, fondant and gum paste. And it rumbles like a real bike. It's my favorite cake that I've ever made," I answer with apparent pride.

"It's a girl's bike," he retorts.

"I'm a girl, Chubs," I laugh.

He sits down and grins at me. Then he notices the selection of treats in front of him and dives into them. After a few minutes, he comes up for air.

"Wow. Not sure what all I just ate, but every bite was fucking awesome! And that bike cake is the shit! The detail on it is amazing, Ava. Do you have a bike?"

"No, I don't. I haven't even ridden on one. But I have a thing for Harleys, and I've looked at a lot of them. I decided I wanted to make one myself, and when I got done, I loved it so much I had a case made for it and put it on display."

"I'd let you ride with me, but I'm pretty sure Gunner would get nasty over that," he chuckles.

"I have no idea why, but he did warn me that I'm not to get on the back of anyone's bike during the cookout. I had asked him for dos and don'ts at the party, and that was a big DON'T from him. I'm taking his word for it since he seemed sincere."

"He was sincere, believe me. But if you want to ride, I'm sure the Prez would give you a ride on his bike," he grins.

"It would be okay for me to ride on his bike, but no one else's?" I try to clarify.

"Yes. He can explain the whys of that to you. He's the Prez."

"Okay. Good to know. Thanks, Chubs."

"No, Ava, thank you. For the snacks and the company. The Prez wanted someone to come here and help you load up your supplies. I volunteered. Who wouldn't want to come where all the food is at?"

Chubs is incorrigible and adorable.

Chapter 8

Gunner

I'm getting irritated standing here in a strip club listening to this whiny bitch when I know Ava is at the clubhouse already. Freddy, an older club member, manages the club-owned strip club, Dreams. I was making my rounds of the various businesses the club owns and got hijacked here listening to Kristy—I think that's her name—whine about the other dancers getting more stage time than her. Normally, Freddy would handle this kind of shit, but he has a soft spot for Kristy, and now I'm playing the bad guy.

"Look, here's the way it is. You dance when you're scheduled to, and that's it. You don't get to choose when or how long. Don't like it, leave. Dancers are a dime a dozen, and you're not special. I don't want to hear about this shit again, or you will bounce on out of here," I growl at her.

"But I'm the best dancer here, and you said you loved it when I did that little thing with my tongue and…"

"Not even sure I know your name or if we ever fucked. And I love all tongue action, so that doesn't make you memorable. You need to get this and get it now—dance the schedule you are given or pack up. I'm done with this conversation."

As I turn to leave, she busts out crying and starts stomping toward the locker room. I glare at Freddy, and he gives me that shit-eating grin of his and salutes as I walk by him. Yeah, he's happy because I dealt with his bullshit.

I prowl outside and swing my leg over my bike. It's a black and chrome H.D. Dyna Super Glide that's been customized. I have floorboard extenders because of my height. T-bar on my handlebars. Anything that can be chromed is on this bike, and it is sharp. I have several bikes, some for long-distance riding, but this bike is my go-to for short runs. I want Ava on this bike wrapped around me soon.

As I ride up the driveway to the clubhouse, I try to see it through Ava's eyes. It was a huge old warehouse that's been updated, remodeled, and turned into a clubhouse. It's set back far enough off the road that it can't be seen until you're halfway up the drive. It's a white cement block building, and it was built to last. It sits on 300 fenced acres, and we like the privacy the extra land gives us. There is a large paved forecourt on the end closest to the main door.

It has a full basement that we use for a gym, storage, and a room at the far back corner that is used for more nefarious things. The basement also contains our arsenal of weapons and a large common room in case of a lockdown.

The ground floor is divided into a large common area with tables, couches, chairs, pool tables, bar, and the kitchen/dining room area. In the back-right corner is the room we hold Church in. It's a large rectangular room with a huge, twelve-seat table in the center and chairs scattered around it and along the edges of the room.

There are stairs in the center of the main room against the back wall that go upstairs to club members' rooms. Off to the left of the staircase is my office.

If you drive across the forecourt and follow the road that goes beyond the clubhouse, you will see several homes, set on five acres each, on both sides of the road. The homes belong to the club members that want to live on the compound. No one has to but most do. My home is the second one on the left.

I pull my bike around the back of the clubhouse to where the kitchen has a back door that leads to the forecourt. I don't see Ava's Camaro, and a jolt of disappointment hits me. But I do see an unfamiliar gunmetal gray SUV and Chubs' bike nearby.

I notice the kitchen door is open, just the screen door closed, and I can hear singing coming from the kitchen. As I walk in the door, I see Ava off to the side, arranging things on a worktable. She has her back to me and is singing softly while shaking her hips and tapping her toes. She's wearing faded jeans and a light blue t-shirt that has crept upwards—a strip of tanned skin is showing above that round ass of hers.

Her hair is pulled up into some messy-looking thing involving a clip, and strands are already falling down around her face. I see the earbuds in her ears and the iPod strapped to her arm and smile. She doesn't notice me standing here, and that's to my advantage. I creep up behind her, lean down and run my tongue along the side of her neck. At the same time I do this, the swinging door that goes to the common area opens, and in walks Axel.

Unfortunately, his entrance distracts me just long enough for Ava to scream and swing her elbow back and up just enough to hit me square in the nose. While I'm reeling backward, she whirls, and pulls her leg back, ready to make me wish I didn't have balls.

Thank God she realizes it's me before she lets that kick fly! The look of shock on her face would be amusing if I could see it clearly through my watering eyes. She rushes forward with one hand over her mouth, and the other gets slammed onto my chest.

"Oh my God! I am soooo sorry! Oh my God! I didn't know it was you!" she's shouting over Axel's laughter.

I'm not sure why, but she's hopping around on her feet and patting at my chest frantically. Then she throws her arms around my waist and hugs me, chin on my chest, looking up at me with wide eyes while apologizing. I'm still dumbfounded that she elbowed me, but I have to admit, her pressed tight to me is fixing all my pain fast.

My concern at this point is that Axel's going to have an aneurysm from laughing so hard. He's doubled over and doesn't appear to be able to get a full breath. He's almost on his knees and is hanging onto a table for support. Okay, so I'm not so much "concerned" as hoping.

I take advantage of the situation, wrap my arms around Ava, and pull her tighter to me. She quiets down and leans into me. I enjoy the moment, lean back, and put my hands on each side of her head. I look down into her eyes and speak quietly.

"Ava, don't ever apologize to me, or anyone else, for protecting yourself. I was fooling around, and I should've thought more about how it would startle you. No harm, no foul. Okay?"

"Okay," she whispers back.

I put my forehead against hers for a moment and then pull back when the door opens, and several brothers come in to see what all the noise is about. Ava doesn't pull away, though, and I like that. She's not embarrassed by them seeing me holding her.

"Holy fuck! I think I pissed myself," laughs Axel, while groping his nuts to see if he's wet down there.

"What the fuck, Gunner? You hurt her?" bellows Petey.

Chubs barrels past those in the doorway, grabs Ava's arm, and pulls her away from me and behind him. He looks at me with a steady gaze. I guess he's loyal, but it's to Ava first, me second.

"Oh, crap. I'm a bit damp down there in the wonderlands," chortles Axel.

"No, guys, no. Gunner didn't hurt me at all. He, um, he startled me, and I swung first and looked to see who it was second," Ava says, looking a little proud and a little embarrassed at the same time.

Everyone stops making noise and looks at Ava and then me.

"You hit the Prez?" questions Petey.

"I wouldn't have if I'd known it was him! I didn't hear him come up behind me!" she exclaims, waving her arms in the air.

"Jesus, fuck, Petey, of course, I didn't hurt her," I grumble.

"Where did you hit him, our little avenging angel Ava?" asks Pooh.

She looks up and gives me big eyes. I don't think she wants to embarrass me by admitting that she got me good, so she's leaving it up to me to explain. I'm not embarrassed in the least. I'm proud as fuck.

"Her classes are paying off. She did great. If she hadn't realized who I was after the elbow, she would have sent my boys into space, and I would have been on the floor," I tell the guys while looking at Ava.

She smiles at me and mouths, "thank you."

"Damn! I wish this shit was on video for our viewing pleasure. The Prez taken out by a tiny, blond baker," says Pooh, smiling huge. "That would be good shit!"

"Hey, let's ask Rex if the security camera in here was recording! If so, make us some popcorn, Ava. We got a fight to watch," laughs Petey.

He turns and hobbles out on his crutches. The other idiots follow him. It's just Ava and me left in the kitchen. She steps closer to me.

"I'm not sorry I didn't hesitate when I thought I was in danger. But I am very sorry it was you I hit and not Axel. He's been itching for a beatdown since I got here. Are you sure you're okay, Gunner? Can I get you anything?"

I walk over to a stool and sit down.

"A kiss would make all my boo-boos go away," I smirk.

She just shakes her head at me.

Because the world hates me, the guys find out the camera was working fine. They have enjoyed watching, and re-watching Ava elbow me. They're having fun, and it's good to see everyone relaxed after a busy week, even if it's at my expense.

Earlier today, I received a phone call from Rex, and he told me what little he could find about Ava. She's 27, soon to be 28, raised in 32 foster homes and orphanages for the first 14 years of her life. And then nothing can be found until she was employed by a restaurant in Bozeman, Montana, at 18 years old. At the same time, she enrolled in college, taking classes in business administration. She's not had it easy, but she's proved she has a strength not many have, to have survived foster care and the system, and to come out doing so well.

I feel a little guilty about having him dig around in her personal business, but she's good at dodging personal questions or re-directing the conversation when I or Petey ask too much. Usually, that means someone has something to hide, but if she does, Rex hasn't uncovered it yet.

One thing Rex found that has been bothering me is that she was admitted to a hospital in Montana, at the age of 23, with serious as shit injuries, and it was all hush-hush. He found a medical chart by hacking the hospital's system, and it was all there was in her file. That in itself isn't right. But he said it looked like the file had been wiped, and this one single chart wasn't wiped well enough, and he retrieved it.

The chart didn't say what the injuries were exactly, but by reading it, you could tell that they were serious, and there were many. Also, it mentioned a head injury and that she was in a coma.

I asked Rex if it was possible she was in a car accident, but he said he doubts that because why would the hospital try to wipe the file for injuries from an accident. It was fishy as hell, and I have to agree with him. He said he checked for accidents in that area around that time frame and came up empty.

I'm sitting at the bar with a beer, but I've positioned myself so I can see Ava moving around in the kitchen through the pass-through window between the kitchen and the dining area. She's a flurry of movement, and her knife skills are impressive. I just watched her chopping vegetables like you see on those old Ninja Knife commercials. She's been at it for about three hours now and hasn't slowed down yet.

I'm a little annoyed with Chubs because he's sitting on a stool in the kitchen chatting her up and keeping her company and has been for hours. Of course, he's not going to leave any time soon because she keeps handing him bite-size pieces of food and waits for his opinion. Like he'll ever say anything negative. If it's not moving, he'll eat it.

I glance around the room and find Petey kicked back in a recliner but smiling my way. He's been shooting grins my direction ever since the elbow incident. I start to get up to go over and give him shit when Ava comes walking out of the kitchen wiping her hands.

"Hey, Gunner. I need to run home real quick and let the pets out to go potty. Is it okay if I leave everything where it is until I get back in about 30 minutes?" she asks.

"Yeah, sure, that's fine. Want some company? I could stand a change of scenery," I say.

"Perfect! You can drive, and I can relax for a few minutes.'"

As we're leaving the kitchen, I tell Chubs to stay out of the food and that we'll be back soon. I'm hoping that's enough to keep him from scarfing everything down.

Ava tosses me her keys; we get into the SUV and pull out.

"So, again, I am sorry that it was you I hit," Ava states.

"No worries, babe. I'll let you make it up to me anytime you want," I grin at her.

She laughs. She has the best laugh.

"So, tell me, Ava, what type of classes do you take that gives you mad skills at taking down MC Presidents?

"I started with basic self-defense classes and kind of got hooked. But those didn't seem to be as well-rounded as I wanted, so I moved on to different martial arts. I'm currently taking Brazilian Jiu Jitsu and Muay Thai, but I've taken kickboxing, Krav Maga, and Judo classes before."

"Holy shit. That's damn cool. But I thought Muay Thai and kickboxing were the same thing," I state.

"No, not really, but they're very similar. I started with kickboxing, but the instructor said one day that Muay Thai allowed low kicks and strikes with elbows and knees. From a self-defense viewpoint, I felt Muay Thai would be better, so I switched."

"What got you started taking the classes?" I ask, hoping I haven't pushed too hard.

She's quiet for a moment and fidgets with her purse strap before saying, "I don't have any family to speak of and thought it would be smart to have some knowledge." She pauses for a moment and then continues, "Ugh, that's not completely true. I had an injury and was going to physical therapy, and the therapist mentioned that it might help me rehab my injuries. And that it would help mentally if I felt like I could protect myself if necessary. When I was well enough, I signed up for the first class."

I can tell that was hard for her to say, and I reach over, grasp her hand and pull it to my thigh. She startles for a moment and then relaxes, leaving her hand there with mine covering hers. I rub my thumb back and forth over the back of her hand, and I am thrilled she's not trying to jerk it away.

We're about five minutes from her place, and I don't want to lose this time with her. We've texted a lot the last week, and we've joked around quite a bit, but we haven't had time alone, and she fascinates me.

"Did taking the classes help?" I question carefully.

"Yes, they helped a lot with building core strength, and they gave me confidence, so that helped mentally. I want to work toward a black belt in some of them, but I'm not concerned with getting one as long as I have the techniques down pat. I just hate having to make the drive to the gym. It's quite a way from here, and I don't always have much time to get there."

"You should talk with Axel then. He manages the club gym, and he's great about finding instructors for whatever members want to try. And the gym is only about ten minutes from your house," I tell her.

"What gym does he manage?" she asks.

"Jax Gym," I answer.

"I drive by that on my way to work. That would be so much more convenient. I'll hit him up about the classes he has available."

We pull into her driveway, and I hate having to let go of her hand. I think she forgot all about it sitting on my thigh, but I certainly didn't.

She exits the vehicle first, and before I can get it shut off and get out, I hear shouting. I quickly climb out, shut the door, and turn toward the voice.

It's Ralph. On her side of the street again and charging toward Ava. He suddenly skids to a stop and looks at me. His eyebrows rise as I walk in his direction.

"Ava, go inside and do what you need to do. I'll deal with Ralph this time," I say, irritated that he continues to harass her.

I half expect her to argue or say that it's her problem to deal with, but she doesn't. She looks at Ralph, tells him, "Good luck, asswipe," and heads inside.

I turn to Ralph and put the meanest look I have on my face. He starts back peddling toward his place, but I stop him when I speak.

"Ava's warned you to stop bothering her and her pets. Petey has warned you, and now I'm going to warn you. And I don't warn someone twice. The next time you say shit to Ava or any of her pets, you will not be found. I'm not joking. That woman deserves to live in peace, and you are going to give that to her. I'll bring down a world of hurt on your scrawny ass before I end you permanently. Have I made myself clear, Ralph? I don't want any confusion on what will happen if this shit continues. Do you understand?"

"Are you threatening me?" he asks, trying to pull the cloak of righteousness around him.

"No. I'm promising you more violence than you can handle."

"You… you can't threaten me. That's not legal and I know my rights," he states while stepping back again toward the street.

"Not threatening, Ralph. Promising. What part of that escapes your fucked-up little brain?"

"That ain't right. Just because you're bigger than me and all that doesn't mean it's right to try to scare me," he foolishly continues.

"Not trying to scare you. I'm educating you, and this conversation has run its course. You bother that woman, and you know the consequences of those actions. Now get on home before I decide to finish this tonight."

I turn and walk to Ava's front door. When I glance back, Ralph is gone from sight. I sigh. You can't fix stupid.

Walking into Ava's house, I see her standing at the back of the house near the sliding doors. She smiles at me and asks, "He still alive or do I need to break out the latex gloves and bleach?"

"He's still breathing, but you may want to keep those items stocked up," I answer.

I walk further into the living room and see Loki and the pig outside in the backyard. I look around, curious about Ava's space, and see the biggest motherfucking cat I have ever seen laying on his back, belly in the air, sleeping on the couch. He's gray with a white belly and paws. He's completely unconcerned with everything going on around him.

"He looks relaxed," I laugh.

"He generally is, but he's the one you never want to piss off," warns Ava. "He can hold a mean grudge."

"Who's he, Mom?" I hear in a comically cartoon-type voice. He sounds like he's been sucking helium.

"This is Gunner. Gunner, meet Mac," says Ava, waving her hand between Mac and I.

I turn and see a large bird standing on a perch near the window. He cocks his head sideways and checks me out.

"Big MoFo," he cackles.

"Mac! Be nice," shouts Ava, irritated.

"He is," insists Mac.

"Yes, he's a big guy, but you don't have to say everything you think. And saying MoFo wasn't necessary," she replies.

"Not a swear," Mac maintains.

"It was implied," Ava says.

I have to laugh at these two. They're like an old married couple bickering back and forth. You can tell this is a daily occurrence.

"Hey, Mac. So, you're the one that keeps Ralph bent out of shape," I interrupt them.

"Ralph sucks donkey dick," states Mac.

I bark out a laugh at the same time Ava screeches, "Mac! Oh my God! Do you need a timeout?"

"No! Mac be good!" he screeches back at her.

"Man, you have got to bring him to the clubhouse someday. The guys will love him!" I laugh.

"Can you imagine what his language would be like after that?" asks Ava. "Petey has not been a good influence as it is, but I can only cringe at what he would be like after spending time around Axel."

Ava opens the slider and in comes Loki and Gee. I've never considered having a pig as a pet, but I have to admit he is a cute little bugger with his reddish and black spots. He rushes in the door and runs straight to a box in the corner of the living room, sliding to a stop and bouncing off the box a little.

Loki walks over to me and bumps my hand with his head. I lean down and give him a good head rub. He's a beautiful dog. The club raises and sells some pitties and shepherds for protection services, and I know Reno is going to love Loki.

Reno is the brother that raises and trains the pups. He's an odd man but has a soft spot for all animals. He's very fussy about who buys our dogs too. He has Rex check out all their backgrounds and credentials. And he insists on meeting with the buyers personally. Usually more than once. And he does follow-ups to be sure that the dogs are being well treated. The whole club supports him on this because we've, on more than one occasion, taken it upon ourselves to shut down dog fighting rings. It's not something we'll tolerate on our turf.

Gee waddles over to me, carrying what appears to be a shirt in his mouth. He drops it at my feet and stares up at me, obviously expecting something. I look at Ava questioningly, and she laughs softly.

"He wants you to put his pajamas on him. He doesn't realize he's a pig and expects to be treated like a human child. I'll do the honors," Ava informs me as she walks over to me and Gee.

Ava drops to her knees next to my thigh, and Gee instantly rolls to his back. She picks up his pajamas and wiggles them over his head, sticking his front legs through the armholes. She tugs the shirt down his belly until it reaches his hind legs. He rolls over, gets up and shakes himself, and then trots off to the rug near the couch and lies down. I notice that on the back of his shirt is a picture of a sleeping piglet.

Ava, still on her knees next to me, looks up and meets my eyes, and smiles. And I am instantly hard seeing her where she is with her perfect mouth so close to where I really need it to be. I reach down, grab her hand, and pull her up off the floor. When she's standing, I use her hand to pull her into me. I place my other hand on her hip and pull her front to my front.

Her gorgeous green eyes meet mine. I release her hand and cup her jaw. She's right where I've needed her to be for a while now.

"You're so beautiful," I say quietly.

Her eyes widen slightly, but she doesn't move. I lean down slowly until our lips are barely touching and tell her, "I'm going to kiss you now because I've been waiting awhile to get this chance."

I pull her tighter to me as I claim her mouth. I kiss her soft at first, and then my tongue traces her full lips before I push it into her warm, wet mouth. The kiss turns hard and demanding.

I feel her arms as they slip around my waist, and her hands lay flat against my lower back. I place both hands on her face, cupping it, and continue the kiss.

It's hot, it's deep, and it's affecting me in all the right ways. This is where she should always be. Hands on me, mouth at my mercy. My cock is harder than hell and wants his chance at her wet warmth.

I change the angle of our kiss and move my hands to her neck, placing one on each side. She moans low and long and moves her hands lower, nearly on my ass. She's feisty and takes what she needs. I love it.

I pull my head back a few inches and wait until she opens her eyes. I tell her in a low tone, "I want you. It's not going to happen now, but it is going to be soon. I can wait until I know you're ready for this, but it's going to happen, and you need to get your head wrapped around that fact. I need to be inside you. I need your body naked and wrapped around mine." Then I slam my mouth back down on hers before she can respond.

She stiffens for a moment, and I fear I may have scared her too much, too fast. But after a short breath of time, she relaxes against me and responds to the kiss again. Her hands slide up my back, and her mouth starts fighting mine for control. She pushes her tongue into my mouth and explores. I just jumped a few notches on the hardness scale.

I pull the clip from her hair and toss it aside, not caring where it lands. Then I'm running my hands through her hair. It's so soft and thick. I can't get enough, and I know I need to stop soon, or I will for sure scare her off.

As I'm fighting to slow myself down, she leans back, pulling her mouth from mine.

"You are beautiful too, Gunner," she whispers. "And I can't believe it's me you're kissing, but I'm not sure if I'm ready for more than this."

Her eyes turn sad, and she slowly pulls away.

"I'll be here when you're ready, honey," I reply, regretfully letting her pull away.

"Maybe we should be heading back to the clubhouse so I can finish up for tonight," she replies.

"Okay, babe, we'll head back. No pressure. But I'm not going away, just so you know," I state.

"Hot kiss, MoFo," hollers Mac.

"Glad you approve, Mac," I laugh. He has effectively broken the tension.

Lola Wright

Chapter 9

Ava

The ride back to the clubhouse was quiet but not strained. It was a comfortable silence, and I didn't pull back when Gunner grabbed my hand and put it on his thigh once we were back in the SUV.

As I got back to work in the kitchen, Gunner placed a soft kiss on my temple and proceeded into the main room to hang with his brethren. That left me with work to do and a lot of things to think about.

I know I'm attracted to Gunner. You'd have to be a nun not to be, and they probably still would be, but would never admit to it. He's very tall, built, and simply drop-dead gorgeous. He's also kind and sweet and protective. But he's still a man and a club president and has beautiful women around him at all times.

How faithful can someone like that be to one woman? Is it possible? Am I judging him unfairly? And why would he want someone like me? I'm average at best with a whole load of baggage.

I've had a few boyfriends over the years, but I've never been in love. And I'm apparently easy to cheat on because it's happened in the past. I was angry when I found out but never heartbroken. And I'm worried that with Gunner, things would be very different, and I could be heartbroken.

As my hands fly about getting things done, my brain is working overtime with all things Gunner. I wish I had someone I was close enough with to ask advice. I've always kept a small distance between myself and others because I learned in foster care, it was easier that way. Us kids were moved around so much it was better not to become too attached to anyone. Now it's biting me in the ass.

I glance at the clock and realize it's time to eat something. so I start making a quick dinner. Being a type 2 diabetic from such a young age, I've learned to pay attention to my body's warning signs. It's not easy being a baker and a diabetic, but I make it work.

After making some French Dip subs, au jus, and homemade potato chips, I assemble a few plates. I grab one and walk out to the bar where the prospect bartending hands me a beer, and I look around until I spot Petey. He's sitting in his favorite chair watching a ball game on the huge-ass TV hung on the wall.

As I'm making my way toward Petey, I see movement off to my left and glance that way. Gunner's sitting on a couch with his feet up on a coffee table with Pooh sitting on the other end in the same position. The two men are looking at each other, laughing about something, and a semi-naked black-haired woman is swinging her leg over Gunner's legs, and she sits down, straddling him. She's not wearing a top and only has on a G-string for bottoms.

Gunner's right hand comes up, just above the G-string, and rests on her lower back as she gets comfortable. He continues talking and laughing with Pooh.

A stab of disappointment hits me hard. We were just kissing an hour ago, and now he's casually letting a semi-naked woman straddle him. I realize then that it was best I saw this, so I didn't let myself get in any deeper with him.

I straighten my spine, put a small smile on my face, and walk up next to Petey's chair. I place the food and drink on the table next to him as he looks up at me.

"Hey, I had to eat something, so I thought I'd make sure you did too," I say.

"Darlin', you don't need to feed me all the time. But I'm sure as hell glad you think you do," he laughs at me.

I lean down and give him a kiss on the cheek and turn for the kitchen. I keep my eyes straight ahead because I refuse to give anyone the chance to think I'm jealous of Gunner's whore. I may feel gutted, but I have no right to feel that way. We're not a couple. He said he wanted me, not that he wanted me forever. I should've realized what he meant and not read more into it. Just because I'm not a one-night stand kind of person doesn't mean he isn't. Or that I'm right and he's wrong. I just read too much into his saying he wanted me. My mistake, not his.

Now that I realize what his goal was, I can deal with that mentally. His type of "relationship" is not my cup of tea, and it's best we just stay friendly. But damn, what a shame because he lit me up like nobody has ever done before.

I feel someone come up beside me, and I turn towards them. It's Axel, and I know this isn't going to end well. I just wanted to escape back to the kitchen, and he's not going to let that happen.

"Once again, woman, why does he get food and a kiss, and I'm left out in the cold?" he loudly asks. The schmuck is smiling ear to ear.

I feel all eyes turn our direction, but I keep mine on Axel only.

"Because Petey is hot," I say, knowing that will get a rise out of Axel.

"I'm hot," he declares, puffing his chest out. He's such a goof.

"But Petey is manly-hot," I goad. The chuckles are starting up, and since there are a lot more people, club brothers and club sluts, than there were before, it's getting loud.

"Oh shit, woman! I'm very manly-hot! I'm the manliest of hot!" he replies, louder than ever.

"Well, you could be if you weren't sporting those moobs," I say, grinning at him and pointing to his pecs.

He looks down at himself and then back at me, confused.

"Moobs? What the fuck are moobs?" he asks.

"Those man boobs you're carrying around, Hoss," I grin at him.

"Fuck! Those are hard-earned pecs, witch! Not moobs," he snorts.

"I call bullshit. If they're bigger than mine, I consider them moobs. But hey, whatever helps you sleep at night, girlfriend," I wink at him.

I start to walk away, but he quickly pulls his shirt up, showing off those fabulous pecs. He is something to see and definitely spank material. But I can't let him know I think that.

He's flexing his pecs at me as I reach for them, but he jumps back and slams both hands over his nipples.

"You got me once but not again, woman!" he says.

I lean into him and pull his head down to my mouth, and whisper in his ear.

"I will admit you do have the best moobs in the room, but I will get you again when you least expect it. And if you're hungry, and you admit they're not manly pecs, I'll feed you."

He pulls back an inch or two, looks in my eyes, and declares loudly, "I have the hottest moobs in the world! Feed me, woman!"

I laugh as he follows me into the kitchen.

Lola Wright

Chapter 10

Gunner

Fucking shit balls! I wasn't paying attention and was laughing at Pooh when Katey straddled me. I'm so used to the girls rubbing up against us brothers or climbing in our laps, I barely registered that she'd done that. I realized what had happened at the same moment I saw Ava in the room. I promptly picked Katey up by the waist and moved her toward Pooh, but Ava never looked in my direction.

Now I'm sitting here wondering if Ava saw Katey all over me or not. Do I say something to Ava? How do I even bring up that subject? What if she hadn't seen it, and I say something about it? I don't want her getting the idea that our kiss meant nothing to me, but I don't want to start a fight if she never noticed Katey. Well, shit, what's a man to do?

I look toward Petey and see he's glaring in my direction. He's become very fond of Ava and would love to see us become a couple, but at the moment, I'm sure he's rethinking that thought. He's already told me that he doesn't think I'm good enough for her but that he'd rather see her with me than someone outside of the club. And this is coming from a guy who's been like a father to me since my parents were killed in a car accident several years ago.

He gets up out of his chair, grabs his crutches, and stomps off toward the kitchen. And to make matters worse, I see Chubs and Rex giving me the same look as they follow him.

I turn to Katey and I growl at her, "Don't pull that shit again. Let the other women know it too. I don't want you all crawling on me or even in my space."

I've already had this chat with her, but she's a determined one and the ringleader of the club sluts. I get up and stomp off to my room to get away and think for a while.

I didn't realize at the time that my disappearing would look worse to Ava when she later noticed both Katey and I missing from the main room.

I spend a restless night in my clubhouse room, not even having the energy to ride to my house. I shouldn't have escaped and faced things down like I normally would have done. But I am finding that I don't react the same to Ava as I do everything else in my world. I know she needs to be handled with care. And that's not something I've ever had to do before. I usually just bulldoze through obstacles to get my way.

Ava isn't the kind of woman you spend a night with and get up and leave, never looking back. She's the type you build something with. And that's not something I've ever thought about doing before. But now I am. I want to build something with Ava. And I know that's crazy as hell since I don't know her that well. But it just is. And I find I'm not freaked out by it but looking forward to getting to know her better and seeing her face every day.

And knowing this, I know I have to speak with her about last night and Katey. If she did see it, I want her to know that it wasn't wanted and wasn't acceptable. I'll find a way to speak with her about it one way or another.

I know that Ava will be here early today to get most of the cooking out of the way for the poker run tomorrow. I'll find time today to spend with her and have a chat. I'm not sure what time she'll be here, but I need to get a move on so I can get some club business done beforehand.

I jump in the shower, dress, and head to the kitchen for a cup of coffee to start my day.

As I arrive outside the kitchen door, I have to wait a step because Katey is trying to enter it also. I notice her hair is wet, so she must have spent the night here with one of the brothers. I nod to her as we hit the swinging door.

I see Ava at the counter pouring coffee for Petey and Pooh at the same time as her eyes glance my way. She looks at Katey then me right behind her. Her eyes rove from my hair to Katey's hair and then back down to the mug she's filling. Not an ounce of expression on her face. Nothing at all.

This isn't looking good. This is bad. Very bad. I may be sunk before I even get onboard.

Without looking up, she states, "Want coffee, grab a mug."

Turning to Petey, she goes on to say, "Want some cinnamon rolls? They're fresh from the bakery. I stopped there on my way here to pick up a few things and snatched some for you."

"Yes, darlin' please," replies Petey in a bland tone while glaring daggers at me. If looks could kill… well, you know.

"Oh, those look great! Get me one too and a coffee. Three creams, one sugar," demands Katey in her annoying whiny voice while plopping down on a stool.

Before I can say anything, Ava replies to Katey, "I'm here to cook for the poker run. I'm not your waitress. The coffee and rolls are right here. Want some, get up and get them."

"You're the caterer, so cater," snips Katey. And then goes on to say, "You served Petey, you can serve me."

"Petey is injured, my neighbor, and my friend. You are none of those things. You want coffee and a roll then get off your back—sorry, I mean ass—and get it yourself," Ava replies, once again with no inflection in her voice.

Pooh chokes on his coffee and covers his laugh with a cough.

Katey screeches, "You bitch!" as she scrambles off her stool and stalks toward the coffee and rolls—and Ava.

I know I should intervene, but I really want to see how Ava handles this herself. If she is to become my woman, and she is, then she needs to make her own way in some things concerning the club. And Katey is known for testing the limits with anyone that is new.

Ava turns to face Katey as she stomps her way.

"You are nobody here! You do as you're told! Your job is to cater, which means serve, so get to serving!" snarls Katey, leaning into Ava's face.

"My job is to cook for the poker run. Not serve coffee and rolls to sluts, cunts, and wannabe women. Want some, get it. Now, get out of my face," replies Ava, once again as calm as can be.

Katey makes a sudden grab for Ava, and Ava catches her wrist before it gets to her. Holding Katey's arm in between them, Ava calmly states while looking Katey in the eye, "It's only fair to warn you before you do something stupid that I don't fight like a girl. I don't pull hair and scratch and scream. I punch, strike, and go for the most damage possible. I'd end up fucking up your face so bad you wouldn't be able to suck cock unless you can do it through a straw. I'll fuck you up worse than polio if you so much as lay a finger on me. Nobody touches me. Nobody hits me anymore without feeling a shit ton of pain."

Pooh once again chokes on his coffee, only this time he wheezes through it to spout, "And here comes a chubby!"

Ava pushes Katey's arm away from her and releases it.

Katey hesitates. You can see her trying to decide if Ava is full of shit or not. Katey's known for loving a good fight, so this will be interesting. She's also used to intimidating the other women and usually gets her way.

I notice we have a few extra bodies in the kitchen now, and everyone except Ava appears to be holding their breath, waiting to see how this turns out. Ava is very calmly staring directly at Katey.

Petey speaks up and shocks the shit out of me when he goads Katey by saying, "What's up, Katey? Found someone who doesn't back down from you? You know the smart thing to do would be to tuck your tail and leave, right?"

That's all it takes to make up Katey's mind, and she lunges at Ava, grabbing for her hair and screeching at the top of her lungs. Ava sidesteps easily, throws up her arm to block Katey's, and lands a hard punch over the top of Katey's arms to her cheekbone. When Katey stumbles back half a step, Ava grabs the back of Katey's head with both hands and slams her face down onto her rising knee. There's a loud crack and a scream from Katey, but Ava is merciless. She pulls Katey's head back up, slides to the side, and re-slams Katey's face into the worktable. Katey melts to the floor at this point.

Ava isn't even breathing hard. She's still as calm as she was before Katey rushed her.

Petey leans over the table and looks down at the bloody mess that is now Katey's face, and says, "That's going to leave a mark."

Ava looks up and points her eyes at Chubs and says, "Would you please take the trash out, so I can get back to work? There seems to be a slutty shit pile laying in my way."

Not one person says a word. We're all just staring at her. Chubs walks over to her and says reverently, "Chubs loves Ava!"

Ava smiles warmly at him and gives his cheek a pat, and he then bends down and throws Katey over his shoulder and walks out with her.

Ava turns back to her worktable and asks, "So, anyone want coffee and rolls?"

Walking back into the kitchen later, I'm happy to see Ava is alone for once. She's busy rolling out some kind of pastry crust, and there are pots and pans cooking and bubbling on the stove. It smells amazing in here.

"Can you take a break for a minute, Ava? We need to talk."

She raises just her eyes to me, hesitates a moment, then says, "Fine. Talk."

Okay, so now I'm a little nervous because anytime a woman says the word "fine," every smart man knows that means nothing is really "fine."

Ava stops what she's doing, wipes the back of her arm over her forehead, picks up a bottle of water, and sips from it while staring at me, waiting patiently.

When I still don't say anything, she speaks up, "You have a problem with what went down with Katey?"

"Uh no, that's not it. Though you did leave her with a broken nose and two loose teeth."

"She was warned. That was me being nice. I don't make a habit of warning people ahead of time, but I was making an effort at being respectful of club property."

There is absolutely no inflection in her voice. I can't tell if she's mad, happy, or just stating facts. She has the best poker face I've ever seen before.

"Be that as it may, she asked for what she received. I don't expect you to take shit off of anyone here. But that's not what we need to speak about."

Her eyebrows rise slightly, and she waves her hand at me in a "get on with it then" motion.

"Katey and I are not a couple. We're not…"

"I get that. You don't have to explain the workings of club slut and club president or even club member," she interrupts to say. "It's none of my business, and I don't need it to be my business. You're a big boy and live your life according to the rules you are comfortable with, as I do. But I'm not sure why you are bringing this up?"

"I'm bringing it up because I didn't want you to get the wrong impression last night," I answer.

"If I did get the wrong impression, it was quickly cleared up when she mounted you half-naked an hour after you and I, well, we uh… it's cool, Gunner. We're very different people who have different goals in life. That doesn't make me right or you wrong. It's just the way it is. No worries. I'm clear on what you want and what I need. They don't mix. We need to friend zone each other and move on."

"Wait. You don't understand what I'm saying," I blurt.

She's now looking at me like I'm a bit slow.

"I told you last night that I want you. And I do. Not for just a night. I want to see where things could go with us. I'm serious about that, honey," I say.

"Sorry, Gunner, but that's a bit hard to believe considering we were making out one hour and the next you have your arm around a half-naked slut grinding on your lap, you both disappear from the room at the same time, and then enter the kitchen early the next morning, once again together, both with wet hair. I may not be very experienced, but this blond hair doesn't mean I'm stupid," she snorts at me.

She looks a little pissed, and I realize she is getting angry thinking I'm trying to play her.

"Look, we don't hardly even know each other. Hell, I don't even know your real name. This"—she points from me to her—"hasn't even become a 'this' yet, and it's probably best that it doesn't. I cook and serve the meal tomorrow, and then I go back to my safe little life, and you continue on with yours however you see fit. No hard feelings," she states.

"Michael Walker. My parents were great parents, and I had an awesome childhood. I grew up in the club; my dad was the president; Petey was the VP; my mom was the best Ol' Lady ever. I'm thirty-three years old, and Axel was raised with me, close as real brothers. When my parents were killed in a car accident eight years ago, Petey stepped down as the VP because he said he couldn't do it without my dad. They were tight as hell. Petey was also going through a mean and messy divorce and had too much shit going on to handle the club too. So, the brothers voted me in, and I asked Axel to be my VP. It's been a hard uphill climb, but we're happy, and we work hard."

I stop for a moment and take a few breaths. She hasn't said anything, but she hasn't run out of the room yet either. I take that as a good sign.

I continue tossing information at her, but a little calmer than before.

"I was an only child. I've never been in a serious relationship. Not once. Never wanted to be, but now I think I do want to try one. With you. I don't know why because you're right, we don't know each other that well, but that doesn't seem to matter to me. I want you to try one too. With me. I can't make promises that we'll be together forever and never have a bump in the road, but I can promise I will try damn hard to make us work, be faithful, and treat you with respect. If it doesn't work out, I'll tell you to your face and not just let things go bad."

"I know that shit last night looked like I was just aiming for a one-night fuck with you, but that's not true. I didn't leave the room with Katey. I went to my room, angry and confused and just needing some space. I should have spoken with you then, but I fucked up. I will fuck up in the future too, but I will never lie to you, and I will never cheat on you. I don't know where Katey spent the night because I don't keep track of who the brothers are fucking. I swear to you, I was not with her. She's clingy and determined to be someone's Ol' Lady, but she will never be mine.

When I run out of things to say, she is still staring at me, but I can tell she was listening intently. There is hope for me yet.

"So, you're saying you want us to be an 'us'?" Ava questions, eyebrows raised.

"Yes, that's what I'm saying, and yes, it's a little surprising to me too, but I want just that," I reply firmly.

"We've never even been on a date," she states skeptically.

"I've never been on a date, period. But if you want a date, we'll go on dates."

"Would you ever raise your hand to me?" she asks.

"Jesus, fuck no, never!" I shout.

"And you can look me in the eye and promise you'd never cheat? Because men cheat and especially ones who have naked women sitting in their laps and offering anything they desire," she challenges me.

"Baby, I've grown up with naked women sitting in my lap. It's old news. I want something real and someone who's there for me, not whichever brother gives them attention. I'm tired of knowing that every single woman I've fucked has also been with half my brothers."

She walks slowly towards me and stops when she's directly in front of me with only an inch separating us. She tilts her head back and looks me in the eye.

I'm dying to touch her, but I know this moment is important to her and for us.

"Why me, Gunner? I'm not looking for empty compliments. I want to understand why a ten would want a five? It does not compute in my brain," she asks very quietly.

"A ten and a five? What the fuck, Ava? Does your mirror not work like others do?" I am dumbfounded that she doesn't see what the world sees when they look at her.

I see her eyes start to narrow, so I go on to say, "Numbers don't matter. You're real, and regardless how you see yourself, you're gorgeous to me. Down to the bone. No fakeness, no bullshit. I like you. Who you are and how you look. A lot."

"I'm not sure I know how to have a healthy relationship. I've not had many examples," she mumbles more to herself than to me.

"We can learn together. My parents had a great one, so I do have an example," I whisper.

"I'm scared to rush into this and then regret it later. Sex hasn't always been a good thing for me. You're beyond experienced, and I have very little good experience with sex. How the hell am I supposed to compare to the women you've been with before. Fuck, Gunner, they're pros, and I'm barely an amateur," she says worriedly.

I can tell she's starting to get panicked, and all I want is for her to stay calm and realize that her lack of experience is a huge part of the draw for me.

"Baby, calm. You just be you. That's what I want. You! I don't want experienced moves. I want heartfelt ones from someone who wants to be with *me*, not the club president. I want someone who isn't going through the motions but actually feels passionate towards me as a man. Their man."

She thinks about that for a moment and then shocks me with how quickly she sorts through her doubts and places her trust in me. Trust I never want to break.

"You better kiss me then, and do it like you mean it, before I get up the courage to walk away like I should," she whispers back in a determined voice.

My mouth slams down on hers. I don't need to be told twice. I'm all over her in a second's time. I grab her by the waist, set her on the table, and move between her legs pushing them wide enough to accommodate my body. I pull her tight up against me, and I know she can feel me getting hard. She runs her hands up my chest and grabs onto my t-shirt.

She's just as aggressive as I am at getting what she wants. She kisses me back just as hard and takes as good as she gets. She's not timid, and even though she said she's not very experienced, she has a naturally talented mouth.

Things are getting hot, and I'm thinking about picking her up and heading for my room when we are interrupted.

The door swings open and in walks Axel and Pooh. Huge smiles on both their faces as I pull my mouth from Ava's and glare in their direction.

"Axel, I swear to God, if you don't get the fuck out, I'm going to hurt you," growls Ava.

"Okay, okay, little sister, we'll leave. No need for violence. But FYI, I'm not eating whatever your ass is sitting on," laughs Axel, holding his hands up and backing out the door.

Lola Wright

Chapter 11

Ava

After Axel and Pooh left the kitchen, Gunner was called away on some club business. We didn't get a chance to finish our conversation or make-out session. I'm back to work on making appetizers for the party tomorrow, and I'm making great progress.

I notice out the back window of the kitchen that several of the members are setting up picnic tables, long tables for the food, and setting up an area for a band. Others are tinkering with their bikes in preparation for the poker run. I see Gunner chatting with his brothers, and the relaxed look on his face looks good. He smiles easily and jokes around with the other men. They're all looking like they enjoy their time together.

I'm bent over a worktable piping filling into hollowed-out cherry tomatoes when I hear the back door open. I look up to see a short, wiry guy about forty-five years old saunter in and stop to stare back at me. He's about my height, 5'8", with long gray and brown hair that's been pulled back in a ponytail. He's got a few days scruff on his face and the usual biker gear of jeans, boots, t-shirt, and black leather cut. A patch reads Reno.

"You Ava?" he asks in a gruff voice.

"Yep, that's me," I answer while setting down the piping bag and wiping my right hand on my apron.

"I'm Reno," he responds, reaching out his hand and gently shaking mine.

"Hi, Reno. Can I help you with something?"

"Gunner said you own a dog I would like to meet. Not sure why, but he said to ask you about him."

"Loki. He's a Native American dog. He's beautiful, and I've had him for almost four years now. He's big and furry and lovable unless he needs to not be lovable. Then he's a force to reckon with at about 190 pounds," I tell him.

"No shit. A Native American dog? I haven't seen many of them over the years. Beautiful dogs. Smart too. I raise dogs for the club. Sell them for protection services. I also work at the club's garage and tow service. But the dogs are my babies," he says.

"Do you train the dogs before selling them?"

"Yeah, I do. None are sold before they're at least two years old. I don't like to rush them," answers Reno.

"Oh God, I would love for you to meet Loki. I trained him, but I've never trained a dog before, and I had no idea what I was doing. I researched training online, read books, and watched videos, but I have no idea if I did things the right way. Would you be willing to meet him someday and assess how I did and what needs to be changed?" I ask, on the verge of begging.

"Hell yeah, I'd be happy to. Petey seems pretty attached to him and mentions him a lot, so he must be well-behaved. Sounds like you did a good job with him, but I can watch you put him through his training and see if there is anything that can be improved upon," he agrees.

"That would be awesome! Thank you, Reno."

The back door opens again, and Gunner strolls in, lightly punching Reno in the shoulder on his way past. Eyes to me, he walks straight up into my face, bends down so we're on eye level, and brushes a light, sweet kiss on my lips. He straightens turns back to face Reno while slinging his arm over my shoulders and pulling my front to his side.

I place my left hand on his stomach and relax against him. Gunner is so big and so solid that it's very comforting to have him wrapped around me. I watch as he leans against the table, reaches down, and pops a stuffed tomato in his mouth. He chews, looks down at me, and winks.

"Did I overhear that you're going to evaluate Loki for Ava?" asks Gunner, directing his question to Reno.

Gunner swipes another tomato as Reno answers in the affirmative.

"You're going to love him. You might want to get on Ava's good side if you get ideas of breeding Loki to some of your bitches, though. He's bonded tight with her," says Gunner.

Reno steps forward and swipes a tomato nodding his head at Gunner.

After swallowing, Reno looks at me with a surprised look on his face.

"Fuck! Those are good! What the hell's in those?" he asks me.

"Mayo, cream cheese, seasonings, green onion, bits of lettuce, and lots of bacon," I answer.

"The ones I had before had a tuna taste to them. Much better this way. Hope you're making plenty," laughs Reno.

"I've fed Chubs a few times now, so I know enough to make plenty, and then even more, of everything," I smile at Reno.

"Chubs loves his food," chuckles Reno.

He looks at me carefully and then says, "Why do you look familiar to me? Have we met before?"

"Not that I can remember. Have you been in Sweet Angel Treats before?" I ask.

"No, I haven't. I will be now that I know you do the baking there, though," he laughs.

I smile in response, but I don't see anything familiar about him.

Once again, the back door swings open and in walks a person I do know, though. Chris Hagen. I know him from a band he plays in at a local bar called Splash. He looks up and stops with a shocked look on his face when he sees me standing snuggled up to Gunner. Something crosses his face, but it's gone quickly. I can tell by the way Gunner stiffens that he saw it also.

"Hey, Ava. What're you doing here? Are you signing up to be a club girl now?" he asks with a snipe to his voice.

"No, Chris. I'm catering the cookout. Is that a problem?" I snipe back.

Gunner and Reno both have the same look on their faces. Confusion, but also a bit irritated, and that irritation is directed at Chris.

"Oh fuck! Now I know why you look familiar!" exclaims Reno. "You've sung with Chris and his band before. That's where I recognize you from. Splash."

"Yeah, a couple of times she has, but she's too good for us to actually join the band," replies Chris.

"I have never said, or implied, I was too good for the band, Chris, and you know that. I have said several times that I don't want to be in a band, and I'm too busy for that kind of a commitment. But you don't listen to what you don't want to hear. Not my problem if it hasn't sunk in yet," I spit back at him while leaning toward him.

Gunner keeps his arm wrapped around my shoulders and gently pulls me back to his side.

"You sing?" questions Gunner while looking at me.

"I do. Yes, I can. But it's not something I like doing in front of crowds unless it's for survival, so I don't do it much anymore. I don't have to because the bakery is doing great, and I don't need money from performing to buy food or cover rent. But I have filled in before when the lead singer in Chris's band couldn't sing. I met Chris and the band at a karaoke bar after I'd had one shot of Jack too many and sang," I mumble.

"If she doesn't want to join the band, then why the attitude Chris?" asks Reno.

"Because we get huge crowds when our social media sites announce she'll be singing with us. She's good, and we need her to get better gigs and go somewhere with our music instead of just staying stagnant here in Denver," he grumbles.

"That's not true, Chris. You guys just need to get your shit together. You want to party like rock stars before you've become rock stars. Suck it up, work harder, and make your own way. Then, when you get to where you want to be, party as much as you want to. Nobody can hand you success. It's earned through hard work, but you all want to skip that part," I respond to Chris.

"That's easy for you to say. You have the contacts and the inside track, but you won't put yourself out there to help anyone, you bitch!" he bellows at me.

Gunner instantly lets go of me and steps into Chris's face. Right up tight to his face.

Chris looks up, a bit leery of having all that is Gunner scowling down at him.

"Do not EVER call her that again, you little shit! You will live to regret it if you make that mistake again," Gunner growls low.

Chris puts up his hands in a placating manner and steps back from Gunner.

"Sorry, man, I shouldn't have said that. Won't happen again."

Gunner steps back to my side, but he hasn't softened in the least. He's angry, and I shouldn't, but I feel a little warmth of happiness to know that he was so quick to defend me. I think I might like it a little too much.

"So, if I understand this correctly, you expect Ava to fix your band's problems and make you all-stars instead of putting in the work yourself. And you're mad at her because she sees the problems and doesn't want to risk her reputation for a group of guys who won't appreciate it anyway," states Reno while looking at Chris.

"I shouldn't have lectured you, Chris," I speak up, trying to calm the situation.

"Actually, it sounds like you told him exactly what he needs to hear, Ava. The same kind of shit his mom and I tell him," says Reno.

"Uh, what?" I ask, confused.

Reno chuckles and informs me, "His mom is my Ol' Lady. Chris is my stepson."

Chris won't meet my eyes, and I don't care. His band wants to show up late for gigs, be high and drunk while playing, forgetting lyrics, messing up notes, and yet think that just natural talent will get them stardom. It won't. It takes hard work and long hours of practice and being a responsible adult. And not one guy in that band wants to do all that.

"What-the fuck-ever, I gotta get going. Shit to do. See you tomorrow, Reno," says Chris while heading back out the door.

"Yeah, I have to get a move on too. Sorry about that, Ava. He's always been a pain in the ass, and just so you know, his mom still treats him like he's five years old, so don't be surprised if she's not your biggest fan if he's on his way to cry to her," states Reno, looking aggrieved.

"No worries, Reno. Sorry about the drama," I say back to him, smiling.

He waves low and walks out the door.

Gunner turns me by my shoulders until we're facing each other and says, "Has he caused you any problems other than being a cry baby?"

"Nothing I can't handle."

"So, the answer is yes, he has. What kind of problems, Ava?"

"He has quick and determined hands. He has an ego much bigger than his actual appeal. But like I said, it has never been anything I couldn't handle."

"If it becomes something you can't handle or something you don't want to handle, you tell me. No hesitation. Reno would never tolerate him being disrespectful to a woman, but especially to my woman, and neither will I. Okay, babe?"

"Okay, honey," I answer quietly.

I suddenly find my feet off the floor. I throw my arms around Gunner's neck, legs around his waist, and I hold on tight while we head to the nearest wall. My back meets the wall and Gunner's mouth hits my neck right below my ear. It's hot and wet and doing crazy shit to my stomach.

"I know you're nervous about there being an 'us,' and I understand your reasons, babe. But we're going to do this at your pace. What you're comfortable with. Each step we take will be when you're ready to take that next step. And FYI, in case you haven't noticed, I love hearing you call me honey," says Gunner quietly in my ear while pushing his hard lower half into my most sensitive place.

"Okay, Gunner. And thank you for saying something when he called me a bitch."

He pulls his head back and places his forehead against mine while saying, "I will always say something. You are mine. Mine to care for, mine to protect. And thank you for letting me do that when I need to, baby girl."

He kisses me then, and it's just as belly twirling as the others we've shared.

"And I will be hearing you sing. I have no problem pushing shots of Jack at you until you do," Gunner chuckles.

After a quick trip home to check on my babies, I'm almost finished prepping and cooking for the day. I go to check on Petey and make sure he has everything he needs. He'll be keeping me company tomorrow since he can't ride in the poker run.

There are a lot of people hanging out in the main room and around the bar, but I don't see Gunner, so I sit down next to Petey. He looks tired and a little cranky. I know he's frustrated about not being able to ride yet.

"Hey, Petey," I say while leaning back in the chair and sipping from my diet Coke.

"Hey, darlin'. You doing okay? You've been working damn hard the last few days. You ready for tomorrow?" he asks.

"Yeah, I'm ready. I have a lot to do tomorrow yet, but I'm as ready as I can get."

"Where's your mind at about Gunner?"

"Being honest, Petey, I'm nervous. I'm not good at letting people get too close, and he's not going to let me keep him at a distance. He's being very understanding about that, though," I say thoughtfully.

"He's good people. Be honest with him, and he'll listen to you. And if you ever need an ear or a shoulder, I have two of each," he smiles at me.

"Thank you. I'm sure I'll be in need of both at some point," I laugh.

"I can tell you from experience, hon, don't let things fester. Don't sit on something that's bothering you. Speak up."

Petey continues quietly educating me. "Gunner is a hard man. He's had to be and especially since his parents passed. But he's fair. He cares strongly for the club and takes his responsibilities seriously. He needs a strong woman that can take his burdens off his shoulders sometimes. Someone he can rely on and knows is always in his corner. He needs that kind of loyalty and trust in the woman at his side, and he's always been smart enough to know that he wouldn't find that in one of these women," he says, waving his hand around the room.

"I think I want to try and be that woman. And I understand what you mean about these women. They've chosen a different path than I ever would, but I'm unsure if I am the best choice for Gunner. I have my own baggage. Gunner has so much responsibility now, I'm not sure he needs to take on more that comes with someone like me."

"That's just nerves talking, honey. Gunner has very large shoulders and an even larger heart. He needs to feel needed. He likes taking care of people. That's why he was the perfect choice as President. But from you, he needs your strength, but also your softness. He wants to take care of you, so you need to let him do that when he feels he needs to. You'll find a balance. Just be honest with him about the things that make you nervous or worried. He'll listen. He won't judge."

"Thank you, Petey. This has helped calm my overactive brain," I say.

"Always here for you, girl. Always here," he replies while patting my hand.

I spot Gunner heading in our direction, and he takes my breath away. He's just too gorgeous to be real. I'm in awe that someone like him would look twice at me, but I'm too selfish to warn him off. I want him. I want him to be mine, and I want to know what it's like to be cared for and protected. I also want him naked and not knowing the word "no" for a week, but that will have to wait for now.

Gunner stops in front of me while staring down at me with a small smirk on his face and massive arms crossed over his chest, he asks Petey, "You trying to steal my woman, Old Man?"

Petey snorts and spouts back, "I would if I thought I could, but she seems to think you are the better choice. Can't explain a woman's thinking, that's for damn sure. Make sure you don't fuck that up, boy."

"Don't plan to, Petey," says Gunner.

Without warning, Gunner leans down and plants his shoulder in my stomach, and lifts me, squealing, and shocked. He then tosses me over his shoulder and turns, striding out the main door and down the walk. He has one arm around my legs holding me in place and the other comes up to slap me gently on the ass and then gives it a good rub.

"What the hell, Gunner?" I holler at him.

He chuckles and continues walking toward the long line of bikes. There are a few catcalls and whistles on our way. He stops, bends over, and gently sets me back on my feet beside his bike.

"We are going for a ride. Not a long one because I know you still have things you want to finish tonight. But we…" he starts to finish when I let out a loud WOOP, throw my arms around his neck, and pull his head down for a kiss.

He complies with my not-so-subtle demand for his mouth and gives it to me. And it is hot! He takes without a second thought and then lets me explore his mouth in ways that are leaving me breathless. He tastes delicious. Minty and manly. Two of my favorite things. The kiss deepens and becomes serious. My hands slide up into his hair—it's silky and soft. I tug gently on the strands of inky blackness, he groans, and pulls me tighter to his body. And he's hard. Everywhere. I can't help but to rub against him, and again, he groans. I moan at the feeling of knowing that I made him that way.

He pulls back slowly while cupping my backside and smiles huge at me. I'm still in the kissing Gunner zone, and it's obvious he likes that he put me there.

"So, I take it you're okay with being on the back of my bike?" he says quietly.

"I still don't know why that's a big deal to you biker boys, but, hell yes, I want to be on the back of yours with you," I answer. "I want my first ride to be with you. Only you, Gunner. Is that okay?"

He growls and pulls me closer. He puts his mouth next to my ear and says low and serious, "I've never had a woman, ever, on my bike. Most bikers only allow their woman to ride with them. I'm one of those that have that belief. No woman, except my woman, will ever be on the back of my bike. It's a code I have always lived by, and now I want you on my bike. And the fact that this will be your first bike ride ever, and it'll be on the back of mine, means something to me. Does that clear things up for you?"

"Yeah, baby, I get it," I whisper back to him.

He steps back, picks up a black brain bucket, and places it on my head. He does up the strap for me and leans in for a quick kiss. Then he puts his own on and mounts the bike. He looks incredibly sexy sitting there in his worn and faded jeans, t-shirt, and black leather cut.

He holds his hand out, and I take a hold of it and swing my leg over the seat and settle down behind him. He reaches back, grabs both of my thighs, and tugs me even closer to him.

"When I lean, you lean. Your body follows mine at all times, sweetheart. And you hold onto me and hold on tight. I don't want to lose my precious cargo. Hold onto me tight, okay, baby?"

"Always, Gunner," I answer him as I wrap my arms tightly around his waist.

Best thing ever! I'm so in love with the feeling of riding his bike. It's wind, power, and freedom all wrapped together. I understand the pull to these machines now better than I ever have. Loud, rumbly, and powerful. I'm hooked. I don't ever want the ride to end. Feeling all of this, and doing it while wrapped around this sexy man, is almost more than my brain can compute.

Gunner rides with his left hand on my knee. It's warm and comforting. I have no fear because I have that much trust in Gunner and his skills. I lean with him, and I feel like we're a single entity.

Like all good things, though, the ride comes to an end back in the lot of the clubhouse. I dismount and remove my helmet as Gunner does the same. I hand him my helmet, and he places it on the seat with his and turns to me with a heart-melting smile.

"Wow! Just fucking wow, Gunner!" I exclaim. "That was amazing! Thank you for the ride."

He leans into me and places both hands on each side of my face with his fingers sliding into the hair at the sides of my head.

"I'm glad you liked it, honey," he says.

"Babe, I like sunny days and picnics. I like lingerie and great-fitting worn-out jeans. I like The Voice and country music. But I love riding your bike like I love cooking and chocolate and coffee and puppies. Big difference. Humungo difference!" I nearly yell.

He tosses his head back and lets out a throaty laugh that has my girl parts singing. He looks back down into my eyes and slowly leans in for a kiss.

Then he leans back again and says, "You like lingerie?"

"Seriously, Gunner? That's what you took from all that I said?" I laugh at him.

He nods. "I'm a man. I didn't hear much past lingerie." He grins at me.

"Who's wearing lingerie? You or Gunner?" asks a snarky voice nearby.

We turn to see Axel and Rex sitting in lawn chairs nearby.

"Most likely you, cockface," Gunner says to Axel, knowing it was him stirring shit.

Axel and Rex both cackle at Gunner.

"I have a nice lacy, robin's egg blue bra that might fit your moobs, Axel. But no way are you getting that ass into the matching panties," I add my two cents.

"Are you saying I have a fat ass, baker girl?"

"I'm not saying it, but I am implying it wouldn't hurt for you to push away from the table a little sooner."

Gunner and Rex are laughing like hyenas.

"You're just jealous that you have to settle for the likes of Gunner, and you know you're missing out on all that is me," declares Axel.

"If you were my only choice, Axel, I'd buy stock in Duracell and live happily ever after with BOB," I laugh at him.

"Oh, you filthy girl! You have a battery-operated boyfriend. Does Gunner know that you get down and dirty without him? He not big enough to satisfy you?" taunts Axel.

"He's the reason I had to upgrade to a much larger model. It's hard to fantasize about all that is Gunner while getting off if I'm stuck using an Axel-sized vibrator. You know, the little bullet one," I toss back.

"Don't talk about Big Al and the Twins like that, Ava! He has a fragile ego," declares Axel as he grabs his junk protectively.

"Seriously, dude? Big Al and the Twins? Oh my God!" I'm laughing so hard at this point I can barely breathe.

I walk away while laughing at the guys and almost make it around the corner to the kitchen door when I hear Gunner shout at me, "You need to FaceTime me tonight with BOB in play, dollface!"

I bolt into the security of the kitchen.

Lola Wright

Chapter 12

Gunner

I wake up early and excited for the day. Things are looking up for the club and for me personally. The club has struggled for a while now. Not financially. We're doing great in that aspect. But we're trying to clean things up and to keep going in a better direction.

We still have some illegal activities that we make money on, mostly guns, but our club has never been involved and has always been actively against trafficking humans or drugs. We work hard to keep our territory free of both. That causes friction with the clubs or gangs that don't believe as we believe.

We have to send messages sometimes, and those can be bloody. We work with other clubs that have similar beliefs, though, and that helps. There will be tension today with so many clubs mingling, but hopefully, it will stay under control. I know I can keep Ava safe, but it's worth noting that I need to keep my eyes open today.

Thinking about Ava, I pick up my phone and text her.

Me: Am I waking you up?

She doesn't answer right away like she normally does, and I assume she's still sleeping. I set my phone back down and sat up.

Ava: Nope, just getting out of the shower.

I read that and immediately hit the FaceTime app.

Ava answers, and I can see her hair is up in a towel, and I can see water droplets on her shoulders, but that's where the view ends.

"I type the word 'shower' and suddenly we're not texting anymore. Why is that?" she laughs at me.

"Mornin', doll. Mind lowering that phone a bit," I grin at her.

She lowers it, and I see her beautiful body wrapped in a short, fluffy, teal-colored towel. She was not lying. She's wet, and I'm suddenly very hard.

She raises the view back to her face, and I notice she doesn't have a stitch of makeup on. She's just as beautiful as any other time I've seen her. Her eyes are an odd shade of green that sometimes have a slight hint of blue in them, and her nose is straight and delicate. Her face is lightly tanned and with her hair pulled up in a towel, I notice a scar that runs along her hairline above her right eye. Even the scar can't ruin the perfection of her face. She's stunning.

"You gonna return the favor, biker boy?"

I lower the phone, so it shows my sitting body. I am only wearing a tight, black pair of boxer briefs, and they are considerably tighter at the moment. I know the moment she notices why they are so tight when I hear a slight intake of air. I grin, knowing she's affected.

I raise the phone back up to my face and smirk at her.

"I'll show you mine if you'll show me yours," I say, winking.

She's flustered and fumbles for something to say for a moment. Then she surprises me once again.

"Sorry, biker boy. I have a morning date with BOB. See you in an hour!"

Then the little witch hangs up on me.

I'm standing in front of the kitchen door with my arms crossed over my chest and my legs spread wide when Ava comes to a stop in her SUV. We make eye contact. She slowly gets out of the vehicle and approaches. She walks up to me, lowers her forehead to rest on my crossed arms, and places her hands on my waist.

I'm looking down at the back of her head and trying desperately to keep from laughing at her trying to act submissive. She's so damn cute. She's wearing jean shorts that have to be favorites of hers because they are soft, faded, and worn-looking from too many washings. They're perfect for her ass and long legs. She has a light green tank top on with lace for the straps on the back side. Black Chucks on her feet. Her hair is up in a messy-looking knot on her head, and it's gorgeous with some already falling out around her face.

"I didn't date BOB this morning. I shouldn't have hung up on you. I didn't handle that well but, dude, you're huge, and my girlie parts panicked. Am I forgiven?"

All of this said with her head still pointing down and resting on my arms.

I bust out laughing, wrap my arms around her, and pull her close. I can't help it, she kills me.

"Your girlie parts? Wow. You hang up on me, leave me hanging, and then try to smooth it over by trying to flatter me about my dick size?"

"Is it working?" she asks as she raises her head and smiles impishly at me.

"Maybe. You got a kiss for me?"

"Always!"

I lower my head and claim her mouth. Now my day is off to a good start.

I help Ava unload her ride, and she gets busy setting out huge boxes of donuts, pastries, and coffee for the guys. When a couple of them started to walk past, Ava informed them, with squinty eyes, that she would be offended if they didn't eat something she set out. And then she said that if they didn't like anything she had brought, she'd cook them breakfast instead. She told them that she was not going to be happy if they decided to go without something in their bellies and then spend the day riding in the wind and sun for charity. Here she is swamped with getting ready for the cookout and yet said she'd take the time to actually cook them a breakfast so they wouldn't be riding without something in their bellies.

The looks on their faces are priceless. First, they look pissed that she stepped in, and then they look a little shocked that she cared enough about men she didn't even know to say what she said. They also walked back to the boxes, and each selected a few treats and ate them. I noticed Trigger, the least friendly one, walk over to Ava when he was done eating, speak with her for a moment, and then give her a kiss on her temple. She smiled warmly at him, and I heard her tell him to be safe today.

"And that is just one of the many reasons why you better not fuck this up with her," warns Petey as he hobbles up next to me.

"I know. I'm not sure if there is another woman out there that would handle all of this as well as she is. She isn't afraid of a bunch of big, loud, obnoxious bikers any more than she's afraid of the club sluts. She amazes me, actually. I'm not sure if I deserve her," I answer.

"You don't. No doubt about that, and you should never forget it either. But since she doesn't know that, grab on and hold on tight because I don't think there are many like her either," he gruffs back at me before walking away.

When it's time for us to roll out, I walk to Ava, grab her hand, and pull her outside with me. I would rather she was riding with me today, but she said she had too much to finish up to ride. She made me promise that she could go on the next one, though, and I'm tickled that she likes riding that much.

We arrive at my bike. I put my helmet on and turn to Ava.

"Take some time off today while we're gone. Get the other women to help when you need it. Any problems with them, let me know when I get back. It'll be taken care of. Also, when you run home to check on your pets, bring Loki back with you. He'll be fine running around here, and it'll give him a chance to get out of the house. Also, here's a key to my room if you need a break from the chaos. Last room on the left. Use it if you want. I'm going to miss you today, babe. Give me a kiss."

Ava leans into me and gives me her mouth. I kiss her hard and ignore the hoots and hollers from the guys. I pull back and look into her eyes. I know I have to get on my bike and get this show going, but it's hard to pull away from her.

Chapter 13

Ava

After watching the guys, a few with women on the backs of their bikes, pull out in a two-wide formation, I walk back to the kitchen. I only have about five hours to have everything ready for the party.

I spend the next two hours getting everything set up and making sure the ribs are cooking slowly in the large homemade grills the guys pulled close to the backdoor. I have the kiddie pools sitting on the tables under canopies, and they are waiting to be filled with ice, then salads and other heat-sensitive dishes. The prospect that was left behind has filled the huge water troughs with ice and placed the kegs in them to get nice and cold. We have everything under control, so I let him know that I'm heading home and will be back in thirty minutes.

I rush home and spend some time taking care of my little furry, feathered, and spotted family members. I change clothes into nicer jean shorts and a different racer-back, lacy tank in black. I add some silver earrings, a few leather and silver bracelets, and a silver chain necklace. I put on some cute sandals and fix my hair in a less messy knot.

I check everyone's food and water dishes and grab Loki's leash. I give Mac a pat on the head, a hug to Gee, and find Duffy sleeping upside down in the linen closet with his head hanging over the edge of the shelf. He gets a belly rub, which he doesn't even wake up for, and I call Loki. He trots over, and we're ready to leave.

Arriving back at the clubhouse in my Camaro, I park way out of the way where Petey told me to park, and Loki and I enter the main room. There are a few club sluts sitting around drinking and flirting with the prospect. He looks up and nods at me, but the women pointedly ignore my existence.

"Where's Big Petey?" I ask the prospect.

"Said he wanted a nap, so he's primed for tonight," laughs the prospect.

That sounds like something Petey would say, so I just laugh and head toward the staircase.

I walk down the hall and use the key to enter Gunner's room. Inside I find Katey and another club slut rifling around through the chest of drawers and the nightstand. Both look up, shocked to see someone in the doorway. I note that Katey's face is messed up pretty bad. Two black eyes, a swollen nose, and a fat lip. The other girl is very short, huge fake boobs, and brassy blond hair with dark roots. Her mouth is forming a perfect O shape from shock at being caught.

I set my bag down near the door and feel Loki brush against my thigh. I ruffle my hand across his head.

"There a reason why you two are in Gunner's room?" I ask, not so nicely.

"None of your business, bitch," snarls Katey while the blond looks like she's trying to find an escape route.

"Better question would be, *how* did you two get into Gunner's room?" I snarl back.

"I've got to get going now," squeaks the blond as she tries to scoot past me.

I grab her by the bicep and stop her exit. Loki doesn't move out of her way either, but he does give a low growl after hearing my tone.

"You're not going anywhere, Toots, until you answer me," I tell her.

"Keep your mouth shut, Marti. We don't have to answer anything Gunner's newest slut asks. Now get out of the way, bitch. We're leaving," sneers Katey.

I turn my attention back to Marti and ask her, "Did you get a good look at Katey's face, Marti?

"Uh, yeah, I did," she squeaks out.

"Want to see how she got that look she's rocking?" I ask Marti.

"No! No, no, no, no, I don't! I didn't even want to be here. But Katey said I had to help her, or she would tell Fang that it was me who gave him chlamydia!"

"Shut the fuck up, you stupid cunt!" screams Katey, grabbing at Marti's other arm.

"Did you?" I question Marti.

"Probably," she answers miserably.

I pull her from the room and give her a gentle shove down the hall while saying, "Get out of here, Marti. And be smart. Tell him yourself, and don't listen to Katey about anything. She's not going to do anything to help you, ever."

Marti scurries down the hallway on her five-inch stripper heels, her ass hanging out of her shorts.

I turn my attention back to Katey and see her standing with a smirk on her face and her arms crossed over her chest.

"Why does it have to be this way, Katey? We can both co-exist here. We don't have to drag each other down or have a spat going like high school girls. Gunner is off-limits, by his own choice, but there are a lot of other single, hot bikers here to choose from," I try to reason with her.

"Gunner was going to be mine," she spits at me. "I was his favorite until you showed up. Just cook your damn food and then go back to your safe little perfect world. You can't handle club life. You're not cut out for it, and Gunner is going to realize that soon enough. He gets his dick wet once or twice, and you'll be kicked to the curb just like the others have been. So, save yourself the embarrassment and get gone, bitch!"

I study her for a moment and realize she really believes what she's saying. But she's wrong. I have never had a safe, perfect little life, and I can handle more than she knows. I'm wasting my time trying to reason with her.

"Get out. Stay out of Gunner's room," I tell her waving at the door.

Katey struts out the door but turns around for one last verbal jab.

"I'll leave now but know this. While you're off baking your cookies, I'll be warming his bed. When you're not at the clubhouse, I will be, and he can't resist a willing pussy. He never has had to, so why do it now? When he gets tired of his little walk on the good side, and he'll get bored of you fast, he'll come back to what he knows best. Are you okay with him fucking you and another at the same time? Threesomes and foursomes are his thing. Do you really think he'll give all that up for one prissy-assed bitch?"

Katey sneers at me and struts off toward the main room.

I walk into the room, shut the door, and flop down on the bed. Loki puts his head on my lap, and I stroke his fur for comfort.

As spiteful as Katey was, she knew right where to aim her arrows. My biggest concern about a relationship with Gunner is that I'm not very experienced, and he will be giving up a lifestyle he's grown up living. He's always had willing women hanging around and has never had to say no before. Does that spell doom for us?

I know in my head and heart that I need to speak with Gunner about this before I bolt. He's made promises to me. I have to have faith and trust in him for this to ever have a chance at becoming something. It wouldn't be fair to Gunner to just believe Katey and not give him the chance to prove her wrong first.

With those thoughts in my head, I head back downstairs to get the cookout ready to roll. I'm not going to worry about all that Katey said today. I'm determined to put on a great cookout, have an awesome night and deal with the rest of that shit another day.

It's going on 4pm, and I can hear the roar of the bikes coming down the road and turning into the club's driveway. I'm outside, Loki laying underneath a nearby table in the shade, flipping and checking on the food cooking on the grills. Gunner had texted me thirty minutes ago and let me know they were on their way, and they were hungry.

I have everything set up and ready to be devoured. I have trays to pass out to each of the tables of various appetizers and finger foods. All the food tables are loaded down with the rest of the meal. They have the option of a full course meal with lots of choices or, if they're not hungry yet, they can just snack on the apps and bowls of chips, dips, candied nuts, and Chex Mix I have set out on the picnic tables.

I watch Big Petey hobble over to a lawn chair near a picnic table and take a seat. I walk over with a full plate of apps and a beer for him. He takes them, smiling up at me.

"I'll bring you a plate of dinner stuff after everyone gets settled," I tell him.

"You spoil me, darlin'."

"That's because you deserve to be spoiled, and I adore you, Old Man."

Petey chuckles as the bikes all start backing into available parking spaces. I spot Gunner. He's standing and removing his helmet while smiling huge in my direction. God, he's gorgeous. And dangerous to my heart.

"Go greet your man, darlin'. He needs to make sure the others know you are off-limits," orders Petey.

"All this caveman stuff is exhausting," I reply, laughing as I walk toward Gunner.

Lola Wright

Chapter 14

Gunner

This day couldn't have gone much better than it has so far. Beautiful weather for a poker run. Not too hot, but also not a cloud in the sky. The ride was relaxing with the weaving in and out of the foothills along the Front Range. And knowing I was coming back to our clubhouse and Ava would be here made it all the better. And the smells coming from the food alone should be worth charging money just to get to enjoy them.

As Ava gets to my side, I swoop down and clasp my hands under her ass and pick her up high. She places her hands on the sides of my head and leans down for a kiss. I love the feel of her in my arms and her lips on mine. I'm also hoping every swinging dick here today sees that she's taken. She's mine. Too bad for them, but I'm not sharing.

I set her down, and she looks up at me and asks, "Good ride?"

"Yeah, doll. It was great. Glad to be back, though," I reply while grabbing her hand in mine and heading toward the tables.

"Everything go okay here today?" I ask.

"Pretty much. I have everything ready, but I better get busy handing out the apps," she says, pulling away and walking toward a table by the grills.

I have this feeling that she's not telling me everything, but she doesn't look upset. I'll have to ask about it, but I know if it's something bothering her, she won't be shy about speaking up about it later. Everyone is heading straight to the kegs, so I walk that way.

I see Ava setting heaping trays on each of the picnic tables and smiling at the various bikers standing around quenching their thirst. It doesn't take long before I have a beer and am sitting next to Petey, who has his own plate already. I reach for a piece of chicken breast wrapped in bacon smeared in BBQ sauce, but Petey slaps my hand as he pulls his plate out of my reach.

"Get your own food, ass," Petey says.

"Too tired to get up, Old Man. Don't be so greedy," I laugh back at him.

Just then, Ava shoves a plate like Petey's in my face and tells me, "Here's yours. I'm only personally serving you two, the others can get their own off the tables. But quit trying to steal from Petey. He can't move around as easily as you." She winks and walks away.

Axel, Pooh, Reno, and Fang all walk up to stand around us with finger foods and beer in their hands.

"How come you two assholes get platefuls handed to you, and we have to walk to the tables to get some?" gripes Axel.

"Because Ava loves me, and she doesn't love you, dickhead," chuckles Petey.

I spot Ava with more loaded down trays heading toward another table when she gets intercepted by Chubs. He smiles sweetly, says something to her, bats his eyes, she laughs and hands him a whole tray then continues on her way. It's a huge fucking tray of food meant to serve several people.

Chubs ambles over to us with his own loaded tray and states, "Chubs loves Ava!"

The guys pounce on his tray, and I laugh my ass off, watching him trying to save his food from the pack.

Suddenly, Chubs starts shouting, "Ava! Ava! Help! Avvvaaaaaaaa!"

Ava arrives and starts slapping at Axel's hands that are still trying to get food from Chubs. This is just too funny. A little blond bombshell is smacking big, badass bikers to save one chubby, curly-headed one.

"You thieving, lazy bastards can walk your tight little asses right over to the tables and get your own damn food! Leave Chubs and Petey's food the hell alone," she demands.

"Whoa! What about my food?" I ask.

"You're big enough to defend your own self," she laughs at me. "Petey is injured, and Chubs is my best buddy."

"I thought I was your best buddy," pouts Axel.

"No, you're my best girlfriend," spouts Ava.

"That's just mean, Ava! Fuck you," replies Axel while grinning huge.

Pointing at Fang, Ava responds smiling sweetly, "Not even with his dick would I fuck you, Axel." I don't think she's forgiven Fang yet for running off her best cake decorator.

"Hey!" shouts Fang and Axel.

Petey, Pooh, Reno, and I are laughing our asses off when Ava just turns and walks away again.

Everyone is filing down the sides of the tables that have all the dinner foods on them. I can't believe how many choices Ava made. I can't even decide what I want to eat, but I know I can't fit it all on my plate. Guess more than one trip is in order.

Ava is standing behind the table helping people and refilling any dish that looks like it's getting low. She's busy and working hard to make sure everyone gets what they want. She's smiling huge and speaking with a lot of people as they file past her.

I'm hearing nothing but high praise for the food and a lot of comments about Ava herself. She's drawing a lot of attention I wish she wasn't getting.

The men have all noticed what I saw right away about her, but she doesn't see in herself. She thinks she's just average, but there is nothing average about Ava. But she is confident in her cooking and baking. She takes a lot of pride in that. I love seeing her shine in her element today, but I still wish the men didn't all take an instant interest in her.

I'm keeping a close eye on her for those reasons. But I've also noticed that not a single club slut or Ol' Lady has stepped up to help. Usually, the sluts don't show up until later after things get rocking, but I'm guessing they wanted a decent meal too.

The Ol' Ladies and the club girls keep their distance from each other when we have these types of gatherings. The club sluts aren't allowed when it's a family meal for club members, though. But several of the other clubs have women with them, so it's kind of a mishmash tonight of women and their different roles in the clubs.

I've ate until I'm stuffed and there were still foods I didn't get to try. I'm kicked back in a chair with a beer next to Petey and a few of the other guys when Chubs walks by with his third or fourth plateful and BBQ sauce smeared across his face. Ava is walking behind him carrying a heaping plate of desserts that she sits down next to him at his table. I guess he's tired of making so many trips to the food lines, and she's helping him out. I have to chuckle at those two.

On her way back to the food lines, she walks up behind me and leans down with her arms circling my neck and her face next to my ear. I reach up and gently stroke her arm.

"Can I get you some dessert, honey?" she asks quietly in my ear.

"Not yet, babe. I ate too much already. But if you could save me a piece or two of your raspberry pie and chocolate and peanut butter cake, I'll make it worth your while," I answer.

"I've already tucked away a couple of pieces of all the desserts for you to have later tonight or even tomorrow," she whispers in my ear.

I reach up and put my hand on the back of her head and pull her down and around for a kiss. She doesn't make it a quick peck but takes her time. Fuck me. I'm going to be hiding a boner in about .08 seconds. She pulls back and brushes a soft kiss on the side of my head and leaves.

Loki ambles over and flops down next to me. I've noticed all the attention he's received today, and yet his eyes haven't left Ava often. He's been fed food from a lot of hands, but his loyalty stays with her. I ruffle his head as he sprawls out on his side next to my chair.

"That's one beautiful dog," says Reno looking down at Loki.

"Yes, he is. Would he be a good cross for any of the females we own?" I ask.

"Fuck, he'd be perfect. I would love to get some pups out of him and see what I could do with them. But your woman is a little resistant to the idea so far. I can't fault her for why she is, though. Maybe you could talk with her. After a good hard fucking, she might be more amenable," chuckles Reno.

I like that idea, but I don't understand why she would be against breeding Loki. He's a spectacular dog, and he's of a breed that is fairly rare, at least in these parts. The club would pay her good money for his services.

I speak my thoughts out loud and Reno explains.

"She hasn't said no. She's just a little resistant. She said she hates to breed for more pups when there are so many homeless ones that can be trained just as well. And she's right about that. But clients are weird about the breed of the dogs they buy. It's a tougher sell when it's a mutt than they are about a purebred. But I do get what she's saying. It's something I'd like to discuss with the club. We do a lot of charity-type stuff for different organizations, and she mentioned that she does the same for animal sanctuaries and rescues. That's where she got the bird, pig, and cat. The only reason Loki isn't fixed is because he didn't come through an actual rescue organization. He was in a bad situation, and she took him out of it on her own."

I realize I need to spend time with Ava, just getting to know each other and not about getting her naked. Some of my club brothers seem to know more about her than I do, and that's bothering me. We need some time to just cuddle and talk. Shit, I'm definitely growing a vagina. I just thought the word cuddle.

Lola Wright

Chapter 15

Ava

After everyone has finished eating, I start covering dishes and clearing the tables. Many of the guys have thanked me and raved about the food. It's been a lot of hard work, but those comments and the gratitude they've shown has made it all worth the sore muscles I'm sporting.

When things are back to order, I set out trays of snack-type foods to keep the masses entertained with their beer. I see Chris and his band are setting up to start playing, so I grab a few things to munch on and run upstairs to Gunner's room.

I wash the day's dust and grime off me and take my meds and insulin shot. I eat my snack and wander back outside to find Gunner. I have time now to just enjoy being with him and my new friends.

I find Gunner standing with several men shooting the shit. I approach, he immediately wraps his arm around me and pulls my front to his side. I wrap my arms around him and enjoy the feeling of his hard body.

I look at the men standing around us and only recognize a few faces. The man standing directly across from me is striking to view. Hispanic coloring, black hair, and eyes, not overly tall, but taller than me. Broad, built, and beautiful. But something about him doesn't sit right with me. He has a gorgeous face but ruins it with a hard and cold look. He makes the hair on the back of my neck rise, and I instantly don't trust him.

The woman standing slightly behind him is stunning. Perfect facial features with arched brows, dark eyes, and full beautiful lips. She has extremely long black hair. So long it brushes her waist.

I'm staring at her in awe as she looks my direction, and our eyes meet. I smile and give a low wave. She smiles shyly and looks back down at the ground. She seems uncomfortable being here.

At that moment, Loki walks up and leans against my leg. I reach down to give him a big body rub, and I hear a small gasp. I look back at the woman, and she's staring at Loki.

"He's friendly. He won't bite," I say to her quietly, not wanting to interrupt the men. "You can pet him if you want. His name is Loki."

She comes forward and puts her hand out to Loki to sniff. He does and then rubs his head against her hand. She smiles huge and is even more stunning than before.

"Hi, I'm Ava," I tell her.

"Maria. He's beautiful! What kind of dog is he?" she says quietly.

We chat quietly for a few minutes about Loki, the cookout, and the poker run. She's friendly but a little shy. And she seems younger than she looks, but I'm not sure of her age. Early twenties would be my guess.

"Maria. Get me a beer," barks the man she had been standing behind.

She instantly stops chatting mid-sentence and walks toward the kegs. I'm a little shocked at how quickly she did his bidding. Not even a half-second of hesitation.

I turn to Gunner and see he's giving me a look. Like one of those "behave" looks.

I smile and tell him I'm going to go sit with Petey for a while and give him big eyes as I walk off. He just smirks a little and shakes his head at me.

The band is starting up, and they sound pretty good tonight. I crash down in a chair next to Petey, suddenly exhausted.

"You okay, doll?" asks Petey.

"Yeah. Just tired. It's been a long day."

"I noticed not a single woman in this club stepped up and helped. That shit didn't go unseen. It'll be brought up at Church this week," declares Petey.

"It's not a big deal, Pete. I'm the new kid on the block. I expected it," I say tiredly.

Axel walks up with a beer in one hand and diet Coke in the other which he hands off to me. I thank him, surprised and a little touched by the gesture. I give him a lot of shit, but he really is a nice guy.

And then he ruins it by planting his muscular ass right in my lap, throwing his legs over the chair arm. He tosses his arm around my neck and plants a wet, noisy kiss on my cheek.

Petey and I bust out laughing at Axel's antics right up until the chair starts wobbling, breaks, and I crash-land with Axel's weight coming down on top of me.

Then Axel throws his head back and laughs hard.

Axel finally rolls off me, stands, reaches down, and helps me to my feet. Pooh, not so helpfully or innocently, darts forward and starts to brush the dirt off my shorts, ass, and legs. I'm trying to swat his hands away when a strong tanned arm wraps around my waist, picks me up, and sets me back down out of Pooh's reach.

I look up to see an annoyed look on Gunner's face, and it's directed at Pooh. Guess someone doesn't approve of Pooh's assistance.

I see Pooh's hands go up in a placating manner as he steps back a few steps.

Gunner stares him down for another moment and then turns to me.

"You okay, babe?" he directs at me.

"Yeah, I'm fine. They were just joking around," I tell him quietly.

"You two asses can go get the bonfire going," Gunner tells Axel and Pooh.

Then to me he says, "You're done working for the night. Do you need to go home and check on the pets?"

"Yes. I better make a quick trip. Be back in thirty minutes," I inform him giving him a gentle kiss goodbye and calling Loki.

I arrive back to the clubhouse, and things are not as quiet as before. I notice most of the Ol' Ladies have left, and more of the club whores have shown up wearing very little and losing more the longer they're here.

I see several couples along the edges of the light from the bonfire. Things are getting hot between them. Petey has a club slut sitting on his good leg, and he's laughing at something she's saying to him.

I look for Gunner and see him in a group of men, plus a few women, standing a little away from the bonfire, chatting. I also notice he has a club slut,

Amy, I think her name is, leaning into his right arm.

She's a cute little redhead. Not gorgeous, not beautiful, but more like a cheerleader type. Short auburn hair, perky nose, and blue eyes. And she's standing a little too close for my peace of mind. And not wearing near enough clothing.

I've never been jealous before, but I feel a jolt of something that feels like it might be jealousy. Ugh! I don't want to be one of those women, but this is new to me. To be in a relationship that matters to me and to feel jealousy over someone standing near Gunner.

"You know payback is a bitch," says a raspy voice close to my ear.

"Excuse me?" I say, jerking around to see the man I'd seen talking to Gunner earlier. The one that Maria was standing behind.

He's standing way too close and smiles a cold and calculating smile at me.

He nods his head toward Gunner and Amy, who is now standing under Gunner's arm with it thrown over her shoulders.

I feel a flash of jealousy and anger at both of them. But I refuse to allow it to show and to give this guy something to use to his advantage. I turn back to look at him and find he's moved even closer to me. I can feel his body heat, he's that close.

"Name's Javier. You're Ava. I asked. Gunner implied you were his, but it's not looking like you belong to anyone now. No Ol' Lady patch. Don't appear to be a club slut but looks can be deceiving. You're fair game according to biker law."

Before I can step back, he takes a hold of my arm above my elbow and pulls me in tight to him. I stiffen and try to step back, but his grip is strong.

"Um, I need you to let go of me, like now. I'm not fair game for anyone here, regardless of what you call biker law. I make my own choices, and this isn't one I want, so please release me," I say firmly.

"I don't think I will. I like you where you are," he says quietly.

"You need to let go and do it now. I don't want a scene, but I'll make one if it's needed. Besides, you have a woman. Maria is here with you, remember?" I remind him.

"Maria is a slut, and she knows her place. It's where I tell her it is, and I care less about a scene than I care about Maria's feelings," he returns with his face right up in mine. "Get this, Ava. I take what I want when I want. That's what bitches are for, but normally, I wouldn't go after another man's woman. But Gunner is making a loud statement that you are not claimed by him by having a slut hanging all over him. So, you're not as special to him as you thought, and that makes you fair game. We'll play a little payback and see how he feels when you're the one wrapped around another. Me. Do as you're told, and we'll both get a little payback tonight, Chica."

I'm starting to realize this is not about me and him. It's about him stirring shit with Gunner and the club. I don't want to be the cause of a more strained relationship between their clubs, but it looks like he's chosen me to be that vehicle. Fuck!

I twist my arm up and circle it back hard at the same time as I step away, and it breaks his hold on me. For a moment, I think about striking him, but he looks surprised that I got free, so I use that moment to step further away from him.

When I'm out of reach and prepared if he tries to grab me again, I tell him, "If you're hell-bent on causing a problem between the clubs, I suggest you take that up with Gunner. Not sure it says good things about you that you would try to use a woman to accomplish your goal."

Javier's eyes shoot daggers while taking a step toward me, anger painting his whole body.

"Have to agree with Ava, Javier," says an angry voice behind me.

Vex steps beside me while placing an arm in front of me and gently pushing me further from Javier. He puts himself directly in front of Javier, and they lock angry eyes.

"Ava, go sit with Pops," orders Axel as he arrives beside Vex.

I don't hesitate to do as Axel ordered. I find Petey, now sitting beside a couple of older bikers with different club patches on their backs and sit down with him on the picnic table. He leans over and gives me a kiss on the cheek and looks at me closely.

"You okay, darlin'?" he asks.

"Yeah, I'm good."

He's looking at me, and then his eyes drift, and they harden instantly. I follow his eyes and see

Gunner, still in the group of men, and still with his arm around Amy. I look away instantly.

"He doesn't mean anything by that, babe," says Petey.

"Yeah, no worries, Petey," I whisper back.

The men Petey was talking with lean over and thank me again for the meal. We get to talking. I keep my attention on them and not what Gunner is doing.

Five or ten minutes pass, and Axel and Vex approach our table. Both are looking me over and looking aggravated.

Axel crouches down next to where I'm sitting and places his hand on mine on the table. I meet his eyes, and I can see a lot of anger in his.

"Tell me what happened with Javier," Axel orders.

"I was coming back from taking Loki home, and he stopped me over near the cars. Nothing happened, Axel. He didn't hurt me. Just ran his mouth a bit, and then Vex showed up, and you came right after that. I'm fine. Really," I answer him quietly.

"Run his mouth about what, Ava?" questions Axel carefully.

"Um, nothing really. Just stupid shit, Ax. I just didn't want there to be a scene, so I was making an exit when Vex showed."

I lift my eyes to Vex, and he's still looking aggravated. I mouth "thank you" to him, and his face softens a little. He walks to our side of the table, puts his hand on the back of my neck and says low, "You're welcome. Anytime."

"What did Javier say, darlin'?" cuts in Petey.

I guess we weren't as quiet as I thought we were. I don't want this to become an issue, and I know the men won't take it well. But I have to trust them to handle it how they see fit.

"He called me fair game. Said he takes what he wants. Said if I'd play with him, we'd both get a little payback tonight. Said Gunner was making a statement that I'm fair game, and not his, by having a slut hanging on him. He said stupid shit that's not worth getting into a fight over, so I broke away from him and was getting ready to either kick him in the boy parts or bolt," I quickly say in a monotone.

Like it hadn't bothered me. Like it didn't hurt that Gunner had kind of put me in that position. Like it didn't bring back memories of another time when I was held by men who took what they wanted also.

Axel rises from the crouch he's been in and sits beside me on the picnic table with his back to the table. He searches my face for a moment. Vex moves back to the other side of the table and sits across from me, also searching my face. All of them are deathly quiet.

"I don't want this to cause a problem between the clubs," I state firmly. "No harm, no foul."

"This isn't on you, Ava. Javier was looking to create a scene to cause a bigger rift between the clubs. And Gunner gave him the ammo by leaving you hanging tonight. You did good, girl," Petey says.

"I kind of wish you had kicked Javier in his boy parts," mutters Vex.

"And Gunner's," spits Axel.

"No, guys, I refuse to let him use me to justify whatever he's up to. Gunner's going to have to clean this up somehow because it's the club's problem, not mine. I don't even completely understand this whole 'fair game' thing, but I know I want no part of it. I'm not into being used, so it was best I just got out of there. Pretty sure Javier isn't the kind of man that would take it lightly if I had put him down," I say, shuddering.

"No, he isn't, and it would have gotten ugly, and you would have been caught up in the middle. You did the right thing, Ava," responds Petey.

"Look, I'm beat. It's been a long-ass day for me. I think it's best I just head home," I say.

"You going to speak with Gunner first?" questions Axel.

"And say what? Thanks for fronting me off by letting sluts hang on you all night? Thanks for leaving me hanging and fair game for your enemy? Yeah, no, I think it's best I just leave. He's a big boy, and he can make his own choices. I don't own him. And he made his choice for tonight, obviously, so I'm making mine. Cooler heads tomorrow may save some bloodshed," I say, again in a monotone, refusing to let anyone see how hurt I am by Gunner's actions tonight.

I stand up and squeeze Petey's shoulder. He pats my hand saying bye.

"Um, would one of you walk me to my car, so I can avoid more drama tonight?" I ask, looking between Axel and Vex.

Axel immediately stands up, and we start walking toward the parking lot together. After a moment of walking, Axel breaks the silence.

"I have no fucking idea what Gunner was thinking tonight, with letting her hang on him, but I do know he cares an awful lot about you, Ava."

"This is new for both Gunner and I. He's not used to having boundaries, let alone what ones to and not to cross. I'm probably making a huge mistake, but I'm going to give him the benefit of the doubt for now," I quietly reply.

"Jesus, fuck, Ava, you are way too good for the likes of us," groans Axel.

"Oh, he's not getting off free and easy. His balls will be busted, and then we'll see how things go from there," I smile up at him as we arrive at my car.

"I want to drive this car, Ava. You have to let me drive this car!" whines Axel while running his hand down the hood.

"Why do I have to let you drive my car?" I question.

"Because that's what lil sisters do for their big, badass biker brothers!"

Chapter 16

Gunner

This has been the best cookout we've ever put on here at the clubhouse. Other than a little tension and some words with Javier earlier, it's been all good. Everyone has been raving about the food Ava served.

The band's playing, and I've been standing with a group of men I know from a few other clubs for a while now. We've been having a slightly rowdy debate on the best touring bike made by Harley Davidson. Everyone has their own opinion, and this is an old debate, but fun, nonetheless.

I know I've drunk way more than I should have, but I have a great buzz and good men to argue with. I'm enjoying myself. I suddenly realize I haven't seen Ava in a while. I look around the bonfire area and still see no sign of her, but I make eye contact with Petey, and he's glaring at me. I'm a little taken aback.

I need to find out why, so I disengage myself from whoever is holding onto me, and I realize with a start that it's Amy. She's snuggled up tight, and I have my arm around her shoulders. What the fuck? Where did she come from?

Fuck me! I wasn't paying attention, and she must have just slid in under my arm, and being an ass—a fucking drunken ass at that—I didn't notice. Now I understand the glare from Petey.

Again, this is bad.

I pull away from Amy, glare down at her as she smirks up at me and walk off looking for Ava. She must be inside because she's nowhere around the bonfire. I pull out my cell phone and shoot off a text.

Me: Where are you?

I wait a couple of minutes, but she still doesn't respond, so I head inside to the kitchen. No Ava.

Just a guy fucking one slut on the worktable while another girl is crouched behind him, sucking on his balls.

Christ, Ava would shit herself if she saw what was happening on the table she has spent so much time at this week. I head into the main room and still don't see her anywhere. My phone vibrates at that moment.

Ava: home

Oh, fuck me! Now I have to wonder if she saw Amy snuggled up to me and left mad or if something else happened. And I'm almost afraid to ask her.

Me: why?

Ava: I'm tired and you looked happy where you were so I left

Oh crap! What do I do? This is so bad, and I have a funny feeling in my stomach. Almost painful. What the fuck do I do?

Ava: quit wondering what to say to that. go enjoy your party.

Me: did you stay home after taking care of pets?

Oh, please God, let that be a yes answer! Maybe she didn't return and never saw a thing.

Ava: no I came back and left again. go away now

Oh, shit balls from hell! I have fucked up, and she's mad. And I'm still too drunk to be smart about this.

Me: If u r mad just say it

Ava: I'm mad. So mad I'm writing down ways to castrate you slowly. None are pretty and neither will your balls be when I'm done. Happy? Now go the fuck away!

Me: Ava baby I'm drunk and stupid. Can I call?

No answer. Still no answer five minutes later. So, being an idiot, I try calling her, and it goes directly to voicemail. She must have turned her phone off. Still being stupid, I leave a message.

"Ava, babe. I'm sorry. I drank too much. I wish you were still here, and I'll grovel properly tomorrow. Thank you for everything you did today. Get some rest, honey, and call me when you wake up."

I hang up and wonder if it would be easier to just kill myself tonight or wait and see what she has in mind for me. Fuck!

I wake up later than normal with a pounding head and a bad feeling in my stomach. Not an "I drank too much" feeling, but an "I fucked up something good" feeling. I shower, dress, and walk downstairs to the kitchen for a much-needed cup of coffee, ibuprofen. Hopefully, Ava will be there too.

As I'm walking through the main room, I see that it's totally trashed. There are beer cans, bottles, and solo cups everywhere. A few naked or semi-naked people are sprawled out on the couches and chairs, and one couple asleep on a pool table. The man's naked ass sticking up, and it's not a good sight to see at any time of day.

I enter the kitchen and see Axel, Vex, and Chubs sitting at a table, luckily not the one that was being used last night, drinking coffee, and eating leftover desserts. Chubs gives me a chin lift, but the other two don't even look up from their plates.

A prospect walks in, and I tell him, "Start waking people up and tell them it's time to leave. They have an hour to get gone. We have Church at 11:00 today, and no non-members need to be on the grounds by then."

He nods and walks into the main room. I can hear him telling people it's time to go.

I sit down at the table across from Axel and sip my coffee. My stomach isn't ready for food yet, though. I pop a few ibuprofen and swallow.

"Everyone have a good time last night?" I ask.

Chubs looks up and nods his head. He then dives back into the two large plates of desserts that he has in front of him.

Neither Axel nor Vex respond. Odd. Neither one is usually this quiet and are usually running their mouths. Hungover probably.

A few more brothers arrive and grab cups of coffee. I check my phone a few times but have no messages from Ava. I know this hollow feeling in my stomach is because I fucked up, and I don't know if I hurt her feelings or just pissed her off. Neither option is good, but I'll feel better once I can see her and do my groveling.

My phone vibrates, and I grab it expecting a message from Ava.

Javier: Great food last night. Ava is spectacular. Will be keeping an eye on her since she's a free agent. Thanks for the shot.

What the fuck? I feel my blood boiling at that fucking piece of shit!

Me: Not a free agent. She's mine. Stay the fuck away from her!

Javier: We had a nice chat last night. Too bad your men interfered or it would have been more than a chat.

Me: Fuck you Javier! Don't push this shit.

What the fuck is he talking about? When did he get a chance to get close enough to Ava to have a chat? My men interfered? Interfered with what? And why the hell has no one told me shit about this?!

"Church! Now!" I bellow to the men in the kitchen. Then repeat it in the main room.

I see Axel and Vex get up, fill their coffee cups, and head toward the room we use as our Church meeting room. Still not a word out of them.

I tell the prospect to make sure all the members are in Church in five minutes, and he makes a run for the staircase to knock on doors.

I push my way through the door to the meeting room and am shocked to see Big Petey sitting at the table already. He doesn't say a word, but he does meet my eyes. And he looks pissed.

Only officers attend Church unless it's an all-members meeting for some reason, and then everyone comes, and the prospects are left guarding the main gate. Today is an all members meeting that we decided on last week. We usually have one of these after a poker run or charity event of some kind. We talk about how things went and what we could do better next time. Prospects are still not allowed.

"Hey, Petey," I greet him.

"Hey, President," he snipes back at me.

Okay, so he has an attitude today, and I am pretty sure I know why. I sigh. Being the Prez can be a real pain in the ass sometimes.

"Look, I fucked up. I know I did, and I've already started trying to fix my fuck-up with Ava. Ball is in her court now," I tell him.

"You don't know the half of it, and I hope she kicks you to the curb," he grumbles.

"What don't I know?" I demand.

Petey is saved from whatever asshole comment he was about to make when the men started filing into the room, taking seats scattered around the table and along the walls.

"Okay, everyone, settle down," I holler, slamming the gavel down.

The room quiets instantly.

"First things first. How's everyone think the poker run and the cookout went? Anything we need to change or improve on?" I ask looking around the room.

There are several comments of how good the food was, how smooth everything went with Ava in control of the cookout, and several comments of praise for Ava. A few remarked on the poker run and the route that had been planned for the ride.

"Any issues we need to discuss?" I ask, knowing this is the opening that Petey is waiting for, and I'm right.

"Yep. I have one. Javier, Prez of The Banditos, cornered Ava last night, put his hands on her, and tried to use her to start a fight between the clubs. She…"

"He put his motherfucking hands on her?" I roar.

"She understood right away what he was trying to do, and she used her head and didn't give him the opening he wanted. But the fact remains, he tried to play and intimidate a woman this club promised their protection. Makes us look weak, we can't protect our own women," continues Petey, completely ignoring my interruption.

"He's playing a dangerous game," spits out Trigger.

"How did she get away from him? Did she hit him?" I bark.

"No, but she had thought about it. I intervened, but she had already gotten herself loose from his grip by the time I got there," says Vex.

"I got there then and told Ava to go sit with Pops," adds Axel. "We spoke with Javier and advised him it was time for him and his to leave club property. That they had overstayed their welcome."

"You sent her to your dad and not to me?" I question. "There a reason for that, Axel?"

"Yeah, Prez. I was hoping she hadn't seen you hanging on a slut and sent her dad's way so she wouldn't. That she wouldn't see what Javier saw and tried to twist to fit his needs," Axel responds with no inflection in his voice but a lot moving around in the back of his eyes.

"Club and brothers first, bitches second!" laughs Fang. Stupidly.

"Shut the fuck up, Fang!" barks Petey. "She was doing the club a huge favor and worked her ass off for us, going above and beyond to make the club look good. And we let her down by not keeping her safe. He could have hurt her, or worse, took her. She means something, or I thought she did, to our Prez, but she definitely does to me. And I want to know why Javier wants a war between our clubs. And to what lengths he'll go to get one."

Several of the guys start talking and discussing Javier's motives, talking over each other, sharing theories and thoughts. I listen with half an ear, but I think I know the answer.

"Okay, guys. Settle down. During patrols last week, we found two pushers selling in our territory. Both were traced back to being Banditos hang-arounds. Pretty sure Javier just wants more turf, or at least some kind of agreement to sell on ours. He's been pushing against us for a while. We need to be more vigilant of our territory, send harsher messages when we're infringed on. Agreed?" I ask.

Several murmurs of yeah and a few hell yesses ring out.

It's late afternoon, long after Church ended, and I still haven't received anything from Ava. No call, no text. I snatch up my phone and shoot off a text to her.

Me: You home?

It's a few minutes later when Ava answers.

Ava: yes

Me: Want to see you.

Ava: I am exhausted. Just taking a lazy day with the pets. Sorry.

Me: I can bring dinner. Watch a movie. Be lazy with you.

Ava: Not sure if I want to hurt you yet or not.

Me: I deserve whatever you decide.

Ava: You wouldn't say that if you knew some of my thoughts

Me: R we going to be ok?

Ava: Probably. Maybe. Trust isn't something that is easy for me to give and you didn't make it any easier. I need a day to think.

Me: I was a drunken idiot. Won't happen again. Promise.

Ava: I'll call you tomorrow. Maybe dinner then?

Me: ok honey. Miss you.

Ava: Miss you too

Lola Wright

Chapter 17

Ava

I'm not sure why I'm so upset. Gunner wasn't really doing anything too bad. But it looked bad, and because of it, I was put in a sticky spot with a rival club President. It being a club slut made it worse. If it had been a sister of a club member or a female friend of Gunner's, I wouldn't have thought anything of it. Whatever. I'm tired of thinking about it all.

So, I've decided today is a do nothing but hang with my babies kind of day. I'm currently in my jammies, a cute pink cami with satin straps, and matching short shorts. I'm lying on the couch binge-watching *Game of Thrones*. I can't help but to compare Drogo with Gunner. A lot of similarities, only Gunner is taller. Yum.

Loki is asleep near the slider, Mac is sitting on his perch near the end of the couch, Gee is snoozing in his little bed by the TV, and of course, Duffy is out cold on his back between my legs and the back of the couch.

None of us have much ambition today. I wore myself out doing the cookout for the club and keeping the bakery going at the same time. Trudy made it all possible, and I'm thinking of giving her more responsibility and a raise.

I hear a Harley coming down the road and assume it's Petey coming home before I remember he's still in a cast. Curiosity gets the best of me. I lean up and look out the window behind the couch that faces the street.

The bike slows down, and I don't, at first, recognize the rider. Shock and worry shoot through me when I realize the rider is Javier, and he's looking at my house while very slowly riding past. There are two other bikers riding behind him.

I grab my phone and get up off the couch after they've passed. I pull the sheers across the window and jog to my bedroom to get dressed, but I hear the bikes coming back, so I scoot into the pet bedroom to peek out the window from behind the curtains.

It's Javier and his men again, going very slowly as they ride past.

This is not good.

I unlock the screen on my phone. Axel and I had been texting after Gunner and I, and my screen opens to our thread. I hit dial.

"Hey, Ava," he answers.

"Javier is driving up and down my street, staring at my house. He's with two other guys, and I have all my doors locked," I rush out.

"Do you have a gun?" he asks urgently.

"No, but I've practiced with knives before."

"Get one, keep Loki and your phone with you, and stay away from your windows," he instructs me. "I'm on my way."

"Be careful!" I order him, but he's disconnected.

I hear the three bikes ride back and forth past my house several times. Then nothing for a couple of minutes, and then the roar of bikes.

I peek out and see Axel, Vex, Chubs, and Gunner pulling into my drive. I open the door just as they get to it, and they brush past me and Loki into the house.

"Did you see them?" I ask, even though they must have met them a few streets over.

"Yeah, we met them on the street. They continued on toward their territory," replies Gunner.

"So, they just wanted you to know that they know where I live. A not-so-subtle threat," I say.

"That's what it seems to be," growls Gunner.

"So, my calling Axel gave them exactly what they wanted. Damn! I shouldn't have called. They weren't doing anything illegal or threatening," I moan.

"No, Ava. You did the right thing," Axel disagrees.

"Actually, I'm wondering why you called Axel? Your first call should have been to me!" demands Gunner. He looks as pissy as he sounds.

"We'd been texting, so his contact info was the first thing I saw when I unlocked my phone. Should I have taken the time to find 'God' under my contacts instead? Or just hit dial and save time, Gunner?" I ask sarcastically, hands on my hips.

Huh. Guess I'm a little angry with him still.

He glares at me while I return the look.

"Hi, Gunner. Bad, Gunner," says Mac from the end of the counter where he suddenly appears. He lifts his wing as if waving.

Everyone's heads turn to Mac.

"Gunner is in troubleeeeee," shrieks Mac.

"Holy shit! That's your bird?" exclaims Vex.

"I'm a Macaw," states Mac proudly.

"Pretty bird," says Vex.

"Pretty biker boy," replies Mac.

Mac's comment breaks the tension, and everyone laughs.

Chubs comes walking up to the other side of the counter carrying one of my very expensive crystal cake stands and a fork. The chocolate and ganache cake is missing huge bites. Chubs is now sporting chocolate around his mouth.

"Uh, Chubs, I have plates if you need one."

"Nah, I'm good, Ava," he replies while continuing to eat right off the stand.

"Who's who, Mom?" asks Mac.

I do the introductions with Mac giving a wing-wave to each guy.

"Look, Ava, you can't stay here with Javier knowing where you live and us not knowing what he's going to do," says Axel.

"If he was going to do something about it, wouldn't he have done it already?" I ask. "He must've just wanted you to be aware that he knew. Or maybe he wanted to see if I would call and you would come? Testing things out. Make a plan based on your reactions."

"Don't know. Can't take the chance on him returning. Grab a bag, babe. You're coming back to the clubhouse with us," orders Gunner. "And put on some fucking clothes, woman!" he adds as we both notice Vex staring at my boobs.

"I haven't decided yet if I'm even speaking to you. Not so keen on being stuck with you until I do," I retort, crossing my arms over my chest.

"You can stay with me, Sugar Tits," offers Axel. That's his latest name for me. No, I'm not impressed.

"The fuck she can! Your decision has been made, Ava. You *are* speaking to me, and you *are* coming to the clubhouse until we get a read on what Javier is up to. You can be mad at me there instead of here. Pack a bag for you and the pets. Do it now," barks Gunner.

I can see the logic behind going to the clubhouse, but I'm not sure I want the joy of watching Gunner and the club sluts being all friendly again. If it happens, though, I can leave, or I can go to Petey's.

"Don't bark orders at me, Gunner. I have no problem staying with Axel if you think you're going to order me around. So, with that being said, I'm supposed to work tomorrow. Will the pets be okay at the clubhouse, or do I need to bring them back here in the morning?" I ask.

"I'll watch them for you tomorrow, Ava. It's my day off, and they can hang with me," offers Chubs.

"Okay, let me get some things together. Vex, could you grab the dog carrier that's in the garage and put it in the back of the SUV for me, please? And the bag of dog food too?" I ask.

"No problem," Vex says, moving toward the garage door that is off my laundry room.

I head to the pet bedroom and start packing things they need into a couple of duffel bags. I don't need a cage for Mac. He usually doesn't use one anyway, even though he has a couple.

After the pets' stuff is ready, I go into my room, get dressed, gather up a couple of changes of clothes, bathroom stuff, and medicine. I grab a small cooler that I carry sometimes for my insulin and put that into my purse.

I carry everything into the kitchen, and the guys start hauling it out to the SUV while I gather a few ice packs and store them in the cooler. I make the rounds and make sure all the doors and windows are locked, and call Loki and Gee. They follow me into the garage, and I see the guys standing at the back of the SUV. I toss my purse inside the vehicle and open the back driver's side door and motion for Loki. He jumps in, moves to the far side, and sits down. Next, I pick up Gee and set him on the seat also.

"We've been waiting to see how you were going to fit Loki in this carrier, Ava," smiles Vex.

"That's for Duffy. He doesn't travel as well as the others and likes to sit on my lap when I'm driving, so he gets put in the carrier. Be right back," I tell them.

I turn, see Mac in the doorway, and scoop him up and place him on the console between the front seats. He loves to be able to see everything.

I return to the house, locate Duffy, and pick him up. He's a hefty boy weighing in around 48 pounds or so. I have no idea what kind of cat he is, but he is abnormally large. I place him on my hip, like you would a baby, and lock and close the door with the other hand.

When I arrive at the back of the SUV, I see four pairs of eyebrows raise at Duffy. I try putting him into the carrier, but he is pushing himself backward, trying to stay out. I have to use some muscle to finagle him inside and get the door shut and latched.

Before I can get my hand away, a fat, furry, gray paw reaches through the door and bats at my hand. And I hear a growl. This isn't my first rodeo with Duffy, so I jerk out of reach and shut the back of the SUV.

"That was a cat?!" asks Axel, eyebrows almost to his non-existent hairline.

"Yes, that was Duffy. He's a little on the husky side, but we don't judge," I answer.

"What breed of cat is that size?" he continues, questioning.

"BFC," answers Chubs before I can.

"BFC? What's that?"

"Big Fucking Cat," answers Chubs with a grin.

Walking into the clubhouse with the guys and pets, I see it's pretty full of men lounging around watching a game on the flat screen, a few club girls playing pool in ridiculous stripper heels, and other men and women sitting at the bar. All eyes turn our way when our strange crew walks in the door.

I'm carrying Duffy, still like a baby on my hip, while Mac rides in on Chubs' shoulder and whistling the *Andy Griffith* tune. Loki and Gee are following the rest of the guys. Loki makes a beeline straight to the chair Reno is in, and Gee starts running in little circles, hopping around like a crazy-ass pig. And grunting and snorting. He's instantly the center of attention, and several are laughing at his antics.

Gunner guides me toward the bar. I gratefully set Duffy on the floor and take a seat. Mac flutters off of Chubs' shoulder and lands on the bar. He immediately spots peanuts in a bowl and helps himself.

As if all of that wasn't enough to deal with, I spot Amy as the bartender. Ugh! She approaches all smiles at Gunner, and asks what he'd like with a wink. Flirty, of course. Not sure if this day could get any worse.

Petey is a few seats down, and Mac walks that way waving a wing and screeching, "Hi, Petey! Hi, Petey!" while Gunner asks for a beer and a diet Coke. Amy moves off to get the drinks.

Amy returns and slides us our drinks and moves down the bar to stand in front of Mac and Petey.

"What a pretty bird you are," she gushes.

"Yup," answers Mac.

Everyone is chuckling at Mac's lack of modesty. Amy apparently likes the attention as much as Mac as she continues to fuss over him.

"I could just eat you up! You're such a pretty bird!

"I am," crows Mac, strutting up and down the bar.

I turn to Gunner. He's standing behind and to the side of me and has his hand on my lower back. When I look up at him, he steps between my spread knees, and he lowers his forehead to rest on mine, and quietly says, "I'm sorry about last night."

"Me too. I wanted to spend some time with you. Get to know each other better, but then shit went sideways," I reply just as quietly.

He cups the side of my face and brings his lips to mine, giving me just a gentle brush across my mouth.

"We'll get to do that tonight. Just us, at my house, with the pets. We'll have a quiet night, yeah?"

"Sounds perfect, baby," I whisper back.

"Hey, Gunner! Wanted to say thanks for last night," interrupts Amy, leaning across the bar with her arms pushing her tits up—and damn near out of her top. She's smiling seductively at Gunner.

"Back off, slut. We're having a conversation here," I snipe at her.

"Fuck you, bitch! He's single and can fuck whoever he chooses, and that wasn't you last night," she spits back at me.

"Wasn't you either, Amy. And you know that. Get to the other end of the bar or leave the property," snarls Gunner.

Shooting me a nasty look, she heads back down the bar. I look back up at Gunner. I'm not happy I have this shit in my face, and I wouldn't if he hadn't been so clueless last night.

"Is this how it's always going to be? We're half-ass together, and I have to put up with club sluts knowing where you spent your night, and I don't? Because I'm not down with that. No man is worth having to fight for his attention," I state to Gunner.

"Fuck no. That's not how I want it either. You just have to weather the shit they'll toss at you until they realize you're not going anywhere. They'll move on to causing other drama then. Promise, babe. Hang tight for me. For us. I'll do my part too, but they won't go away overnight," Gunner answers.

I sigh to myself. Ugh. He's right. Nothing worth having ever comes easy, and he is worth standing strong for.

"Okay, honey," I say, leaning my head on his chest.

We have a moment of peace before hearing Amy's annoying voice.

"Pretty bird! You want a cracker? Polly want a cracker?" Amy is saying repeatedly to Mac while leaning close to his face. Big mistake.

"Polly want a cracker?" she repeats.

"Ho want a dick?" replies Mac instantly back to her.

I see Petey spew a mouthful of beer across the bar, and Axel lose it and starts howling with laughter.

I then see Mac flinging peanut shells at Amy.

"You disgusting bird! Stop that! Now!" screeches Amy.

Mac flings another at her before I can say or do anything. As I get to my feet to retrieve my mischievous, naughty bird, she slaps Mac in the head. Hard!

Oh, hell no!

I push past Gunner, heading toward Amy, when I see Petey scoop up Mac and cuddle him close. Just as I get to the end of the bar where I can go around it to beat the shit out of Amy, I see a blur rush past me. Next thing I see is Loki's front paws hit Amy square in the chest at full speed, and her go down hard on her back. He's got her pressed to the ground—all 190 pounds of him—paws on her chest, his snarling face about an inch from her terrified one.

I stop, lean against the end of the bar, and enjoy her terror. Everyone is rushing up to see what's going to happen, and I feel Gunner press up behind me.

Axel is still howling in laughter when I turn eyes to Petey and check on Mac.

"You okay, Mac?" I ask him.

"Yeah, Mom. Ho hit me!" he answers.

"I'm so sorry, Mac," I sympathize.

"Eat the Ho, Loki!" Mac hollers.

I look toward Amy, who is now crying and begging, and see Loki hasn't changed positions except now his nose is touching hers, and he's still snarling. His drool is dripping into her face, and she's too scared to wipe it away. I'm so mad I'm vibrating, but I have to admit it is kind of fun watching Loki at his best.

"Eat the Ho, Loki!" screeches Mac again.

Loki snarls louder.

"You going to call him off, babe?" asks Gunner, with a smile in his voice.

"Not until she pisses herself," I answer.

I hear a few chuckles. I guess the guys aren't all that upset that one of their willing sluts is being terrorized by a huge dog. Most are animal lovers and most likely feel she has this coming.

"Pissy Ho," shouts Mac. "Pissy Ho! Pissy Hooooo!

"Loki, bring her to me," I say, stepping a few steps back from the end of the bar.

Loki instantly grabs hold of her jean shorts and belt and drags her from behind the bar to my feet. Amy is screaming and flailing her arms around, trying to grab onto something, but Loki is much stronger than her.

I crouch down next to her head, and Loki releases her but doesn't stop snarling at her.

"If you ever lay another hand on any of my pets, I will not call him off. I'll walk away and let him maul you for as long as he wants. Don't look at them, don't speak to them, and never, ever—fucking ever—touch one of them again. Am I clear?"

"Y-y-yes," she stammers.

I stare down at her for a long moment, then stand and hand signal for Loki to step away. He does and comes to my side, but his hair is still standing on end. My beautiful boy is pissed!

I turn to Gunner. He's standing behind me, smiling huge, and petting the top of Loki's head.

"I'm heading to the kitchen to warm up something to eat. Anyone hungry?" I say to the room as I call the pets, pick up Mac, and walk to the kitchen.

Lola Wright

Chapter 18

Gunner

We're at my house, full with good food and cuddling on the couch while the pets explore their temporary home. They've adapted well, and when I mentioned that to Ava, she explained that they, as a family, have moved several times in the last few years.

I'm half lounging on the arm of the couch, and Ava is tucked up against me in a half-laying position. Her head is on my chest. I put my hands under her arms, pull her up, and twist her until she is lying in front of me as I slide down. We are facing each other with our heads resting on the arm.

She's relaxed, and it's a great look on her face. She's so beautiful it makes me catch my breath and realize how lucky I am that she has given me the benefit of the doubt and is here with me now. Not many women like her would want someone like me. A biker, rough around the edges, wild, and willful. I'm a lucky man, and I know it.

"Why did Chris make that comment about you having contacts and refusing to help his band?" I ask.

"Ugh. Chris is so far up his own ass he doesn't know what's going on around him most of the time. What he meant, though, is that we met when I was at a club with an artist named Solene Bridges. I had met her a few months before that, and we got chatting. She wanted to buy a song I had written. We met later, she listened to it, and eventually, her recording label bought the song, and she recorded it on her second CD."

My eyebrows rise as she looks up at me shyly and smiles.

"You wrote a song? And it sold and was recorded?" I ask, confirming what she just said.

"Yeah, I've written tons of songs, but it has always just been a way of expressing myself, not to try to sell. It just happened. It was fun, and it led to me selling a few others to a few different artists. I'm not getting rich by any means, but I did make enough to make the down payment on the bakery. I have a bit of an artistic bent. I learned how to play guitar at one of the foster homes I was in and loved it. That led to writing songs. Mostly just to get emotions out that I didn't dare express any other way. Anyway, Chris knew who she was and was eavesdropping when she suggested that I get with a band and get some of my songs on tape. She said it would help sell them if the artists could hear them as a complete song. Chris jumped in, introduced himself, and offered his band as a solution. We did a few gigs together, played a couple of my songs, and now he thinks I'm his in to the world of music. I'm not. I don't want the attention of being in a band, and writing the songs was never about trying to make it a career. He doesn't get that, though, and gets nasty when he doesn't get his way."

I think that's the most she's ever revealed about herself. I'm grateful and impressed. But I want to know more. I want to know everything about her. It's like an obsession.

"So, you can sing too?" I ask.

"Well, yeah, a little. When I left my last foster home, I would busk on the streets to make enough money to eat. It wasn't something I really enjoyed, though. I looked at it as a job. Like it or not, I had to eat. Don't get me wrong, I love to sing and play, just not in front of a crowd. I get really nervous. I think they threw money in my guitar case mostly because I was so young, and they felt bad for me," she laughs quietly.

"Tell me who you are, Ava," I ask just as quietly as I slip a piece of her hair through my fingers.

"Ava Beaumont. Twenty-seven years old. Mom to Loki, Mac, Duffy, and Gee. I almost own a bakery that I want to expand to include catering. I love martial arts and the UFC. I want to learn to handle firearms and be comfortable with them. I want to own horses, a donkey, and goats. I want to have, adopt, and/or foster kids. And I want you in my life."

God, this woman! I lean into her, and we share a sweet kiss.

"What about your family, Ava? Why are you alone, and why were you in foster care?"

"I was a mistake. I wasn't wanted," she whispers.

"Your parents put you in foster care?" I gently ask.

"No, they put me in a shoebox and placed me at the bottom of a dumpster. Or at least one of them did. A homeless man heard what he thought was a kitten crying, and he climbed in and found me instead. He took me to a fire station, and they took me to the hospital. I was a preemie, and I was a crack baby. I was a few days old when I was found. It was a miracle I survived that long. After I was healthy enough to leave the hospital, I was put in an orphanage. From then until I was fourteen, I was in thirty-two foster homes and orphanages. Nobody wants to adopt a crack baby."

I'm left speechless and just staring at her. I can't believe any mother could do that to their child, but to have left a small and sick baby like that takes a special kind of evil person. I feel an instant hatred toward her mom. I know if she were here, she would be the first woman I'd ever use force against.

"Did they ever find your mom?" I ask heatedly.

"No, and I don't ever want to find her," Ava responds firmly.

This woman, who takes in strays, loves them, and treats them like family, has never had that given to her. She gives of herself without ever having had it returned. How can I not be impressed that she's done so much in her short life, and all without any help?

"You're not alone anymore, Ava. You have me. You have Petey and Axel and Vex and Chubs. You have the club at your back," I vow.

"That's good to hear since I want all of that," she replies. "And I want you. Now Gunner. Please."

I lift up off the couch and help her stand. I get up, bend down, and toss her over my shoulder. She woofs and starts laughing as I carry her to my bedroom.

I push the door shut behind me with my foot and carry her to the edge of the bed. I set her down on her feet.

"Are the pets okay for the night?" I query.

"They're good. Quit stalling, biker boy. Strip!" she orders.

I don't. I push her down on the bed and follow her, half laying on her, half propped on my left forearm. I immediately slam my mouth down on hers while my other hand settles on her neck. I'm not rushing this no matter how badly I want her.

I settle into her and make love to her mouth. I go deep and fall in love with her taste. Her hands are in my hair, and she's pulling me toward her hard. She's not passive. She's taking what she wants from me as I am her.

She moans long and low. It makes my already hard cock tighten into steel. I shift my weight a bit to help relieve the ache. I slide my mouth from hers to her neck. Her unique scent is enough to make me want to give up going slow and start ripping clothes.

"Oh God, Gunner! Please," she moans, sliding her hands anywhere on me she can reach.

"I don't want to rush this, baby. Let me enjoy you," I whisper in her ear as I nibble on it.

"Okay, honey, but I need to feel your skin. Under my hands and on my skin," she pants.

I push up on my arm and reach behind me to tug my t-shirt off and toss it aside. Her hands immediately land on my chest, and her eyes are drooping with passion. She suddenly scoots down the bed a few inches, and her lips land on my pec. Her mouth is warm and wet and feels so good I grind my cock into her hip.

Now I'm the one who is moaning, and my jeans are uncomfortably tight. I slide my hand to her breast and cup its weight. She has perfect tits. I find her nipple and give it a light pinch. I reach down and pull up her shirt, glance down and see a dark blue lacy bra covering my goal. It looks amazing on her lightly tanned skin, but I need to see her nipples.

I drop to my back and pull her over on top of me. Her mouth instantly hits mine, and she's sliding her tongue in and deep. I pull her shirt up, and she lifts her head long enough for me to pull it off and toss it toward mine on the floor. I gently push her shoulders to get her to sit up astride my hips. I need her moist heat rubbing on my cock, and I want to see her breasts bared to my eyes.

She's sitting up but looking down at me with her golden hair hanging in gentle waves around her face. Fuck, she's beautiful!

"I have some scars, Gunner. They're not pretty, but they're mine, and I survived them. They're a part of me now as a reminder that I can survive almost anything," she tells me in a low voice.

"No scar is going to scare me away, honey. Scars or not, you're beautiful to me. You're perfect for me," I whisper back to her.

She looks down into my eyes for just a moment, sits up straighter as I put my hands on her waist, and then slowly reaches behind her and unhooks her bra, letting it fall to the side. Her gorgeous breasts spill out and into my sight. Unbelievable! Her breasts are full and round without being too big, and her nipples are a perfect raspberry color. They're hard and ready for me.

I slide my hands up her ribs and cover both breasts. She pushes them harder into my hands. I sit up, slide my back partially up against the headboard, and then pull her down tightly to my mouth so I can get a taste of those nipples. She runs her fingers through my hair and moans loudly as I devour them. She starts grinding down against my cock, and I know I need to get her naked.

I pull back and bite gently on her collarbone. She pulls back and looks at me with begging in her eyes. I can't say no. I don't have that in me.

I roll her to the side and lean up over her to help pull her shorts off. I look down and see a small patch of blond curls and the sweetest-looking pussy ever. I run my fingers through the curls, and she gasps. I can't wait any longer. I roll off my side of the bed, stand, and grab a condom out of the nightstand. I turn back to her and see her looking me over with a hungry look in her eyes. I push off my socks, unfasten my belt and jeans, push them down, and step out of them.

I look up to see her staring at my cock as I give it a couple of tugs and start sliding the condom on slowly. Her eyes never leave my cock. Christ, that's making me harder than ever. I've never been so grateful for the hours spent in the gym and sparring with the guys as I am right now. The look in her eyes make up for all the blood and sweat I've given up to look like I do.

Ava slowly rises up to her knees and walks on them to the edge of the bed. I step closer, and she puts her hands on my hips, and looks up at me. I lean down and we kiss gently.

"Lie back, baby, and show me that pretty pussy," I order softly as I continue stroking myself, walking to the foot of the bed.

She moves back and turns so she's facing me before dropping to her back, head to the pillow, and bends her legs until her feet are planted in the bed, spread apart.

She's looking at my hand on my cock, and my eyes drift to the best thing I've ever seen. She's bare, except for that little patch of curls, and she's wet. Glistening. I want to bury my face there and stay until morning. I continue to admire her for another moment, and then I start climbing over her up the bed on my hands and knees. I stop when I get to her pussy and watch, fascinated and turned on as all hell, as her hand gently opens herself up to my view. So pretty and so wet and so mine!

"We're coming back to this part later tonight. I want to taste you, but I need to be in you now," I rasp out.

She removes her hand, and I move on up until my face is above hers. She wraps her arms around my neck and pulls my face down to her mouth. She kisses me, giving me a glimpse of the passion she hides inside.

I once again lay half-on/half-off her and give everything to her through our kiss. I slide my hand down and play with her breasts and nipples, squeezing, rubbing, and pinching. She's making the most amazing sounds. She's so responsive. I finally move my hand over her stomach and down to her wetness. I slide my finger up and down her slit gently, and she pushes against my hand wanting more.

I push her legs open a little more and rub my whole hand over her pussy. I find her clit and flick it gently with my finger. She reacts instantly by attacking my mouth even more. I slide my finger slowly down until it dips into her wetness. Ava moans and raises her hips seeking out more from me. I give her what she wants. I push my finger all the way into her and realize how tight she is. It's hot, wet, and very tight. She's going to grip my cock so good.

I pull my head back from her and look into her eyes while slowly pumping my finger in and out of her pussy. I love the look on her face. She's turned on, she's excited, and she is wanting me. No one else. Me.

I pull my finger from her and slide two back in and watch her quiver. I hook my fingers and search for that spot that will push her over the edge. I find it and rub gently.

"Gunner, please, God, I need you in me. I want to come on your cock, baby," she pleads breathlessly.

I pull my hand away and cover her completely with my body. I grab the back of her knee and pull her leg up and around my hip, opening her up completely to me. I guide my cock to her entrance and enjoy the moist heat coming off of her. I push in about an inch and plant both my forearms on the bed on each side of her head. She wraps her arms around my back and pulls on me. My height puts my head above hers, so I lower my face so my chin is resting near the top of her head, and her face is in the crook of my neck. I push slowly into her.

I stop when I'm all the way in and savor the feeling of her wrapped around me in all ways. I move my leg up a bit, and it forces her leg to push up and around my hip a little higher. I brace against my other knee and foot, glide back almost out of her, and then slam back into her heat. I can't help it. I repeat the glide back and slam forward move a few more times before slowing into a rhythm that is demanding but not brutal.

I push up a little on my arms, so I can look down at her face. She is glowing. She's holding her breath for a beat and then expelling it when I'm moving backward. She's pushing up against me with every thrust, and she's moving her hands around my back, smoothing them up and down to my ass and back to my shoulders.

"Gunner, baby, I need you harder. God, please! I'm so close. I need you to make me come, honey, please," Ava begs.

I start thrusting harder, and I feel a tingling at the base of my spine. I need her to come before I do. I lean up on one arm and reach down between us to find her clit. I rub it and thrust my hips, driving my cock home.

Ava leans up a little and curls into me while watching where our connection meets. I love that she wants to see my cock pounding into her. She reaches down and runs a finger along my cock as it disappears in her.

Fuck, she's going to make me come before her. Shit! I slam into her, and she goes off right when I need her to. She cries out, gasps, and clutches me to her hard. I follow right behind her and feel my orgasm in every part of my body. I explode into the condom while planting deep in my girl.

She hangs tight for a few seconds then leans back down into the bed and shudders. Her eyes meet mine just as I start a few slow glides in and out of her while feeling her tremors from the power of our orgasms. She couldn't look more gorgeous.

I stop gliding and stay planted.

Then I plant my face in her neck and breathe in heavily. She wraps her arms around me, and there is no place I'd rather be than right here with her, in her.

After a moment of blissful unawareness of anything but us, I slowly pull out and move on my back next to Ava. I remove and toss out the condom and curl my arm under Ava's shoulders and pull her front into my side. Her head is on my chest and her hand is on my abs. I'm the most content I think I've ever been.

We lay in silence as I caress her lower back and keep my woman tight to my side. I wish we could stay like this forever. It's perfect. She's perfect.

As I run my hand along her lower back, I feel the scars she mentioned earlier. Raised bumps of ruined flesh. I don't hesitate on them because I need her to understand, scars or not, she is perfect to me. And I don't ask about them either. Now is not the time.

"You fuck like a boss," Ava states.

I bust out laughing at her, and I feel her giggle more than I hear it.

"I'm lying here mindless, and you're lying there thinking that?" I ask.

"I'm blissed out and mindless because of that," she retorts, snuggling in tighter.

Lola Wright

Chapter 19

Ava

I wake up slowly and with a smile. Gunner's curled around me. He's warm and hard everywhere. I have to grin at the thought that the big, badass biker is cuddly and likes to spoon. I hate to get up, but the pets need food and to get outdoors. I start sliding out from Gunner's grip, and it suddenly tightens. His face presses up against the back of my neck, and he groans.

"Don't move unless you're shifting my direction," Gunner growls.

"I have to let Loki and Gee outside, baby. I'll get coffee and come back," I tell him.

"I'll do that, and you stay here, stay naked, and I'll be right back," he replies as he rolls out of bed and yanks on his jeans.

I enjoy the view of his back and ass as he leaves the room. I get up, slip on his t-shirt, and head to the bathroom. After brushing my teeth, swiping a brush through my hair, and using the facilities, I go back into the bedroom and climb back into bed.

I no more than get settled when Gunner walks in the door carrying two cups of coffee, jeans still unbuttoned, sexy abs and chest on display, and being followed by Duffy, who jumps onto the bed and flops down across my legs.

Gunner sits with his back against the headboard and hands me a cup. We're sitting side by side, arms brushing together, sipping our coffee.

"What time do you have to leave for work?" Gunner asks.

"Not going. I called Carrie last night when I was packing, and she's working for me today. She wants the extra hours, so this works for both of us. I thought it would be easier to just take the day off than to need someone to babysit me at the bakery all day."

Gunner reaches over and takes the cup from my hand and places it with his on the nightstand. He then turns to me, grasps me by the waist, and sets me on his lap. I place my arms around his neck and lean in for a kiss.

"Good idea, baby. We can spend the day together and just be us. I have to run to the clubhouse and do a few paperwork things, but after that, I'm all yours. Yeah?" Gunner asks.

"Sounds perfect. We haven't had much alone time. And I want that with you," I say as I lay my head on his chest and snuggle into him.

"I want that too, more than you know," he replies quietly.

Gunner's in his office at the clubhouse, and I'm sitting at the bar writing out a grocery list. Mac is standing on the bar in front of Chubs sharing some mixed nuts. Gee is pushing his skateboard around the main room, and Loki is nearby watching everything.

A few of the members are scattered around. A prospect is behind the bar stocking and washing glasses. It's actually quiet in here, and I noticed everyone seems a little more serious than usual.

I'm guessing they don't like the Banditos stirring things up, and they don't like the disrespect being shown to their club.

I'm staring at the back wall of the bar, concentrating on what I need to put on my list when Mac decides to get on my bad side and lighten the mood of the guys at the same time.

"Mom got her some! Mom got her some!" he screeches loudly.

I'm so shocked, I don't even move. Not even my eyes.

"Oh Gunner, harder! Harderrrrrrrr!" he spouts.

O M G! I can feel the heat creeping up my neck and face. I can also hear the laughter coming from the room.

"Fucks like a boss! Fucks…"

"You say one more word Mac, and you will be in a ziplock bag next to the chicken in my freezer! Got me?" I snarl at him. "No more cashews for you—ever!"

I step off my stool, stalking his direction when I see him take off running the length of the bar hollering, "Loki, save me! Save me!"

He gets to the end just as Loki arrives. He jumps off and lands on Loki's back. Loki walks off nonchalantly.

"Whew! Mom is pissed!" shouts Mac.

The laughter and howling in the room is deafening. Before I can find a corner to crawl into, Gunner strides into the room looking quizzically at the guys still laughing. It doesn't take him long to figure out that I'm the butt of the joke. Probably could tell by the flaming red of my face.

Gunner strolls over to me, grinning, hooks me behind the neck, and pulls my face to his chest.

"No idea why you're blushing, and the guys are laughing, so I'll just ask, whose ass do I need to kick?"

"Mac's feathery ass. He outed me. My own damn bird just told the room that, and I quote, 'Mom got her some,' plus a few other juicy comments," I reply, hiding my face.

I can feel Gunner's body shaking with his laughter. Of course, he's not embarrassed. Men have no shame. He hugs me tighter, and I guess it's time to face the men. I pull away, look around the room, making eye contact with each and every one of them, and I take a bow. Then I call Loki, Mac, and

Gee and walk out of the clubhouse with the little bit of dignity I have left.

Gunner's working again, and I'm hanging with the pets at his house. It's a Cape Cod style, dark gray with white trim. It has four bedrooms, three bathrooms, and great closets. I especially like the open floor plan between the living room, dining area, and kitchen. A long slate-gray granite countertop in the kitchen separates it from the dining room and living room areas. The appliances are all top of the line and are a cook's dream. And everything is surprisingly neat, orderly, and clean. With Gunner being a single guy, I guess I was expecting a little clutter. It's nice seeing that he likes order as much as I do.

I love that his backyard is fenced. Loki and Gee are taking advantage of that fact. Duffy is lying across my lap sleeping, and Mac is softly humming to himself on the coffee table. I have a stew bubbling gently on the stove, bread in the oven, and am waiting for Gunner to finish up so we can relax together.

My phone vibrates where it's lying on the coffee table. I pick it up, and my stomach gives a little lurch seeing a text from Gunner. I get that lurch every time I see him, hear his voice, or know he's close by.

Gunner: Almost done. You ok?

Me: I'm fine. Missing you though.

Gunner: Same. Anxious to get home to you.

Me: Make it happen.

Gunner: Be there soon

I set my phone down and get up to check on dinner. Everything's looking good, so I plop down at the table and open my laptop to work on payroll for the bakery. After a few minutes of working, there's a knock at the door.

I open the door, and Fang's standing on the wrap-around deck.

"Hi, Fang, what's up?" I ask, surprised to see him. I stand in the doorway, and I feel a little guilty, but I don't invite him inside. I'm not sure why, maybe it's because I know he screwed over a co-worker, but I'm not comfortable around him. He seems shady, and I don't like the vibe I get from him.

"Hey, Ava. It was decided I'll be the one sticking with you at the bakery tomorrow. Just wanted to know what time you want to leave, so I can pick you up here in the morning," he says.

I'm not thrilled it's him they chose to shadow me. But it's not my choice, and I have to roll with the decision Gunner made.

"I need to leave at 4:30am. I'm usually at the bakery by then, but getting there by 5:00am will be okay," I answer.

"Okay. I'll be here at 4:30 tomorrow morning. See you then," Fang says, then turns and leaves without another word.

I shut the door and realize that during our entire conversation, Fang never once made eye contact. Odd. Obviously, Gunner trusts him with my safety, and I should too, but I am not convinced I can.

My head is thrown back, and my feet are planted on the edge of the bed. I have my hands in Gunner's silky hair, and I'm tugging uncontrollably. Gunner has an extremely talented mouth, and I'm finding out just how talented at the moment.

"I want one more, Ava. Give it to me," rasps Gunner, lifting his mouth momentarily from eating me out.

"I can't, baby! I can't, please, come in me! Gunner, baby, I need you in me now," I moan, thrashing my head on the bed.

Gunner slowly pushes two fingers into me and nips my clit lightly with his teeth. That's all it takes to give him the one more he wanted. I explode, curling my abs for a second, and then flinging myself back on the bed. The whole time, I'm still pulling at his hair.

"That's right, baby! Let me have it all. Fuck, I love the taste of you," he says, pulling back and slowly gliding his fingers in and out of me but giving my clit the break it needs.

I open my eyes and point them toward Gunner to see his satisfied smirk. He removes his fingers, places his hands under my pits, and shifts me to lay with my head on the pillows as he comes down on top of me.

I pull his mouth to mine and taste myself on his lips. I wrap my limbs around Gunner and savor the feeling of his hardness and heat. He's a beautiful man—face and body.

After a moment of kissing me tenderly, he rises up onto his knees between my thighs, and reaches for a condom. I watch with appreciation as he wraps that beautiful cock and then pumps it a few times while staring back down at me.

"I need you on your hands and knees, baby," he orders.

I quickly comply and when my ass is raised right in front of his cock, he rubs the head of it through my wetness while placing his hands on my hips.

"Soft, wet, pink, and mine. Beautiful, baby. I can't go slow this time," he whispers to me as he places his cock at my willing and wet opening.

"Take what you need, honey. I want it, and I want you anyway I can get you," I tell him.

He slams all the way in, and it is fantastic! I push back against him, and he starts pounding hard at me, gripping my hips and using them as leverage and to hold me in place. Every few thrusts, he does a swirl and grinds hard. He's hitting right where I need him to, and I'm getting close again.

"Lift up, baby, back to my chest, now," he orders harshly.

I do as he says, and his arms slide around me, one to my breast and nipple, pinching hard, the other to my clit and our connection. I lay my head back on his shoulder while he thrusts up into me hard.

"Gunner! Now, please! Harder!" I demand.

He pinches and tugs my nipple hard, scrapes my clit with his fingernail, and slams home hard. I come, groaning out my release, and I push down hard on his cock.

His hand leaves my breast. I feel his forearm across the back of my shoulders as he pushes just my upper half down flat on the bed. He repositions his foot and grabs my shoulder, and slams home hard and steady for a few thrusts before he stays rooted deep in me. He pauses for a moment, and I hear him release the breath he'd been holding as he starts rotating in small circles and grinding hard against me. It sets off small aftershocks and a mini-orgasm before I relax into the bed, spent.

Gunner pulls out gently, and I fall flat on the bed. I feel his hand gently rubbing my ass.

"You okay, babe?" he asks with a smile in his voice.

"Not sure. Ask me in a while," I say back, exhausted.

He chuckles and leaves the bed to deal with the condom. He comes back, slides into bed next to me, and pulls me up tight to him. He moves the hair out of my face and places a sweet kiss on my forehead and covers us partway with the sheet.

We lay for several moments, recuperating and enjoying the feel of being alone together. I'm starting to drift off to sleep when Gunner rolls to his side so that we are now face-to-face with his arm lying over my waist.

I reach up and drift the back of my hand across his jaw. He hasn't shaved for a day or two, and I love the scruff. His eyes are so close to being black that it's only in the light you can see any brown in them at all.

"I know you're wondering about the scars on my back. And I appreciate you not pushing about them. It's not something I've ever talked about before. Never had anyone I trusted enough to talk to about what happened… I buried the reason I got them deep. Very deep. I placed it into a box at the back of my brain, and since I don't see the scars very often, I can pretend they're not there," I say quietly.

"Do you trust me enough to tell me what happened? You don't have to if it's too hard. I can wait. I want you to trust me, but I know some things are hard to discuss," Gunner says, just as quietly.

I burrow deeper into Gunner. I need the safety he gives me.

"I was working at a restaurant in Bozeman. A co-worker insisted on setting me up on a blind date with the brother of the guy she'd just started dating. I finally said yes and went on the date. He was nice. Clean cut, good looking, well dressed. It was an okay date, but I didn't feel anything toward him. No spark, nothing. I don't know why either. I was twenty-three and single, and should have been excited about the date, but something was off," I tell him.

Gunner is slowly stroking my side and hip and listening intently.

"At the end of the date, he asked me out for another one. I politely thanked him but said no to another date. He was nice about it but kept pushing for just one more. I finally gave in and agreed to another date," I continue.

"My co-worker was all excited and suggested a double date with her and his brother. I thought that might ease the tension a little, so I agreed. I still knew I wasn't interested but foolishly didn't follow my instincts."

I pause and take a deep breath. Gunner hugs me to him tighter and then eases back, and says, "You don't have to finish. I don't need to know if it's going to bring up bad memories, but I'd like to share your burden and help if I can."

"I went on the date. Met his brother. It was okay, but still, I didn't feel like I wanted to continue seeing him. I just didn't feel anything but wary about him, and more so about his brother. Just a gut feeling. After the date, the three of them drove me home, and he walked me to my door. On the first date, I had met him at the restaurant, and I should've done that again. I was stupid. He again tried for another date, but I was firm this time that I wasn't looking for a relationship at the time, but I thanked him and wished him well. He took it better than I expected, kissed me on the cheek, and returned to the car, and they left."

I can feel my breathing and heart rate starting to pick up speed and get heavier. I was tensing up, and I knew Gunner sensed it too when he again kissed me on the head and then rested his cheek there.

"My co-worker, Tiffy, was a little pissy with me for a few days, but eventually, she got over it, I guess. She continued dating the brother, Mitch, and quit bringing up Mark to me. She told other co-workers that I felt I was too good for someone like Mark, but I just ignored the gossip and kept my head down. It soon blew over."

"Mark would text or call sometimes, but I never answered. I felt communicating with him would be like leading him on that there could be something at some point. But he was persistent. I saw him near the restaurant several times and twice at the grocery store. His brother and Mark lived the county over from where I did, so I started feeling like I was being stalked. I got home late one night from work and saw him parked on the street across from my apartment. I lived on the ground floor, and my apartment faced the parking lot and street. He sat out there for hours."

"I went to work the next day and pulled Tiffy aside. I told her that he was stalking me, and she didn't believe me. Told me to 'get over myself' and walked off. I should have talked to the police, but being a foster kid raised in the system, I wasn't trusting of the police. And as it turned out, it wouldn't have mattered."

At this point, I need some distance. I sit up, place my back against the headboard, and stare straight ahead. I need to be in control of my emotions, so I try to blank my mind and just spit the words needed to finish this story. Gunner sits up, mirroring my position, waiting.

"You think you're safe in your own apartment, and in your own bed, but you're not. I woke up to being punched in the face repeatedly. I tried to fight back, but I was already injured and confused as to what was happening. And I was outnumbered. There were two of them. Mark and his brother, Mitch. One kept their hand over my mouth while the other punched me everywhere he could. They took turns and then worked together once they stuffed a washcloth in my mouth. Long story short, they took turns beating me with fists, feet, and Mark's belt and buckle, and then they did worse. They did the one thing I never thought I could come back from." I shudder hard, eyes dry.

"After a few hours, I was only semi-conscious, and I think they assumed I was dead or would be soon. They stood around me, lying on the floor, laughing, and high-fiving each other. They taught me a lesson for being a stuck-up bitch. Nobody turned down a Carrington. Mark made the comment, 'she's circling the drain,' and then they both spit on me and left my home."

"Fuck me. Jesus. Baby, come here," Gunner says low, sounding like he's in pain while reaching for me and pulling me tight to him. His body circles mine as much as he can, and I can feel his heat soaking into mine. I lean into him and just breathe through the pain of the memories.

I continue talking because I have to finish this now that I've started.

"I woke up six weeks later—five weeks and five days later to be exact—in the hospital. I had numerous broken bones. A skull fracture. Severe bruising to my kidneys and spleen. Lacerations on my back from the belt buckle. If there was anything lucky about the attack, it was that I was in a coma while the worst of the injuries healed. I didn't have to be awake for the stitches or setting of the bones. Rehab was tough and painful. I healed. The injuries healed. Mentally, I was a mess. I was scared of leaving the hospital. I was scared to sleep. I was scared of the dark."

I reach down and take hold of Gunner's hand. I need to lean on his strength a little.

"But the worst part of it all was that the cops wouldn't take a statement or listen to me. They said 'the issue' was resolved, and I needed to return to my life. I called city, county, and state agencies and was rebuked from every one of them. I didn't understand why no one would listen. Finally, the hospital had a social worker come to my room and explain," I pause, staring at the wall.

After a moment, Gunner squeezes my hand gently and asked, "Why, baby? Tell me, and then I'm going to hold you all night, and you'll be safe to sleep. I promise that on my life."

"The brothers' parents died when they were very young in a car accident. Their uncle had raised them. Their uncle is Senator Carrington. He's very powerful and has a lot of friends in all the right places. Mitch, the brother, is the Sheriff for the county they live in, and Mark was one of his deputies. The Senator used his influence to get the charges reduced. Mark took a plea agreement for simple assault and received one year of probation, and part of the plea agreement was that if he pled guilty, Mitch wouldn't be charged at all. Mitch is still the Sheriff, and Mark now works as the jail administrator instead of as a deputy. That's all they got for what they did. It was all signed and sealed by the time I woke up from the coma they had caused."

Gunner is so angry, I can feel him vibrating next to me. I know the feeling—I've lived with it for four years now. But he remains calm on the outside and is what's keeping me grounded.

"The good Senator put ten thousand dollars into my bank account to 'pay my medical expenses,' but it was really to try to buy me off. He also made huge donations to the various police agencies different charities. None were willing to help me because they didn't want to lose the money. He bought them off too. The money is still in my account. I have never touched a penny of it and someday when I can face, really face, what happened, I'll donate it to a worthy cause. I packed up and left and have moved quite a few times over the years, trying to escape my own head. I have a good lock on it most days now. I have not, to this day, shed a single tear over the attack. I refuse to give them that too. I can't control the nightmares I still have sometimes, but I can control my tears. They don't get those too!" I say vehemently.

Gunner is done sitting and doing nothing. He turns to me suddenly, pushes me down on the bed on my side, comes down facing me, wraps me in his strong arms, and pulls me in tight. He pushes my face into his neck and gently rocks us back and forth.

"They should've paid for what they did, baby. Not right how you were treated by the people that are supposed to protect the innocent, not the guilty. But never again! You're not alone anymore, and you have me, Axel, and Petey. You have the others in the club. We're your people now. You belong to me, to us. You just keep being strong, and I'll be at your back anytime you need me," he vows. Then continues, "But if you need to shed those tears, do it for you and not because of them. Heal yourself however you need to. I'm here, and I'm not going anywhere that you aren't. You cry your tears, I don't care. I'll hold you through them and beyond. Always know that."

I hold on tight to the best thing that has ever happened to me. Gunner. My Gunner. My rock. My future. And I sleep tight in his arms, his safety. I sleep peacefully, feeling and knowing I'm safe.

Chapter 20

Gunner

I lay awake long after Ava falls asleep. I'm wrapped tight around her, and my mind is racing. My beautiful girl was attacked and raped by two men. Two cops that are sworn to serve and protect that have an uncle that uses his power and influence to protect them and their lack of morals. They didn't pay for what they did in any way. And that can't stand. I can't let it stand.

So much makes sense now. Ava's obsession with self-defense and martial arts. Learning how to use a knife outside of the kitchen. Wanting to learn how to handle firearms. Loki. Moving several times, most likely looking for somewhere she felt safe. Her not batting an eye at a group of bikers but being nervous around law enforcement. Her wariness around Officer Stanaway. She's learned the hard way the good guys aren't always good, and yet she's found safety with us, the ones that are supposed to be bad. And it definitely explains the wiped hospital records.

My mind races with things I need to speak with Rex about tomorrow. I need his computer skills. I need to come up with a foolproof way to make the Senator and his nephews pay for all they did to Ava. Nothing will make up for everything she went through, but they still need to bleed, and in a way that won't come back on my woman or us. We don't need the kind of heat a Senator can bring, but I'll burn our compound down myself before they're walking away and living easy.

Fang followed Ava to the bakery this morning, and Chubs is here to get the pets. Duffy's refusing to let Chubs pick him up by hissing and swatting at his hands, and Mac is standing nearby on the counter warning Chubs, "Don't piss off the cat!"

I intervene before things get bloody and tell Chubs to leave the cat here at the house. He sleeps all the damn time anyway. We set out food and water, and Ava had set up a litter box, so the cat is set to sleep his day away.

Chubs and I walk to the clubhouse with Loki and Gee following and Mac riding on Chubs' shoulder. As soon as we enter, Chubs heads to the kitchen, and Pooh calls Gee to him. I see Pooh pull a shirt out of his back pocket and starts putting it on Gee. I shake my head at them and head to my office with Loki.

I pull my cell from my pocket as I sit down at my desk.

"Hey Prez, what's up?" answers Rex.

"I need some intel on three people. I need every single thing you can dig up on them. Got a pen to write down their names?"

"Yep. Shoot," says Rex.

"Mitch and Mark Carrington. They're brothers. They live in a county near Bozeman. Mitch is the sheriff. Mark was a deputy but now is the jail administrator. Also, their uncle. Senator Carrington. I want bank records, land or property they own, addresses, marriages, divorces. I want every damn thing on them."

"A Senator. Wow. Okay, I'll get busy. This have anything to do with Ava? Since she lived in that area, I'm guessing it does." Rex questions.

"Yeah, it does. Dig deep, Rex," I tell him.

"On it, Boss. Hey, I did find a few things out that you'll want to know, though. I was going through cell phone records of Javier's. He calls and gets calls regularly from Stanaway. That cop that handled Ava's neighbor's complaint. And Stanaway was pulled off detective duty and put back on the road for some mishandling of evidence. Evidence that would've hurt the Banditos. He's dirty, just like we knew. He's probably how Javier knew Ava's home address. He's worth keeping an eye on too."

"Fuck! I was wondering how Javier found her so quick. Keep an eye on their cell phone traffic. We may need to do something about Stanaway."

"Will do. I'll be at the clubhouse later and will get with you on anything I find out on the other shit then. See ya," Rex says and disconnects.

Gunner: Hey babe. Everything ok?

Ava: Yep, all's well. Busy here today playing catch up.

Gunner: Fang there?

Ava: He left but said he'd be back to follow me home and then to the clubhouse.

Gunner: Don't leave without one of us.

Ava: I won't. If you have time, come here. I need a kiss lol

Gunner: I'll bring lunch. And a kiss (wink)

Ava: Perfect!

Gunner: Call if you need me before that.

Ava: Ok baby

I settle in and get to work running an MC. Loki settles in and decides to take a nap. After a few hours, I get up and head to the main room to get a Coke. First thing I spot when I hit the main room is Gee riding his skateboard around the room wearing a t-shirt that reads: I only ride Hogs!

I stop and watch him, laughing at his t-shirt, when he rides toward me and bounces off my legs. It doesn't faze him. He gets up and starts pushing the skateboard with his snout. He's always the happiest little guy, and I've noticed he's made friends with several of the club members.

I wander over to the bar and take a seat next to Petey. He's looking grumpy today. I nudge his shoulder with mine when I sit down and look him over.

"What's up, Petey?"

"Not much. I'm bored as fuck. Few more weeks with this cast, and I get it off. Think I'm going to take a road trip for a few days. Get out of town and just ride," he states.

"I was at the shop the other day, and your bike looks great. All fixed up. Might do you some good to spend some time on it and away from here," I answer.

"Yeah. I feel useless as hell sitting around with this cast. Shit's happening with Ava, and I'm not even able to be there for her," Petey grumbles.

Ah, now I get why he looks grumpy. Petey and Ava have gotten very close, and he's worried about her. He proves this with his next comments. Ones I knew were coming my way sooner or later.

"People know she means something to you, to me. That makes her a target. That's unacceptable. I'm of little to no help to her right now. But you can be, should be. But you need to keep your eye on the prize. You're like a son to me, always have been, but especially since we lost your parents. And I don't mean to sound like I'm lecturing you like you're a kid, but you need to decide if you want her permanently or if she's just a minute's distraction for you. And if that is all she is to you, then cut her loose. I'll kick your fucking ass for that, but it would be better in the long run if you can't treat her the way she deserves. She's the best thin…"

"She's mine. Period. Not letting her go, ever. And I have my head on straight about that, Petey," I state firmly, interrupting his soon-to-be tirade.

Petey stops speaking. Stares at me for a moment and then nods his head.

"Good. Glad to hear that, son. Real glad. She's got a good heart, and she's given you the benefit of the doubt more than once now. Don't push your luck, though. I learned that lesson the hard way. Cost me my marriage, and I don't want to see you make the same mistake. Ava is loyal. You don't find many like that in today's world. Treasure it, don't destroy it." Petey hesitates for a moment and then asks, "Has she told you why she was in the system as a kid?"

"Yeah, she did. She is a survivor," I answer.

"I want to find her mom if she's still alive. Not for Ava. She doesn't want to ever meet her mom, and I can't blame her for that. But because I want her mom to see what she threw away like trash. I want her to know that her daughter is a beautiful person, inside and out, and not because of her mom, but despite her. I want her mom to feel like the pile of shit that she is. I want to grind her in the dirt and leave her there," Petey says angrily.

"I'm with you on that, Petey. The woman doesn't deserve to know Ava, though, and she doesn't deserve to ease her conscious by knowing she didn't kill her daughter. She doesn't deserve shit," I reply.

"Yeah, true," he agrees.

Chubs walks in from the kitchen with Mac still perched on his shoulder. Chubs is carrying a bowl of fruit and a plate stacked high with chips and sandwiches. He plops down on the other side of Petey. Mac hops onto the bar, and Chubs slides the fruit over to Mac.

"Hi, Petey, Gunner," says Mac waving his wing at us.

"Hey, Mac," chuckles Petey.

"Hey, Mac," I say.

"If you're going to be around here today, Petey, want to watch the pets for me? I got a few things to do at work, but I can take them with me too. Doesn't matter, really. I like the little shits," says Chubs around a mouthful of food.

"Swear!" shouts Mac.

Chubs sets his sandwich down and pulls a cashew out of his pocket and gives it to Mac.

"Thanks," says Mac, eating his cashew that I'm pretty sure Ava told him he could never have again.

"What's that about?" I ask, waving my hand between Mac and Chubs.

"Mac's version of a swear jar," answers Chubs, smiling. "I swear, he gets a cashew. He's helping me clean up my language, so he doesn't learn bad words from me, and Ava doesn't get pissed at me."

"Swear!" shouts Mac again. And he receives another cashew from Chubs.

"That damn bird is training you alright, Chubs," laughs Petey. "He's outsmarting you too!"

"Swear!" screeches Mac.

"Doesn't work on me, Mac," chuckles Petey.

"Fuck!" answers Mac.

I'm laughing at Mac when I turn to Petey and tell him, "I'm taking lunch to Ava in a few minutes.

Want to ride along? We can take the pets so Chubs can go get some things done."

"I'll take Loki and Gee with me. The guys at the shop will love them," says Chubs. "You take Mac. I'm running out of cashews anyway."

"Yeah, let's go. You're buying me lunch too, though," answers Petey while picking up Mac.

I can't believe that Petey has to give me directions to get to Ava's shop. I've never been here, and I should have by now since she's my woman. I pull up close to the front door and park my truck. I feel like an ass for having neglected to see the place that's so important to Ava. But now that I'm here, I have to admit, I'm impressed. It's obviously too girly for me, but it fits her personality. It's cute and quirky. Pink, black, and white signage out front announcing its name—Sweet Angel Treats. The sign has a small angel floating in the corner and holding a cupcake.

I grab lunch, Mac hops onto Petey's shoulder, and we enter through the front door. I notice the bike cake in a display case immediately and head that direction. The detail is amazing. Chubs had told us about it but seeing the cake in person is another story. Ava's talent is evident in every little detail of the cake. Petey's as impressed with it as I am if his "fuck me" is any indication.

"Hey, Trudy," screeches Mac.

I turn and see a cute brunette at the counter. She's got bouncy curls and a huge smile on her face. Ava has spoken highly of Trudy, and I can see why. She's perfect for the front of the store.

Trudy comes out from behind the counter and walks toward us. She's not gorgeous like Ava, but she's nice looking and has a nice full figure. Her personality shines through, and that's what catches your attention the most. And I notice it's caught Petey's as he is standing a little straighter and smiling back.

"Hi, Mac! You're looking hot today," Trudy says as she reaches us.

"Of course," answer Mac.

"Oh my God, you two must be Gunner and Petey! Ava said a hot, badass biker was bringing her lunch today, but she didn't say there would be two of them coming that fit that description," Trudy says, grinning at Petey.

Trudy holds out her hand to Petey and introduces herself.

"Hi, Petey, I'm Trudy. It's so nice to meet you after hearing Ava gush about you all the time."

They shake hands with Petey grinning ear to ear.

"Hi, Gunner! So nice to meet you. You're a big, tall glassful, aren't you? Wow."

"Hey, Trudy. Nice to meet you. And thank you for helping Ava out when she was cooking for our poker run. She told me how much she relies on you, so thank you," I say, shaking her hand.

She beams at me.

"Okay, boys, quit flirting with every pretty girl you see and feed me," laughs Ava as she comes out of the kitchen and walks up to me.

I lean down for a kiss and get a full-body hug at the same time. Ava leans into me and then looks toward Petey and Mac.

"Hi, guys!"

"Hi, Mom!" says Mac, jumping from Petey's shoulder to Ava's in a flurry of wings and feathers.

Trudy smiles, gives a low wave, and walks back to the counter. We all walk over to a table that Ava indicates, and we sit. Mac perches on the back of an empty chair. I sit our lunch on the table and start pulling out our take-out containers of Chinese food. Everyone dives in, and we talk very little as we're eating. As we're finishing up, Petey tells Ava about Chubs' and Mac's antics and their "swear jar" deal. Ava's laughing, and it's a beautiful sight. To know all she has survived and yet seeing her get so much pleasure from little things like her bird outsmarting a club brother. She's strong and positive. She looks forward, not backward. She doesn't dwell on what's been bad in her life but uses those experiences to strengthen herself for better outcomes in the future. How can I not admire that ability?

"I love the bike cake, babe. Unbelievable how much detail you put in that," I tell Ava.

She smiles huge at me. She's proud of the cake, and she should be. It's amazing.

I look around the shop, and my mouth drools when I spot all the different pastries and sweet treats in the various display cases. There are cakes of every flavor displayed on small tables and counters, a full display of every doughnut and bagel you can image. There are pies on pretty plates in one case, while different pastries in small bite-size pieces in another. She's got just about every type of dessert on display somewhere. The old-fashioned counter with the diner-style stools are all full with customers eating treats and sipping coffee. There are small tables and booths scattered around the shop along with an area that has a few couches and comfy-looking chairs. The shop is pretty full, and there's a steady stream of customers coming in and out of the door buying things to take home.

I note that there's a young girl, probably early college age, keeping busy just filling the cases and boxing treats up for the customers that Trudy is collecting the money from and sending them on their way with a smile. My woman has a thriving business. I'm proud as fuck of that, knowing I have someone in my life that isn't afraid of hard work and will go after what she wants.

I tune back into the conversation going on between Ava and Petey, and I move my chair closer to Ava and drop my arm over her shoulders. I lean over and give her a kiss on the temple and tell her quietly, "Love the shop, babe."

Ava turns and gives me a gentle brush of her lips across my mouth and answers just as quietly, "Thank you."

Trudy approaches the table and asks what she can get us for dessert. Ava asks for a coffee, and Petey and I are stumped. There are so many choices to choose from, and I honestly want some of everything.

When I tell Trudy that, she laughs and says to leave it up to her, and she walks away.

"How do you work here and stay so slim, Ava?" asks Petey eyeing all the treats on display.

"Martial arts classes and jogging. Plus, when you're making it all day, you end up taking little bites of this or that so you can adjust the flavors, and you get plenty of it by the end of the day, and that keeps me from eating huge slices of everything," she explains.

Trudy approaches and sets down a tray with about a dozen or so different sweets and cups of coffee for everyone.

"You find something on that tray that you want more of, just holler. I won't be far," Trudy states, winking at Petey and walks off.

"Love you to pieces, Petey, you know that, but you pull a 'Fang' here and cost me Trudy as an employee, and I'll hurt you bad," Ava states calmly.

Petey smiles innocently at Ava as he starts stuffing treats in his mouth.

Lola Wright

Chapter 21

Ava

After the guys and Mac leave, I get back to work. I don't have a lot to finish up before I can leave, so I get it done and go looking for Fang. I find him out front in a booth texting on his phone. As I approach, he turns his phone over on the table.

"Ready to leave?" Fang asks.

"Yes. I'm ready. I need to stop at Whole Foods on the way for a few things, though. Then a quick stop at my house. That okay?"

"Sure," he grumbles, still not making eye contact.

I turn to leave and notice he picks his phone back up, swipes on it, and continues texting. I leave the shop and get into my Camaro parked out back. I sit there with it running, waiting for Fang. I have a bad feeling, and I'm not sure why. I remind myself that Gunner trusts him, and I should too, but I also know that it's my responsibility to keep myself safe. I still feel the hair on the back of my neck tingle.

After a few moments, Fang comes out the back door and heads to his bike, waving his hand at me to go. I pull out and drive toward Whole Foods with Fang following. I pull into their parking lot, check my surroundings, get out of the car, and walk inside. I move through the store quickly, grabbing everything I need, pay, and bag up my groceries. I decide to put them in a cart rather than carry them, following the advice from a former self-defense instructor who said not to weigh your arms down in case you needed them for protection.

I know I sound paranoid. Don't judge me. I ignored my instincts once and paid dearly for doing that. Never again. I may not be able to save myself someday, I can't control other people's actions, but I can do my best not to put myself in a bad situation or be unaware of what's going on around me. Be aware, be prepared, my instructor used to say.

I pause at the door of the store and look around. I see Fang waiting on his bike, once again texting. I keep my head up, eyes watchful, and go straight to my car. I put the groceries in the passenger seat and approach Fang.

"I'm not going home first. I'm going straight to the clubhouse," I tell him.

"What the fuck, Ava? You said you were going home first," he says irritably. "Quit worrying about every little thing, go home, get what you need, and then we'll go to Gunner's. Easy."

I hesitate. He's right. It'd be easier for me to go home, get a change of clothes for work tomorrow, and then go to Gunner's. But I feel this need to get to Gunner. I can't explain it, but I need Gunner close. I can get clothes in the morning.

"I don't need to go to the house," I kind of lie to Fang.

"Jesus fuck, Ava! I don't want to have to get up even earlier tomorrow, so you have time to go home first! My job is to keep you safe. Fucking babysitting. Doesn't mean you give the orders. Fuck!" he snarls at me.

I'm shocked at his outburst, but I'm not backing down, and I'm not standing in the middle of a parking lot any longer arguing with him. I turn on my heel, get in my car, and pull out of the parking lot, heading toward the clubhouse. Fuck him. He can follow or not, I don't care. I see him following me, but he's on his phone, probably bitching to Gunner about his woman. I'm so not going to have him as my babysitter tomorrow. And I don't care what Gunner has to say about that.

I stop at a red light and see Fang a few cars behind me. Light turns green, I drive through the intersection, and take a right onto the freeway. There's very little traffic, and I relax a little until I hear the roar of more than one bike. I look in the mirror and see five bikes coming up behind me. None of them are Fang. All have visors on their helmets, and they're pulled down, hiding the faces of the riders. They're coming up fast, and I see them split, with one coming up on each side of my car. They stay even with my doors, and the one on the right is on the paved shoulder of the road, not even in a lane. This is bad.

I'd set my phone on my passenger seat, so I pick it up, open it, and hit Gunner's contact. I put it on speaker and set it back down just as I see the rider on my left point for me to turn onto the next right-handed exit. Yeah, fuck that.

"Yo, babe. On your way here?" Gunner asks.

I'm starting to get really nervous, but I fight to keep my voice calm.

"I'm on the highway, about eight miles from the turn-off, and I'm surrounded by five bikers trying to get me to pull over," I tell him in a steady voice.

"Fuck! Where's Fang?" he shouts at me.

"Don't know, don't care. Right now, I just care about getting to you," I reply.

I hear Gunner shouting into the room. I wait for him to finish giving his orders, but as I'm waiting, I look to my left again and see the rider holding a handgun in his left hand and riding with his right.

"They have guns. I have to get out of here, baby," I tell Gunner with a nervous tremor in my voice. I know he hears it, and I can tell he's on the move when he answers me.

"Haul ass, baby! Do what you have to do to get here and be safe. Guys are coming to you, but you just drive straight here. They'll deal with the riders. Keep me on the line, honey."

I drop my foot down heavy on the gas pedal, and the car responds beautifully. I pull away from the bikers a little, and then I see them in the mirror gaining on me again. We're at nearly a hundred miles per hour and coming up fast on a few cars in front of us.

"I'm coming up on other cars fast, Gunner. I'm going to try to use them to scrape the bikes off of me," I'm telling him more to keep my mind busy and to keep from thinking about the bikers chasing me.

"Be careful, Ava. All I care about is you getting here in one piece," he growls.

I know he has to be frustrated and angry because he can't help me at the moment.

The bikers are next to me again, and I slowly ease over toward the one on my left, making him swerve into the next lane, I hit the gas again and pass the car in front of me. It forces the biker on my right to slow down and use the shoulder to pass the car. This gives me a little breathing space to speed up more and get ahead of them a bit. I know in a few miles, I have to slow down and turn right to get to the road that leads to the clubhouse, but I know they're aware of this also. I want to get to that road before they do, but I'm also nervous about being on that road because there won't be anyone but us if shit goes south.

We leave that car way behind as we're now up to over one-hundred-twenty mph. Suddenly, a biker flies past me and pulls over directly in front of my car. The other four are on my sides and rear bumper. The biker in front waves a handgun in the air in warning.

"I recognize their patch, Gunner. It's the Banditos. I saw it on their cuts at the cookout."

"Okay, babe. Just concentrate on your driving," he replies.

"I'm almost to the turn-off. Take it or not?" I ask.

"Yes, if you can. If not, we'll get to you," he answers tensely.

Suddenly, there's a gunshot. It's loud and terrifying. I don't bother to look for who shot at me. I push harder on the gas pedal, and now I'm so close to the back of the biker in front of me I can't see his rear tire. Whoever shot either missed my tire, or it was just a warning.

Another shot and my back window explodes. I hear Gunner hollering, but I can't listen. I jerk to the right and refuse to acknowledge that I just sent a biker into the ditch at a high rate of speed. I don't even look. I jerk back into my lane and slam on the brakes as I duck my head instinctively.

I hear tires screeching, and I feel the impact of a bike or bikes hitting my back bumper and a thump on what's left of the back window or roof. Just as fast, I pull my head back up and gun it hard. I look in the rear-view mirror and see a bike sliding, riderless, down the highway.

"Two down, three to go," I mutter to myself.

Another shot, a loud explosion and glass flying all over me as my driver's side window disappears. I feel a sharp stinging pain in my arm, but I don't look down. I see my turn-off, and I take it as fast as I think I can to make the turn. My car's rear-end slides to the left hard, but I keep control and keep hauling ass. I have one job, and that's to get to Gunner.

"Ava! Ava! Fuck! Ava!" I hear Gunner shouting.

"I'm on the road to the clubhouse, and I'm coming in hot. Make sure the gate is open because I'm not stopping for it, Gunner!" I shout back.

"Jesus fuck, Ava! Jesus! Drive until you see me, baby. Don't stop for anything!"

Just then, I see one lone biker coming up behind me, but I don't know where the others have gone. I see four bikers coming toward me on the two-lane road we're on. As they fly past, I see Axel in the lead, and he's waving me toward the clubhouse. I don't even slow down. I'm doing ninety mph on a side road and don't care. I see the clubhouse driveway, and I slow barely enough to make the turn. As I slide sideways, I see the prospect that mans the gate jumping out of the way, and I gun the gas again going straight toward Gunner, who's running down the drive toward me.

I lock the brakes up and slide to a dusty stop and throw the gear shift into park. I go to open the door to get out, but I can't get my arm to work right, so I just wait for the few seconds it takes for Gunner to reach me.

He throws open the door and pulls me out and into his arms. My feet aren't even touching the ground. I don't know which of us is shaking the hardest. I bury my face in his neck and hang on with my right arm.

I feel and hear others gathering around us, but I'm not letting go of Gunner. He moves his one arm down and gathers my legs and cradles me against his chest, and starts moving toward the clubhouse. He takes us inside and to a couch where he sits and keeps me close in his lap.

I feel him dropping kisses to the top of my head, and I finally pull back far enough to see his face.

He's pale and worried. I know he was as scared as I was.

"I'm okay. I'm here. You're here. All's good now," I murmur.

"Yeah, baby, yeah," he says back to me while rubbing his cheek against the side of my head.

There's a commotion around us, and I look up to see Loki and Gee standing nearby. Petey's hobbling toward us on his crutches, and he's as pale as Gunner. Mac's on his shoulder.

"Mom, you okay?" screeches Mac.

"Yeah, Mac, I'm good."

"The fuck you are!" shouts Petey as he gets to us. "You're bleeding all over the place!"

Gunner stands us up and then sits me back down on the edge of the couch. He gently takes a hold of my arm and examines the wound.

"Get me some clean towels, a wet cloth, and call the doc. Now!" he bellows.

"Hospital, Gunner! She needs to go to the hospital!" hollers Petey.

"Fuck! Yeah, let's go," Gunner says as he bends to pick me back up.

"No! Stop! Check it out first. I might just need stitches. Please, Gunner, I don't want to go to the hospital. Those places skeeve me the fuck out. Please!" I insist.

I'll beg if I have to.

"I go in with a gunshot wound, I have to answer questions. And explain why there are bikers spread out down the highway in bits and pieces. And I don't do well with cops, Gunner. You know why. I will freak out and throw the biggest hissy fit you've ever seen if you make me deal with cops!" I threaten, more than a little hysterically.

"Okay, baby, calm down. We'll get the bleeding stopped and decide then," Gunner soothes.

Gunner drops to his knees in front of me, and Petey takes the seat next to me on the couch, gently takes my arm, and places it on his leg. Someone hands him the items Gunner demanded, and Petey starts clearing away the blood to find the wound.

It hurts now that I have time to think about it. I'm trying hard not to flinch and pull away. I was hit in the bicep. It went through the very top part of the muscle. More than a graze, but it didn't hit bone. I was lucky. Gunner has a tight grip on my other hand, and I think this is hurting him more than me.

I realize I'm shaking all over. Shock. I try to conceal it, but that's not going to get past Gunner and Petey. Gunner stands and then sits down on the arm of the couch next to me and leans over me, holding me close.

"I'm sorry. I'm trying to calm down. God, I'm sorry. I've had worse injuries. So sorry! I'm a mess," I whisper.

"You're doing fine, honey. Just fine. I know this hurts but hang in there," says Petey overhearing me.

"Get a shot of Jack over here. Fuck, bring the bottle," shouts Gunner.

A prospect, the one they call Bozo, comes running up with a bottle of Jack and a shot glass, handing them off to Gunner.

Gunner pushes a glass full of Jack into my good hand and orders me to drink.

"I don't really drink much, babe," I educate him. "I can't handle booze and get talkative as hell when I drink."

"Fine. Get talkative, but drink up," he orders.

"Okay. You've been warned," I say as I down the shot.

Coughing, wheezing, and watery eyes commence. Shit! That hurt.

"Gunner! Doc can't come for several hours. He's tied up at the hospital," says a member I don't know yet. I think his name is Pigeon, but I'm not sure.

Petey chuckles as Gunner places another full shot in my hand.

"Looks like you're going to be the first person I've ever stitched up that's going to be talking my ear off, aren't you, doll?"

"Probably, Petey. Prepare for a serious case of word vomit," I warn. "And giggling. And truths you probably don't need to hear. It's like truth serum to me."

"Before that happens, let's move her to a table, so I can get this sewed up. I need to clean it out and get the bleeding to stop first, though."

Gunner helps me stand up and leads me to a table. He sits me down, hands me another shot, and sits next to me.

The door flies open, and in walks several of the men, Axel in the lead. They walk to our table, and Axel comes around to my side and gives me a one-armed hug from behind and a kiss on the top of my head.

"We need to talk," says Axel, turning to Gunner.

"After Ava gets sewed up," dismisses Gunner.

"Go, Gunner. I'm fine. Hi, Reno! Petey can handle this, and you have a club to run. Problems to solve. Hey, Trigger! Haven't seen you in a while! People to maim. Shit to do. Ass to kick. And you…"

"Fuck. She wasn't kidding about the booze," laughs Petey.

"Little Ava can't handle booze?" asks Axel.

"Not in the least. Makes her chatty. And truthful. This could be fun," Petey replies.

"I'm fine, Axel. Thanks for asking! Hey, Gee! Love the shirt! Shit! I have groceries in my car. If my eggs got broke, heads are going to fucking roll!" I inform them seriously.

"Think they already did, Ava," says Reno, looking at Gunner meaningfully.

"You got this, Petey? Bozo, help here if needed. Office, now," Gunner grunts out while turning and leaving the room. Several of the guys follow him.

Lola Wright

Chapter 22

Gunner

"Talk," I order as soon as the door closes. I sit on the edge of my desk with my arms crossed.

"Ava was right. Was the Banditos. Highway's a mess. No way the cops aren't going to be here to talk with her soon. Someone was bound to have called it in and probably a description of her car," Axel says, sighing and running his hand over his non-existent hair.

"Trigger, take Ava's car to the shop. Use the back roads. Have the guys drop everything and get it fixed and re-painted. Make it gray. Keep it out of sight for now. We'll figure out what to do about that at a later date," I demand. Trigger gets up immediately and leaves the room.

"Anyone with an Ol' Lady or family members might want to get them somewhere safe until we see how this is going to play out. They can come here if needed. Send a prospect for groceries, water, that kind of stuff," Axel suggests.

"Good idea. Let the men know that when we're done here. Where was Fang during all of this?" I ask.

"When we passed Ava, Fang was behind her, but a little in the distance. I don't know why he wasn't on her ass. Haven't spoken with him yet," replies Axel.

I walk to the door and bellow out of it, "Fang! Get in here!"

"How serious is Ava's injury?" asks Reno.

"Shot in the bicep. Bleeding like hell, but no bone was hit. Will need stitches but should be okay if infection doesn't become a problem. She was pretty fucking calm on the phone with me during the whole shit storm, and I got some Jack in her just as the shakes were setting in. She's tough as hell and has survived worse than this. She'll be fine."

Fang walks in the door and shuts it quietly behind him. He looks old suddenly for a 30-ish man in his prime.

"I'm asking this once, and I do not have the patience for bullshit, Fang. Where the FUCK were you when my woman was being shot?" I growl.

"We got separated at a red light, and then they were on her before I could catch up. Shit went down fast. I'm sorry, man. She was hauling ass, and by the time I got near her again, she had already taken out two of them. When she hit the turnoff, the others kept going straight, and I barely made the turn to follow her here."

"Did she have a tail when you left the shop?" I ask.

"No, I would have noticed if we did," answers Fang.

I look at him skeptically. I'm not sure if I believe him or not.

"Fine. We'll talk more about this later," I say, indicating he can leave.

Fang walks out of the room, and I notice Axel is looking how I'm feeling—unsure about a club member.

"Boss, check this out," says Pooh, pushing in the door and holding out a cell phone to me.

I take it and notice it's Ava's phone. It's got an icon blinking, and it's vibrating. I swipe on the icon and a message pops up.

"Northwest window breached."

"Get Rex!"

"I'm here, Gunner," says Rex as he pushes in past Pooh.

I hand him the phone, and he starts swiping and clicking on stuff.

"I need to go to my room where my equipment is, but someone has broken into Ava's house. I don't know if this system is wired to the police so they respond automatically or not, but her cameras are on, and I think we can get video of whoever is there. This alarm has been going off for quite a while, by the looks of things. She must not have heard it vibrating, maybe had the radio playing. I'll let you know what I find. Might want to send a few guys there, though. See what's up," Rex advises.

"I'll send Cash and Reeves," says Axel, leaving the room.

"Where did you get her phone, Pooh?" I ask.

"It was lying on the seat of her car. I grabbed that and her purse before Trigger took off with it. I noticed it was vibrating and saw the message."

"We need to call Church. Open meeting, everyone is required to be here except for those that just left to clean this mess up," I tell the room.

After making a few phone calls, I need to find Ava and check on her. It doesn't take long to find her when I hear the laughter near the bar and see her sitting on a stool, head in her good hand, elbow resting on the bar. Obviously, Petey has sewn her up, based on the large bandage wrapped around her left bicep. And based on the look on her face, he's kept the Jack flowing.

I notice Loki is staying close to her, laying right at her feet, but his head is up, and his eyes are watchful. Mac is strutting up and down the bar loving the attention, and Gee is crashed on his side near a couch.

I approach, put my forearm around Ava and place it on her upper chest, pulling her back up against my front and dropping a kiss on her head. I've got some time to kill until Church, and I need to spend it with her. I need to see with my own two eyes that she's okay. I see several of the guys are hanging close, including the usual ones, and unfortunately, it's Katey behind the bar with the prospect keeping the men in beer and whiskey. She has a nasty look on her face, and I'm tempted to just kick her out, but I have more important shit to worry about today.

"Well, I think it's just stupid! What biker is going to want an Ol' Lady who can't have a few drinks without becoming a dumbass motor mouth," says Katey disgustedly.

Obviously, I've walked in during an ongoing conversation that's just starting to get good.

What? Shoot me. All men like a good catfight!

"Well, I think it's just stupid that any man would like fake boobs! Who wants to have a mouthful of plastic? I mean, seriously, think about it. They could just chew on an empty milk jug. Where's the thrill? I don't want to have a mouth full of a plastic dildo! The real thing is always better, if you ask me," declares Ava, slurring her words a bit. Yep, she's hammered.

The guys are laughing their asses off at this debate. I have to admit that Ava has a point when you think about it that way.

"You wouldn't know what to do with a cock in your mouth," Katey says back.

"I might not have your experience, Thunder Cunt, but not everyone can aspire to having a calloused back. Some of us prefer quality over quantity," returns Ava.

"Thunder Cunt?!" roars Katey.

"I'm sorry. That was rude. How about Kneepad Ninny?" asks Ava trying to look innocent.

Petey pours another shot of Jack for Ava and pushes it over to her. She looks at it like it has the answers to life at the bottom, but she tosses it back and slams the glass down. She turns to Petey and just stares at him for a moment.

"What?" asks Petey.

"You're pretty damn hot for an older guy. You should totally hook up with Trudy. She might end up being my manager some day, and her boobs are real too. Like mine. And no variety of V.D. has ever been named after her. And that's a good thing!" she whisper-shouts the last part to Petey.

My girl has had way too many shots of Jack, and I see hair holding and projectile vomiting in our future. But she's not in pain or freaking out over being shot, and above all that, she's gorgeous, keeping the guys laughing during some stressful times, and she is a hilarious drunk.

"And speaking of stupid, Ava, what the hell kind of name is Gee? Can't think of anything more original than a letter?" interrupts Katey with a sneer.

"His name is Magnum P.I. —G. I call him Gee for short," returns Ava.

"His name is Magnum P.I., and you call him Gee for short? I don't get it. It makes no sense," smirks Katey.

"His name is Magnum P.I.G... Gee for short," repeats Ava very slowly.

"Stupid. I don't get it," sniffs Katey.

Ava looks up at me, gives me big eyes, and says, "I guess it's truly possible to get your brains fucked out."

I roar. I can't help it. She's adorable. I lean down for a quick kiss, and Ava grabs the back of my neck and makes it a long and sensual kiss instead. Yay me!

Ava pulls away slowly, gives me an exaggerated drunken wink, and looks down the bar to Axel, who's smiling huge at her. I guess it's his turn for her attention and drunken chatter.

"You're pretty hot too, Axel. If you weren't brother material, or so damn feminine, I would definitely hump your leg," laughs Ava, pointing at him.

"Quit saying I'm feminine, you witch!" shouts Axel with a big grin.

"Dude, you are so totally a dudette. You manscape like a motha. You have fake boobies. You moisturize everything. Total chick," Ava says smugly.

Axel jumps to his feet and starts flexing his muscles, changing up his bodybuilder poses. He turns his back to us, flexes his ass at Ava, and says over his shoulder,

"You wish you had this ass! It's tight! No jiggle in this wiggle!"

"Your ass would be a cum dumpster in prison, Nancy," laughs Ava.

She's laughing at Axel so hard, I'm afraid she's going to topple off the stool. I step closer and keep her steady.

"I could kick anyone's ass that tried touching my goodies," retorts Axel.

"You'd get twat punched!" declares Ava.

I feel my phone vibrate in my back pocket. I grab it and tune out the ongoing slugfest with Ava and Axel.

"Yo, what did you find?" I ask, turning away from Ava.

"Her bedroom window was broken into. They entered there, and not much else was disturbed. Not sure what they were looking for or if they were waiting for her to come home. No clue as to what their objective was, but we got the window boarded up for now," Reeves informs me.

"Shit. Alright, you guys might as well come back to the clubhouse. We have Church in under an hour."

"Okay, Prez. Be there soon."

I tune back into the nonsense going on in the room, and I have no idea how the subject turned to the one I'm hearing at the moment.

"No, really. I want to know. You claim you know everything so tell me!" shouts Ava.

"I have no idea why other men name their cocks! I can't speak for them, but I named mine because he's so big it's like he's his own person! He thinks, reacts to stuff, and has a massive appetite," answers Axel, doing his best hyena impression.

"It's just weird when men talk about their dicks in the third person. I have two boobs, but I didn't name them, and I don't talk to them as individuals," muses Ava. "And something else that makes zero sense to me is why would any man eat Rocky Mountain Oysters? I mean seriously, Nancy, I would not, under any circumstances, go into a restaurant, order and eat, an animal's who-ha."

At this point, Petey drops his forehead to the bar and bangs it several times. He looks up at me, laughing.

"She hasn't stopped talking since her first shot. Your woman cannot handle her liquor in the least. She's hilarious, adorable, and exhausting."

My phone vibrates in my pocket again.

Rex: It was Banditos. I tapped into her camera. They entered and were waiting for her to come home.

Me: Fuck! How'd they know she'd be there at that time? She was coming here.

Rex: Not sure but one got a call and they left immediately. There were five of them.

Me: Same number that chased her.

Rex: She called you 8 minutes after they got a call.

Me: See you at church

I pocket my phone and hear the last comment made in this wild and crazy conversation.

"I jog or run on the treadmill, and I wear a bra to stop the bounce. When men run, do they wear something to stop the swing?" Ava asks into the laughter. She's totally adorable.

I took Ava to my house and put her to bed. She was hammered. I fed and watered the pets and left Loki in charge. When I left the bedroom, the pets were all in there with her.

I left some painkillers on the nightstand for her and a bottle of water. I have to get back to the clubhouse for Church, but I was hesitant to leave her alone. I wrote a short note, letting her know where I was and that I would be back as soon as I could, and left it next to the water.

I find the clubhouse full when I get back there. It's quiet and tense. Word has gotten around to everyone about what's happened, and we all know it means bad things for the near future.

"All club members head into Church. Anyone not a member, except for the prospects, needs to leave. The clubhouse will be closed to everyone but members, prospects, and family for now," I tell the crowd.

I hear the grumblings from some of the club sluts and hang-arounds, but I'm not concerned with them. They know the score. They just hate giving up the free food, booze, and sex. Too bad. We have bigger fish to fry right now.

I walk into Church and take my seat. I bang the gavel down, and the room goes quiet.

"Is everyone up to speed on what went down today?" I ask the room.

All heads nod, and I hear several yeahs.

"Rex. What have you found out?" I aim my eyes his direction.

"Ava got the attention of Officer Stanaway through a complaint from her neighbor about her dog. Stanaway's rubbing shoulders with the Banditos. Not sure if he's getting cash for favors, but I do know he gets free rein with the club sluts. Willing or not. Javier's aware that Ava is the Prez's. Stanaway has fed Javier the info on where Ava lives and works. And you all know that five Banditos tried to run Ava off the road today. Most likely to take her as leverage. Instead, she took out two of them. Both dead. The Banditos will not be happy that their mission failed, and it cost them a few brothers."

"Most of this we already know Rex. Anything new?" interrupts Petey.

"Yeah. Prior to Ava seeing five bikers bearing down on her, five bikers had broken into her house and were lying in wait for her to come home. Ava changed her mind about stopping at her house before coming here. Right after she changed her mind, one of those bikers got a call. They left her house and found her on the road. I tapped into her security cameras and have this on video. Somebody tipped them off," Rex continues.

"There must have been a tail on her right from her shop. Stanaway, maybe?" Axel questions.

"Also, Ava has a powerful enemy. A Senator. By digging into her background, I found a link between the Senator and the Banditos. That link is Stanaway. It's a small world, gentlemen. Stanaway attended some specialized training out of state just before he was pulled as a detective. He took that training with the Senator's nephew, Sheriff Mitch Carrington. According to cell phone records, they have stayed in contact. Water seeks its own level," Rex says, shaking his head.

"What does this all mean? Are the Banditos starting a war with us over Ava and the Senator or because they want more turf?" questions Reno.

"Both. A joint objective. Banditos get more turf if they take us out and gain a powerful contact, the dirty Senator gets Ava, and with us out of the way, she has no protection," I interject.

"Why does this Senator have a hard-on for Ava?" asks Petey.

Rex hesitates and then looks at me. He doesn't want to tell Ava's story. It's hers to tell or share with who she wants to know. I'm not sure how he even knows, but Rex has a way of finding a lot of things out that people want kept hidden.

"Ava had a run-in with his nephews a few years ago. The Senator has held a grudge. Let's leave it at that. I know you're all smart enough to know there's more to the story, but that's Ava's to share if she chooses," I tell them.

"That doesn't matter at this point. What I want to know is how are we going to handle this with the Banditos?" barks Trigger.

"No. What matters right now is finding out how the Banditos knew Ava was not going home and was heading here instead. If she had a tail, why didn't Fang clock it? Why didn't she? And why is everyone here except for Fang?" Cash, our club enforcer, speaks for the first time.

Cash is a huge man. An inch shorter than me but twice as broad. Quiet, thoughtful. Smart as hell. Never says ten words if three will work. He's the perfect enforcer, and I can see by the look on his face he's taking the blame upon himself for Ava being hurt.

"Brother, Cash, what are you trying to say here?" asks Reno carefully.

We don't just accuse our brothers of some wrongdoing without proof. And that sounds close to what Cash is implying.

"I'm not accusing Fang of anything, if that's what you're thinking, Reno. But I've been thinking on this today, and I've been sitting in that main room watching everything. I was also at Ava's house today. This was planned out. It wasn't a coincidence that they found Ava on the road. I don't believe in coincidences and certainly not one where they wait at her house and suddenly leave just to find her on the road. Someone told them she was coming straight here instead of going home. Who knew she'd changed her mind? Gunner and Petey didn't know, and neither did the woman who works at the bakery. I called. I asked her. She said Ava told her she was going to the store, then home, and then coming here. So, Ava changed her mind at the store. Why?" Cash says, saying more words than I have ever heard out of him in an entire week.

"Petey, did Ava say why she changed her mind when you were sewing her up?" I bark at him.

"No. She was hyped up on Jack and said a lot of stuff but nothing about the incident," he answers, getting up out of his seat and hobbling toward the door.

"Where are you going?"

"To ask Ava what, or who spooked her!" snaps Petey.

"Take a seat, Pops. It'll be quicker for me to run to the house. And Cash is right—Fang isn't here—and I personally told him to be here for Church," says Axel as he takes off out of the room.

A few minutes later, my phone goes off. Axel. I guess we'll find out our answer now. I hit the speaker button, but before I can say a word, Axel says the one thing I never wanted to hear.

"She's gone! And there was a struggle. There's blood in the kitchen, and the front and back doors are unlocked. Shit knocked off the counters, screen door is broke. Loki's missing. Looks like whoever it was come in the front and went out the back."

"Fuck! She's gone!" I roar. I grab the back of my neck and bend over at the waist. I failed her. Someone got to her in my own damn bed.

"Go find her, Gunner!" shouts Petey.

Several of the guys and I haul ass to my house. She was so close and yet not close enough. As we crash inside the front door, I slam to a stop when I see the blood near the back door. Please don't let that be hers! I can smell pepper spray. Fuck!

Gee is snorting and running around the kitchen tracking through the blood. Mac is standing on the kitchen counter, clearly agitated.

"The blood goes out the back door, across the deck, and down the steps. Whoever it was, parked around the side of the house, just out of sight of the clubhouse. Ava fought hard," Axel says.

She was attacked while in bed and sleeping. Attacked again while in a bed. I will make them pay. Whoever they are, they will burn in hell, but it will take them a long, painful time to get there.

"Get me the prospect that was working the gate!" I bellow.

I stalk back out to the kitchen again and hear Mac screeching.

I try to calm him down, but he's not having it. He's flapping his wings and screeching nonsense. Duffy is lying on the couch, but his head is up, and his eyes are open. That, in itself, is strange. I reach down and snatch up Gee and cuddle him close. Surprisingly, it calms both of us.

Chubs comes hustling in the door and starts gathering up the pets' supplies. Ava has an actual diaper bag with their things, so he grabs that and then puts Mac on his shoulder, he picks up Duffy in one arm and takes Gee from me with the other.

"I'm going with you all to find Ava. But she would want these guys safe, so I'm taking them to the clubhouse to be with Petey. They're used to him. They'll be fine," Chubs says as he walks out the door.

Reno and a nervous-looking prospect come in as Chubs leaves.

"Who's left through the gate in the last hour," I ask the prospect.

"When you first called the meeting, the club girls and hang-arounds all left. And then about 20 minutes ago, Fang and Katey left in her car," he nervously tells us.

"What does she drive?" I demand.

"A yellow Corolla. Beat up with rust. The plate hangs on at an angle."

"Notice anything odd about Fang or Katey? Anything out of the ordinary?" I question.

"Not about Fang or Katey. Um, but, uh…" he stammers to a stop.

"What? Spit it the fuck out!"

"That big ass dog of Ava's charged at me when I was shutting the gate. I jumped out of his way, and he ran out the gate following Katey's car down the road."

"And that didn't clue you in enough to call one of us?" I say quietly to him. I'm shaking with fury.

"I didn't really think about it, I guess," the prospect admits.

"Get back to the gate, and call me if you see that car again tonight."

The prospect rushes out the door, and I turn to Axel, Cash, and Reno. We're all stunned to suspect a club member, but all clues point to Fang. What the fuck!

"Why would he do this to Ava, to the club?" Axel asks, rubbing a hand over his head.

"He has to know his life will be short and painful if he has tossed in with the Banditos," murmurers Cash.

"How did they get past Loki?" Reno questions.

I turn toward my bedroom and notice for the first time that the door is busted all to fuck. It's open and barely hanging on by a hinge.

"They didn't get past Loki. Look around. Think. Loki wouldn't have attacked Fang for coming in the house. He's used to seeing him around, and he's been here each morning to get Ava. There's no blood in the bedroom. Just here by the door," I say, thinking out loud.

"Fang got Ava to come out of the bedroom and then shut the door leaving Loki in there. At some point, Ava realized something was wrong and started fighting. Loki broke the door down and got his teeth into someone. The blood may not be Ava's like we thought," Axel says, following my line of thought.

"We'll know exactly who took Ava when we find them because, chances are, they're chewed to fuck," I say out loud.

Chapter 23

Ava

This cannot be happening. Not again. I'm trying hard not to panic. I have to stay calm and figure out a way to save myself this time. It's so dark in here, but I can feel around without lights. Maybe I can find a weapon, an escape. Something, anything, is better than just giving into fear.

I take a few deep breaths and hold before slowly releasing them. I clear my mind. I think about what I know instead of worrying about what I don't. I need a plan.

When I woke up to find Fang standing over me, I froze in terror. I was still drunk and confused, and having him in my face was scary. But he wasn't beating me, and I started to calm down and to actually wake up.

When he told me Gunner wanted me at the clubhouse and sent him to get me, I should've been sober enough to see through his lie, but I wasn't. My arm was hurting pretty badly by then, and my mind was still fuzzy. So, I got out of bed and didn't even notice I was only wearing one of Gunner's t-shirts and my panties. At least the t-shirt hung almost to my knees. I had followed Fang out of the bedroom door, and he closed it before I saw Katey in the living room, and I knew. I knew something was wrong and that things were about to go south. I was right.

Before I could move, Fang wrapped his arms around me from behind and pinned mine to my sides. It hurt like a bitch where his arm was squeezing on my wound. I tried kicking, but he was prepared. Katey darted forward and took advantage of my disabled arms, and punched me square in the jaw. Boom! For a whore, she packed a punch.

I drew my legs up and kicked as hard as I could. I hit her in the chest and sent her flying. She flew back, her legs catching on a coffee table, and landed hard on the floor. I continued fighting, kicking, and knocking things over everywhere I could. I tried to make it as hard as possible for Fang to get me outside and in a vehicle. I knew my odds of survival decreased if I was moved to a new location. Here, at least, I had the chance of someone hearing or seeing something and help arriving. I'd be on my own somewhere else.

I bent my head down and made contact with Fang's arm, and bit down. I didn't let go until he ripped his arm away, bellowing. He kept hold of my injured arm and punched me in the side of the face. It scrambled me for a moment, and that gave him enough time to get another good grip on me. By then, Katey was back in action. We were almost to the front door when Loki broke down the bedroom door and came charging, teeth flashing. Fang swung around and tried keeping my body between his and Loki's but had to change directions to do so. With the kitchen counter on one side of him and me in the front, Loki was having trouble getting a hold of Fang.

I tried head-butting Fang, and I did make contact, but not enough to get loose. It gave Loki the opening he was looking for, though, and he grabbed onto Fang. Katey got the back door open, and we were in it when Loki took Fang to the ground. Fang struggled to hold onto me and to fight off Loki, and we went down hard. The last thing I remember is going down to the deck with Fang and Loki on top.

When I came to, I was in the trunk of a car, and by the feeling and sound of things, it was hauling ass down a rough road. I hurt everywhere, and the bouncing around isn't helping. I brace myself the best I can and assess my injuries. My arm is hurting, and my head is pounding. My legs feel okay, so I can still run if needed. I'm feeling nauseous, but that can't be helped.

I gingerly feel around for a release latch for the trunk lid. I find it. Whew. That knowledge may increase my chances of being able to bolt. I look and feel around until I find the taillight closest to my head. I push on it, hoping to knock it out. It's not budging. I keep trying, but I'm not hopeful. After a moment, I give up and start feeling beneath me for the spot where the spare tire should be. Hopefully, there will be a tire jack or tire iron I can use as a weapon.

I find where the seam is to the trunk carpet and peel it back. I feel around and find a tire iron. Oh my God, thank you! I fight to get it loose, it finally comes out, and I feel a little better about my chances. Not great, but a little better.

After several long moments, I feel the car slow a little. I try to decide if I should open the trunk and prepare to jump or wait until it's opened and come out fighting. Running is always better than fighting if the odds are against you, I think to myself.

I lie on my back and grab onto the trunk lid with one hand and carefully pull the release with the other. The lid gives, but I hold it down, so I won't give up my advantage if someone's looking in the mirror. I very carefully let the lid open just an inch or two and lift my head to peek out.

It's completely dark outside, and I don't see any lights anywhere. No houses, streetlights, or cars. We must be far from town. The road is more dirt than gravel, so I'm not sure if it's a private lane or a maintained county road. I can feel the incline of the car changing, so I do know that we are in the mountains somewhere. Going up, then down, but mostly up. I just don't know how long I was out, so I have no clue how far from the clubhouse I am.

Being in the mountains is bad for me. I'm not dressed for it, and the weather can change rapidly. I'm also barefoot, have no phone or water, no idea where I am, and alone. But I'd rather face those challenges than whatever Fang and Katey have in store for me.

Like that old song says, I'd rather die standing than begging on my knees.

The car suddenly slows down more and then hangs a slight left. The road is suddenly a lot rougher. I can barely hear voices, and I'm assuming they belong to Katey and Fang, but I'm not positive. I don't want to wait around long enough to find out either.

So, I prepare to jump out as soon as the car is going slow enough that I can survive the jump and fall. I know it's going to hurt, but I block that out and think only of seeing Gunner again. Of his hugs. His kisses.

With the moonlight, I can see trees. A lot of them. That's good. That'll give me some cover if I can make a run for freedom. I wish I had my cell phone, but I don't even remember the last time I had it on me.

I feel the car slowing a bit more, but then I hear a motorcycle coming up the road. I peek out the back of the trunk and can't see a headlight, so it must be coming toward us and not from behind. The car comes to a stop, but I'm afraid to jump out now since the rider would be able to see me. I wait, tense, and try to hear anything I can hear.

The car and bike both shut off, and it's silent for a moment. Then I can hear voices, and I strain to make out what they are saying.

"You have her?" asks a voice I don't recognize.

"Yeah, she's in the trunk. Knocked out, but alive," replies Fang. His voice sounds strained.

Then I find out why when he says, "Her fucking dog chewed my leg all to shit. I need to get the bleeding stopped and get stitched up. Is there anyone at the cabin that can do that?"

"Don't know. Don't give a fuck. Just get her to the cabin, and Javier will take her from there. You can deal with your shit after that. The cabin's only about two miles up the road. You can't miss it," says the biker.

"You can't take her now? I have to get patched up, man!"

"Fuck no. I'm on my way to town to lead the attack on the Devil's clubhouse," answers the biker as he starts his bike.

I hear the bike roar off.

"Fuckers! I need fucking help!" screams Fang.

"I'll patch you up when we get to the cabin," says Katey.

As they start the car and put it into gear, I slide out of the trunk. I'm wobbly on my feet, but I crouch down and head for the trees. I just get to them when I hear the car stop and doors opening. I look back, and Fang and Katey are getting out of the car.

Shit! They can see the trunk's open. I turn and run. I hear shouting and someone is coming after me. I don't look back. I don't know if it's Fang or Katey, but I can probably outrun either one of them, considering Fang is injured too.

I hear a gunshot, and a bullet strikes a tree, but it's not too close to me, so I keep running deeper into the woods. It's dark, and I'm getting scratched and slapped by limbs, but I keep pushing ahead. I hear a few more gunshots, but they're not hitting me, so I know they can't see me.

After a few minutes, I don't hear any sounds. I slow and take a quick few breaths and do a mental shakedown of myself. My head is pounding, and I feel a little off-balance. My arm is burning where the gunshot wound is, but it's been slapped by a few branches, so it's bound to feel bad right now. I listen closely, but I can't hear a thing in the woods. I'm guessing they are driving for the cabin for reinforcements. I can't wait around for them to show.

I have no clue where I am, and I don't want to wander too far into the woods and get completely lost. So, I turn around and move back toward the road. I want to be close enough to be able to see it occasionally, but not so close to be seen by anyone looking for me. I want to kind of follow the road back the way we came, if possible.

When I was running, I knew I was going uphill, so I move downhill slowly and carefully. When I can see the road in the distance, I turn slightly to my left and stay in the trees and stay parallel to the road, and move as quickly as I can without falling. Thank God we have almost a full moon tonight as it helps me see where I'm going.

After about ten minutes, I hear vehicles approaching, coming from behind me. I move deeper into the woods and keep moving. I can see headlights in the distance. They stop, and I hear car doors slamming. I can hear voices, but I'm too far away to make out what they are saying. I dip down behind a tree and stay still. I don't want to be spotted in the moonlight.

I see several people walking up and down the sides of the road with flashlights. I carefully move further away from the road, keeping trees between myself and them. I have the advantage because I can see them, but I am vastly outnumbered if I get caught.

When several of them move into the woods and are coming my direction, I get up and get moving again. I'm hoping all the noise they are making will drown out any sounds that I make moving through the woods. I'm moving uphill, though, and it's hard without a flashlight to see clearly.

A few are getting close enough I can hear them hollering back and forth. They are looking for tracks. I'm hoping my bare feet that are taking a beating are not leaving much of a track, but I have no idea.

It's cold but not freezing and with me on the move. I've been warm enough so far, but I know that's not going to last. I need water, shelter, clothes, or a miracle. I'm hoping that they think that I would take the easiest route, and that would be downhill, on the road and leave for that direction soon. But so far, they are still here and searching.

I keep moving uphill and to the side away from them. So far, I've been lucky that I haven't been spotted. I'm trying to move from tree to tree and to stay out of the open areas as much as possible.

After what seems like forever, but is probably only twenty or thirty minutes, I hear them fading away. Their voices are further in the distance and less clear. I'm breathing hard, so I slow a little. Luckily, there isn't a lot of underbrush, and that's made it easier to move, but I have been steadily climbing in elevation.

I stop and sit when I find a fallen log. My legs are shaky, and I'm totally lost. I have no clue where the road is at this point, but I can't hear anyone following either. I'll take these circumstances over whatever Javier had planned for me, though.

After a few minutes, my breathing has slowed down to almost normal again. I still haven't heard anyone and haven't seen any flashlights, so I get back on my feet and start moving again. I have to keep pushing until I find help.

Lola Wright

Chapter 24

Gunner

It's been over forty hours since Ava was taken, and we still have no idea where she is or who has her at this point. I haven't slept, and neither have the men. Everyone is busy doing something, trying to locate her. I can't even wrap my mind around what could be happening to her at this moment. I'm sick knowing that she woke up to a threat again.

"Prez, Reeves found Loki!" Petey shouts from the main room.

I leave my office just as Reeves comes in the main door with Loki limping beside him. I rush over and kneel down next to Loki and start looking for injuries. He's covered in dried blood, and I can't tell if it's his or not. I look at the bottom of his feet, and they are raw and bleeding. And he reeks of pepper spray.

Reno bends down next to me and starts examining Loki too. Loki has his head hanging and looks exhausted.

"I'll take him to the kennels and get him fed, watered, and washed so I can fix anything that's wrong," mutters Reno as he stands and calls Loki to follow him.

I stand and turn to Reeves, who just walked in the room.

"Where'd you find him?" I ask.

"I was leaving to go to town and found him about 200 yards from the main gate heading this way," Reeves answers.

"Wish he could talk," I say.

"Gunner! I got something!" hollers Rex as he rushes up to me.

"What? You know where she is?"

"No, sorry. But when we went to your house last night, we found a cell phone lying just off the porch. I picked it up, not knowing who it belonged to, and wanted to find out. It's Fang's. He must've dropped it during the fight. I didn't get a chance to really look it over until a little while ago, and there isn't anything on it that helps us find Ava, but then it got a new text."

Unknown: If you don't find A, your little momma is smoke. So is the kid.

Holy shit! Maybe Ava got away. Sounds like it, and Fang's ass is on the line for her escape. Or is he hiding her, maybe holding out for more from the Banditos? I'm hoping it's not the latter.

"Any luck tracking Katey's phone or location?" I ask.

"No, she must still have it off," answers Rex. "What do you think about this? Is Ava out there somewhere loose or what? Should we try answering this text in hopes we can get more intel?"

"Fuck yeah, we should! What're we out if it doesn't work?" shouts Petey.

I take the phone from Rex and think for a moment. Then I type:

Fang: I'm looking! Fuck! Anything to go on?

Before pushing send, I hold it out for Rex and Petey to read. They both nod their heads.

I push send and hold my breath. A moment of tense silence passes before the phone vibrates with an incoming text.

Unknown: Dirt bikes combing the area near the cabin. She can't be too far on foot. Keep checking the back roads. Attack on DA clubhouse off until bitch is found. This is on you!

Fuck me! That doesn't help us, but at least it kind of confirms that Ava escaped. Now we just have to find her before they do. So, I send another text.

Fang: Not familiar with these back roads. Which ones should I check out?

Unknown: All of them fucker!

Shit! I was hoping for a road name. A location of some sort. I turn to Rex, "Look for any cabin in the mountains around here that belongs to any member or family member of a Bandito. Also, check to see if the Carringtons own a hunting lodge around here. Try tracking the location of the phone texting Fang's too."

"On it, Prez!" Rex says as he turns and leaves the room.

I put Fang's phone in my pocket as my phone rings.

"Yeah?"

"Lady here at the gate wants to speak with you or Petey. Name's Trudy. Send her up?" asks Bozo, the prospect manning the main gate.

"Yeah, send her through," I answer and disconnect.

"Trudy's at the gate. Know why?" I ask Petey.

"Fuck. Yeah, when I called her this morning and told her she'd have to manage the shop, she demanded to speak with Ava. I had to tell her that Ava's missing. She's probably here to demand answers or try to help. She was pretty upset. She thinks the world of Ava and is probably worried out of her mind."

Trudy walks through the main door and heads straight to Petey and I, minus the smile she usually has gracing her face.

"When you say 'missing,' do you mean kidnapped or ran away?" she demands as she reaches us, hands on hips.

"Club business, Trudy. We can't tell you much. We just need you to run Ava's shop until she's back here," Petey says gently.

"Fuck club business. This is Ava's business which makes it my business. I'll run that shop, no problem there, but I want to know what happened to Ava," she returns heatedly.

I have to give her credit for bravery. She marched into an MC clubhouse and is facing down two big, intimidating bikers she doesn't really know, all to look out for her boss. And by the looks of it, she's not going to back down any time soon. I find that I like it a lot that Ava has this kind of loyalty in the people around her.

"She was kidnapped out of my house night before last. We know who took her, but we're not sure why or where they took her. Please believe me that we're doing everything we can to find her. She's mine. Every club member is doing all they can to bring her home," I say to Trudy, looking her in the eye so she can see the truth in them.

She stares me down for a moment and then a bit more calmly asks, "Was that Fang guy involved in her coming up missing?"

"Yes, he was. Why? Did you notice something?"

"Neither Ava or I liked him around much. He made us feel uncomfortable. I kept a close eye on him when he was in the shop, and I felt like something was off with him. He seemed a bit too friendly with that cop, Stanaway. I saw them behind the shop, chatting. It seemed odd."

Maybe we should find Stanaway and have a chat. I turn to leave to do just that when Trudy speaks up again, stopping me in my tracks.

"Do you know if Ava has her kit with her or not?"

"Kit? What kit? What do you mean?" Petey asks, just as confused as I am.

"Her insulin kit. She always carries it with her, in her purse in a small cooler bag, or puts it in the fridge," Trudy answers, looking at us like we're stupid.

"Fuck! I didn't even know she was diabetic. She never said. But I did notice her putting small ice packs in the freezer before and a cooler in the fridge. I just never asked about it," I answer, feeling like a fool.

"Well, she needs that insulin, or she's going to be in trouble soon. She takes shots every day," says Trudy, now looking scared.

The implications of what Ava is facing suddenly hit me. She isn't just running from her captors, she's running out of time because of her not having her medicine. Fuck me! We have to find her and soon.

"Put the word out, Petey. Everyone needs to know that she's a diabetic," I tell him.

"If she was at your house, her insulin and cooler bag will be in the fridge. The oral medicines will be in her purse. Whoever finds her will need her insulin and meds, and probably orange juice or glucose tablets," Trudy informs us.

"Come with me to my house. You know what to look for better than I do," I tell Trudy, turning to leave for the house and thanking God that she showed up here tonight.

Chapter 25

Ava

My feet feel raw and are very painful to step on now. I'm cold and shivering, thirsty, and tired, but I have to keep moving. I know if I stay still, they'll either find me or I will die from the cold.

I'm a long way from the road we were on when I ran, but I have heard what I think were dirt bikes in the distance a few times. I thought about going toward them, but I was afraid it might be the men looking for me, so I kept on moving the way I was going. Away from the sound of them. I'm lightheaded and getting dizzier. I keep moving, but I have to stop more often to keep my balance.

I found some wild berries a few times now and ate them, but I'm still not sure what they were or if I should have ingested them or not. My main concern right now is not falling and rolling down the hill I'm on. It's not so steep I can't walk, but steep enough I might roll a long way down.

I also need water. My mouth is so dry I couldn't spit if I wanted to. My situation is not good, but I'm not in the hands of Javier either, so it could be worse. So, I keep putting one foot in front of the other. It's almost daylight. I can see the sky lightening up, and I'm hoping I'm high enough I can see something when it's light enough.

I stop and sit on a stump and pull my knees to my chest and pull Gunner's t-shirt down over my legs. I huddle into myself for warmth and rest my head on my knees. I know I can't stay long, but I need a moment.

I rest longer than I intended to, but when I look up, it's much lighter, and I take a moment to look around. I'm not far from the top of this hill, so I get off the stump and start climbing more directly toward the top.

When I reach the top, I'm winded and hurting. I turn and start searching the surrounding area now that I'm above the tree line. And I spot what looks like a small road, more of a one-lane track not too far away. It's off to the side of where I'm standing, and it's downhill from here. I can also see what looks to be the beginnings of a valley a long way off in the distance, and I wonder if that's the direction of Denver. I realize now how high I've climbed over the last couple of days.

I decide to walk down to that little road and hope it takes me somewhere that has water. I have no choice at this point. I don't want to run into the men looking for me, but I have to get to help at some point. It's a risk I have to take.

After about forty minutes of trudging toward that road, I see it right in front of me. When I popped out of the trees again, there it was. It looks like a driveway more than a road. I start following it, and the walk is much easier now. After walking around a curve, I see a small cabin tucked into the trees. It's not big, and there are no vehicles around it and no garages or barns that could hide one. I move off the road and stand in the trees just watching the cabin for any kind of activity.

I approach it slowly and carefully, but it looks deserted. It must be an old hunting lodge. I peek in a dirty window and see that it's a one-room building, and no one's inside. I try the door, but it's locked, and I can't push it open.

I walk around the cabin and spot an old pitcher pump and rush to it and start pumping. Nothing comes out at first, and I'm tiring out fast. But a few pumps later, I hear a gurgle. I continue and a little water trickles out with rust in it. I keep pumping until clear water is rushing out, and I drop to my knees and use my hands to cup some and drink. I pump, I cup, I drink. It's so cold and refreshing. I splash some on my face, and even though it's cold as hell, I feel instantly better. I stand and look around me. I see a telephone pole and wire leading to the cabin. Please let there be a phone!

I try the few windows, but they will not open. I look around until I find a rock big enough. I pick it up and throw it at the window. The window breaks. I use another rock to pound out the remaining pieces of glass and carefully pull myself up and through the window. I cut my hand and legs but not seriously. I stand inside, looking around.

It has a tiny kitchen in one corner, a fireplace, living room/bedroom in the other corner, and that's about it. There's a small two-person table and two chairs. Bed, couch, and one chair in the living area. It's rustic but relatively clean. It hasn't been years since someone was here.

The Devil's Angels MC

I spot an old phone on the wall with a long cord. It's so old it still has a round wheel for dialing. Rotary phone, I think it's called.

I pick up the receiver and almost fall to my knees when I hear a dial tone. But now I freeze and stand there staring at the phone because I don't know Gunner's or Petey's numbers. They're stored under contacts, and I just tap to dial. Oh shit, technology has bit me in the ass!

I'm shaking all over from the cold and from not eating. I want to just lie down in that bed and rest. But I know I have to call for help first. No way am I dialing 911. I dial my own cell phone and cross my fingers. I'm lightheaded and need to sit down, so I stretch the cord and plop down on the edge of the bed. I have no idea where my phone is at, but last I saw it, Gunner had it in his hand. I'm praying he still has it.

"Yeah?" answers a male voice I don't know.

Fuck! What if Fang had grabbed it, and Javier has it now? Oh shit, what do I do?

"Yeah? Who is this?" says the man.

"Who's this?" I ask instead of answering.

"Ava? Ava? Is that you? This is Rex!" he shouts.

Before I can answer, I hear fumbling, and it sounds like the phone is changing hands, and I finally hear the voice I need to hear.

"Baby? Ava? Honey, is this you?" Gunner demands loudly.

"Yes. Oh my God, Gunner. Yes, it's me!" I holler back.

"Where are you? I'm on my way!"

"I don't know, Gunner. Oh shit, I have no idea where I am. I was unconscious when they put me in the trunk and when I got away from them, we were in the mountains somewhere. I don't know where I am! I found a cabin and saw this phone! I've been running and hiding in the woods until now. They've been hunting me, so I have kept moving."

"Oh God, baby, I've been scared shitless about you. Are you injured? Did they hurt you?" Gunner questions, almost babbling his words, he's talking so fast.

"Small injuries. No serious ones. I need food and clothes and you. Please come get me!" I am almost whimpering now.

I hear voices in the background and then Gunner again.

"Stay calm, honey. Rex is trying to track your location through the phone. Just stay on the line with me and stay calm."

"I'm high up in the mountains above Denver. I can't quite see Denver, but I think I saw the plateau this morning when I was at the top of the hill this cabin is sitting on. I'm partway down the hill, and it's tucked off a little two-tracker type road."

My teeth start chattering ,and everything is starting to hurt now that I've stopped moving. I'm not feeling good, and I know my sugar has dropped to dangerous levels. I need food immediately.

"When you were standing on the top of the hill, which direction was the plateau you think you saw, honey?"

"West of me, I think," I answer slowly. I'm not sure, though. Things are getting cloudy in my mind.

"Hang in there, Ava. Rex'll figure it out soon, and I'll be on my way for you. Just keep talking to me, baby."

I stand up slowly and painfully and start looking in the cabinets for something, anything. The only thing I find is a small box of animal crackers way to the back of the cabinet. They haven't been opened and don't look like mice have found them yet, so I rip open the package and start devouring them. I'm starving, and I would have eaten them even if the mice had had a head start.

I hear Gunner talking, but I'm not really listening. I'm too busy filling my face. I finally tune back in to his voice.

"How's your sugar levels, Ava? And why have you never told me you're a diabetic?" he asks, growling a little.

I realize he's annoyed, and I know he's going to be more annoyed if I answer that question.

"Ava?"

I speak around a mouthful of crackers, "Sugar's low. Need juice and food. Found some animal crackers, and I'm eating them, but they won't be enough for long. Ate berries when I found some, but I have no idea what they were, but they helped."

"And what about the other part of my question? Why have you never told me you were diabetic?"

"I didn't want..." I start to say, but I then hear dirt bikes in the distance.

Fuck! Are they now on the same road as the cabin? How close are they?

"Ava! What's going on?" Gunner shouts.

"I can hear dirt bikes. I don't know if they're looking for me, but I can't stay here and find out. There's nowhere for me to hide. I have to go," I tell Gunner.

"Fuck! Go, Ava! Go somewhere and hide. Be safe. Rex has a lock on where you are, and we're coming. If you get cornered, fight, baby. Fight hard! Don't go anywhere with anyone but me or a club member, okay?" Gunner says quickly.

"Okay, Gunner. Bye!" I hang up and look around quickly for any kind of clothing but see nothing. Out the window I go as I hear the bikes getting closer. I quickly get another drink of water and take off over the hill behind the cabin and back into the trees.

I don't get very far when I know the bikes have made it to the cabin. I hear them shut off, and I can hear voices. I carefully get a little closer and try to hear what's being said while staying hidden. I know it's risky, but I need to know if these are guys out for a ride or guys hunting a lone female.

I can just barely see the backside of the cabin through the trees, and I see two men walk around the back of it looking around and in the broken window. One walks over to the pump, and I hear him say something to the other guy. They split apart and start walking toward the woods in two directions. I turn and try to quietly get some distance between us.

I know I'm depleted. I know the odds are against me. But I'm smart, strong, and I'm not going down without a fight. I have a great life, and I've finally found a great man, and I'm not giving that up easily. So, I keep moving regardless of how worn out I feel. The water and crackers have given me a second wind, and Gunner knows where I am now. I have to stay safe until he gets here.

The guys are hollering back and forth to keep track of each other, and that helps because then I know where they are too. They know someone, most likely me, has been at the cabin. With water still on the ground by the pump, it's likely I'm not far.

I hear one shout to the other that he's trying to call the boss, but he has no signal. The other hollers back to him to keep trying, and I realize the second guy is very close to me. I look around frantically and find a downed tree nearby. I get down behind it and burrow under as far as I can. I feel around for a broken limb or a rock, anything to use as a weapon, and I find a limb about the size of my wrist and about four feet long. I grasp it and pull it toward me as I push even further under the tree's cover.

I try to slow and quiet my breathing when I hear movement close to my hiding spot. He's only a few steps away when he stops moving. I don't know if he's spotted me or not, but I'm not coming out unless I have to, and then I'm coming out fighting.

I hear him taking a piss and am grateful he's pointed the other direction. I hear him zip himself back up and take a step or two. I'm shaking like a leaf and praying he hasn't spotted me.

Suddenly, he hollers loudly, "We know you're here, little girl. More guys are coming, and we're going to flush you out, and you'll pay dearly for making us look for you. Come out now, and it'll go easier for you."

Yeah, right! Like I'm going to believe that shit. I actually quit breathing, though, when I hear and feel him sit on the log I'm hiding under. It shifts down an inch or two that it didn't have room to shift with me under it. The bark is scraping into my back and legs, and it hurts like hell. I bite back a groan and try to hold my breath as much as possible.

After a few painful minutes, he gets up and walks in the general direction of the cabin. I wait until I can't hear him moving through the woods, then climb out from under the tree, but I carry my wooden weapon with me. I start moving away from the cabin again. I get a short distance from where I was hiding when suddenly a man is stepping out from behind a tree. Directly into my path. We're about five feet apart, and he looks as shocked to see me as I am to see him. I've no idea where he came from, but he's wearing a leather cut, and it has a Bandito patch on it.

I jump forward and swing with all my strength hitting him in the side of the head. He hasn't made a sound, and he goes down that way. Before he can move, I hit him again. Hard. This time, his eyes close, and I think he's out cold, not just dazed. My weapon broke in half on that last swing. I feel no remorse.

I quickly feel around his pockets and belt and find a knife in a sheath. I remove the knife and bury it deeply in his thigh. He jerks and I pull the knife free and stab him again. This time, his eyes open, and he bellows out in pain.

I jump out of his reach and take off running as fast as I can. I know he's not going to be able to catch me with those wounds, but he's making enough noise his buddy will be at his side soon. I have to scoot.

I don't care about making noise at this point, and I move quickly downhill, hoping to find the road to the cabin, and hopefully, Gunner. My feet are on fire, but I have a goal to meet. And that's to live long enough to see Gunner's beautiful face again.

I'm slowing down, even though I'm moving downhill. I'm exhausted, and I'm not sure how much farther I can go. I'm stumbling more, and it's very difficult to traverse the terrain in the condition I'm in. But I make it to the road and move away from the cabin. I'm not moving fast, but I keep moving. I also keep listening for a vehicle or bikes, not knowing if those men got a message through to Javier asking for more men.

After about ten minutes, I hear engines. Cars, trucks, or bikes, I can't really tell. I stumble off the road and hide behind a large tree, and wait to see if it's friend or foe. A large black truck comes into view, being followed by another truck, and then several bikes, then a van. I wait until they're closer, and I recognize Gunner's truck in the lead. I almost collapse right there, but instead, I stumble out to the road and then drop to my knees in exhaustion and relief.

The truck slams to a stop and Gunner is bailing out the door before it's even completely stopped moving. He's on the ground in front of me in a second and wrapping me in his warm, strong arms.

Gunner picks me up and carries me to the passenger side of his truck where Axel is standing with the door open. He places me on the seat and hands me a bottle of water. While I'm guzzling it down, several of the men crowd around the door.

"There're two men still up by the cabin. One is stabbed twice in the leg. The other was calling for reinforcements. More may be on their way already. Don't know," I gasp out.

"Is the cabin straight up this road?" asks Axel. I nod my head yes.

Gunner issues some orders, and Axel and several of the other men run to their bikes and roar on around us and go in the direction of the cabin.

I'm suddenly so tired I can hardly keep my eyes open. I lean my forehead on Gunner's chest and drift off. He gently shakes me awake and slides me into the seat facing forward. He puts a seat belt on me, closes the door, walks around to the driver's side, gets into the truck, and turns to me.

"Ava, baby, listen to me, okay? I don't know much about being a diabetic. You need to tell me what else you need right now? I have your medication, your insulin kit, food, and more drinks. Help me out here, honey, okay?"

"Cold. Thirsty. Hungry." I manage to say.

Gunner immediately grabs a blanket from the back seat and tucks it around me as he hits the heater controls to my seat. He hands me my diabetic supplies and watches closely as I test my blood and take the meds I need at that point.

He then opens and hands me a chocolate granola bar and a bottle of water. I'm shaking so bad I can't hold onto the granola bar, so he takes it and helps by feeding it to me. Then he tips the water up to my mouth and lets me drink deeply. I'm too exhausted to do much more than sit there and let him take care of me.

"We need to get to the clubhouse and get you checked over. I have a doctor waiting there. He's a club member's brother, so he knows to keep his mouth shut, and he helps us out when he can. Are you okay enough for me to start driving home? Do you need anything else?" Gunner asks quietly.

"Loki? Is he okay?" I mumble.

"Yes, he's at the clubhouse, and Reno patched him up. He's going to be fine. The other pets are okay too."

I look up at Gunner and notice for the first time how tired and ragged he looks. This was just as hard on him as it was for me, I realize. I shakily raise my arm and put my hand on his cheek and just enjoy the moment, knowing I'm back with him and safe.

"I'm okay for now. I just need sleep and you. Thank you for finding and rescuing me," I whisper to him.

He uses his hand to grip my chin and raises my face to his. He places a gentle kiss on my lips.

"I didn't rescue you. You rescued yourself. So sorry, baby. I can't believe a club brother did this to you. I'm so, so sorry. I trusted him, and I was wrong, and it cost you. I can't…"

"Shhh, honey. It's over for now. I'm going to be fine, and I'm with you. I'm safe now. Take me home, Gunner. Please," I interrupt him quietly.

And he does just that while holding my hand the whole way. Even though I don't know that at the time because I pass out within seconds of him starting his truck.

Lola Wright

Chapter 26

Gunner

Ava's asleep and my heart is back to its normal pace. I have a hold of her hand, and I'm not letting go. I called Petey and let him know that we found her. He's going to call Trudy. I could hear the relief in his voice. He's been a bear during this whole ordeal. I have to smile a little knowing how much he cares about Ava. She may have been born without a father, but she has one now, whether she knows it yet or not.

As I pull into the clubhouse lot, I see Petey on his crutches hobbling our way. Guess he couldn't wait a few more minutes to check on his girl. He opens the passenger door as soon as I come to a stop.

Ava's passed out with her head resting on the window, and Petey holds her steady as he pulls the door wide. Her head lolls around for a moment and then her eyes slowly open.

"Hey, Petey," she mumbles, eyes blurry.

"Hey, baby girl. And it's Pops to you," he replies. "Good to see you, doll. Missed that face," Petey replies quietly as he leans in her door and hugs her tight.

He stands there, just holding his girl, her head on his shoulder. I move in and unbuckle her seat belt. Petey steps back reluctantly, and I pick her up. I carry her into the clubhouse and lay her on a couch. Petey hobbles over, lifts her head, and sits down under her, resting her head on his lap. He wraps the blanket tight around her again and sits there, brushing her hair back out of her face.

"Doc got held up with an emergency at the hospital but will be here soon," Petey says quietly to me. Then he asks, "Have you heard yet if Axel found those guys that found her at the cabin?"

"He called just before I got here. They have both of them. Ava fucked one of them up bad, and Axel said the guy hasn't stopped whining yet, so they gagged him," I chuckle.

"Ava was kidnapped and hunted like an animal for two days, and that guy thinks we care if she fucked him up? Or that he's hurting?" Petey asks incredulously.

"Yeah. He's going to wish Ava had finished him off in the woods by the time we're done with him," I growl, no longer amused.

"Any sign of Fang yet?"

"No, but that will happen at some point, and it will be a club decision as to what happens to him."

"I think everyone has already decided what that should be, Gunner. Everyone is feeling the betrayal and that he used a woman, your woman, to betray us. Not acceptable. We don't involve women and children. No innocents. We've always held that belief until him. He will be dealt with harshly."

I nod my head, knowing this is true. The door opens and in walks the doctor. He looks as worn out and tired as we all do. I shake his hand and thank him for coming. He nods his head and then looks toward Ava.

"That her?" he asks.

"Yes," I answer and then explain to him what has happened the last few days.

By the end of the explanation, his eyebrows are at his hairline, but he walks over to the couch with his bag, grabs a chair, and pulls it close to her. Petey gently wakes Ava up and helps her to sit.

"Hi, I'm Dr. Harrison. Call me Seth. Can you tell me what injuries you have and what you know about your blood sugar levels?"

I listen carefully as Ava groggily explains everything the doctor needs to know. She's slowing waking up, and I grab another water bottle for her. When the doctor starts examining her feet for injuries, I head into the kitchen and make a pot of coffee. I know Ava needs her java to wake up. After it is brewed, I walk back into the main room just in time to see her trying to stand and wincing.

I rush over and pick her up. The doctor informs me that she wants and needs a shower, so he can disinfect and bandage the injuries she has. He quickly explains the dangers of infection for a diabetic, especially in the foot area, and I carry her to my room. Once inside, I set her on the bed and go into the bathroom, turn on the shower, and return to her side. She's asleep while sitting up on the bed. My girl is exhausted.

I bend down and pull my t-shirt up and over her head carefully and then help her stand enough to pull her panties off. I toss both in the garbage can by my bed. I carry her to the shower and sit her on the bench inside. She's just out of reach of the spray. I quickly strip and step into the shower, lift her back up onto her feet and stand her in the spray. I wish I had a tub here like I do at the house, but I didn't want to take the time to run her up there, so this will have to work.

I bathe her carefully because of the nicks, scrapes, cuts, and her gunshot wound. I wash her hair, and it takes twice to get it clean. She tries to help, but I just move her hands back to the wall and continue washing her. Once she's clean, I move her back to the bench, and I wash up quickly.

I dry us off and find a pair of boxer shorts and a t-shirt for her to wear, and get us both dressed. I step out the door and shout down to the doctor that he can come up and finish treating her injuries.

I stand by while he treats each and every injury and explains to me in detail about diabetes and how it affects her body. He says he can't re-sew the bullet wound because it's been too long since the stitches were torn out. He removes the few stitches that remained hanging loose, and bandages her arm again.

By the time he's done, so's Ava. She hasn't complained a single time, even though having disinfectant poured onto all those wounds must have hurt like a bitch, but her eyes are drooping again. I reposition her in bed, kiss her forehead, tell her to sleep, and I close the door behind me as I leave.

When I hit the main room, I see the guys have returned. A few of the guys have stayed in the mountains, hoping to spot some Banditos and find the cabin they were taking Ava to when she escaped. It's war at this point, and everyone knows that.

As I approach the couch where Petey's still sitting, he looks up and says, "Doc has left. Said he'll return tomorrow to check for any signs of infection. He explained what to watch for, and I asked if he could give us a class on diabetes next time he comes. We should all be aware of what to watch for and how to help her if needed. He said he would. I don't expect everyone to attend, but I'll be there."

"Good thinking, Petey. He explained a lot of that to me while he was examining her, but the more of us that are aware, the better for her," I answer.

I turn to Axel and Cash, who are standing nearby with beers and ask about our two guests they brought here.

"They're both in the basement room. Chained down, door locked, and a guard sitting down there just in case. They'll be there come morning, so get some rest, Gunner. Be with your woman in case she wakes. We've got this," says Axel.

"Is the injured one going to die before I get my hands on him?" I ask.

"Probably not. She must have clubbed him because his head and face have damage. Leg was stabbed twice. Deep, and he bled like a pig, but it's stopped now. Mostly," Axel grins.

"She still had a death grip on the knife when I got to her. She dropped it on the floorboard of the truck when I set her down. Not sure where she got it, but glad she did," I tell them.

"He has an empty sheath on his belt, so I'm guessing he got stuck with his own knife," smiles Cash.

"Either of them talking?"

"No. Haven't said a word other than the one whining and crying about his injuries."

"Okay, I'm going to bed. Come get me if anything comes up, and thanks. Appreciate all you've done," I say as I slap them on the shoulder and head back to my woman. "Get some sleep, Petey. She's safe now."

I want Ava at my home, with me. I want her to wake up and see me, not someone trying to hurt her again. So, with that in mind, I return to my room, pick Ava up out of bed, blankets and all, and walk us home. She never even stirs.

I'm pouring my second cup of coffee when I hear Ava screaming. I drop the cup, sprint for the bedroom, and come to a complete stop in the doorway. She's sitting up in bed, hair going every direction, eyes wildly bouncing around the room. When they land on me, I can see that she's slowly waking up from whatever nightmare she had been dreaming. Shit! I shouldn't have gone back for that second cup of coffee. My whole reason for bringing her here was so she'd wake up to my face, and I fucked that up for coffee.

I move slowly to her side and sit on the edge of the bed, facing her. She drops her head into my shoulder and shudders.

"It's okay, baby," I say soothingly while cupping the back of her head.

"God, Gunner, I'm so sorry," she whimpers.

"No reason to be. Just relax," I say. "I'm not going anywhere."

She relaxes into me, and I maneuver us around until we're both lying in bed, her in my arms. We lie quietly together for several minutes before she turns her face toward mine.

I have to catch my breath because even with the black eye and bruising along her cheekbone, she's so beautiful to me. My poor little Ava's battered and bruised, but she still has the power to turn me speechless.

"Where are my babies?" she murmurs.

"Chubs has them. He called, and he's bringing them over to see you in about an hour. They're all fine, but Mac has been asking about you. I think Chubs would like to keep them, though. He's gotten quite attached," I tell her, chuckling a little about Chubs.

I hear the front door open and close and then footsteps, so I assume that Chubs has arrived early. Instead, in walks Axel, and he moves directly to Ava's side of the bed and pushes his way in next to her. He curls into her back and starts petting her hair like you would a dog.

What the fuck?!

"Hey, lil sis. How you doing?" he asks the back of her head.

Ava giggles and turns onto her back to look at big ass Axel sprawled out next to her.

"I'm okay, big bro. You trying to piss off Gunner already?"

"Don't care. Just wanted to see with my own two eyes how you are today. Your face looks like shit, but that's okay. I like being the hot one in the family," he answers her with a cheeky grin.

"Get the fuck out, Axel! Out of my bed! You can see her when she comes to the kitchen. Now!" I bark at him.

He doesn't listen. In fact, he acts like I haven't even spoken. He just continues to lay his obnoxious self next to my woman, grinning at her. Then he has the nerve to say, "We need coffee, Prez. Me and Ava will wait here while you fetch some."

To make the start of my day even better, I hear the front door open again, and the next thing I see is Loki leaping onto my side of the bed and instantly pushing himself between Ava and me. He starts licking her face, and I have to let go of her and move out of the way because of his size. Ava's laughing and rubbing his face. He flops down in the room I made by moving, soaking up her attention.

I hear little hooves skidding into the room, see Gee sliding to a stop and looking up to me. I bend, pick his rubbery little body up, and set him on the bed. He starts rutting around Ava's side and making his weird little grunting sounds of happiness.

I finally just stand up out of the bed altogether when Duffy comes strutting into the room, tail swishing. Thank God for king-sized beds. Duffy makes himself comfortable after he forces his way to Ava's side, moving dog and pig out of his way.

"Hi, Mom!" screeches Mac as the bird walks his way across the floor.

"Hi, Mac! Missed you, buddy," laughs Ava.

"Missed you too!" replies Mac as he flutters up onto the bed.

I look down and what I see is all Ava. She's propped up against the pillows and headboard now with Axel still sprawled on his back on one side, Duffy curled up on her other, Mac perched on her legs, pig and dog stretched out in my spot already settling in for a nap. Pure Ava. She attracts both man and beast.

Chubs appears in the doorway with a doughnut in each hand. And his usual smile on his face.

"Hey, Ava! Glad to see you back and safe now, girl," Chubs says in between bites.

"Hi, Chubs! Thank you so much for taking care of the pets! I don't know how to ever thank you enough for that," gushes Ava.

"Food. Just food. And you're welcome. Loved having them. Just hated why I had them. I want to get a dog of my own. When you're feeling better, want to help me pick one out at the rescue?"

"Oh my God, yes I do! That's a great idea, Chubs!" Ava's eyes are lit up like a kid at Christmas.

I leave the room, glad Ava is home (and I do think of this as her home now) but wishing I had had more alone time with her this morning. We have things to discuss, like this being her new home, among other things, but they can all wait. I'll let her enjoy her pet time, that including the two big humans with her also.

Lola Wright

The Devil's Angels MC

Chapter 27

Ava

The doctor was here earlier and re-dressed my wounds. Then he spoke with several of the men about diabetes. I was surprised at how many of the men showed up to learn about my disease. I was so moved I was almost in tears to see big, badass bikers wanting information on how to take care of me if something arose because of my diabetes. I have this wonderful feeling of belonging somewhere. To someone. For the first time in my life, I feel wanted.

It's afternoon now, and Gunner's at the clubhouse handling club business. Axel and Chubs have left.

Reno, Vex, and Pooh have come and gone, and it's just Petey and me here with the pets.

There's a knock at the door, and Petey hollers, "Come in," and in walks Trudy carrying several boxes from the bakery. She takes one look at my face, drops the boxes on the kitchen island, and rushes to me. She drops down in front of my spot on the couch and just stares at my battered face.

"I'm okay, Trudy. Really, I am. Just sore. Minor scrapes and bruises," I say to her quietly.

"Oh, honey! Your beautiful face!" Trudy whispers. Then she shocks the ever-living hell out of me when she suddenly shouts, "Those pieces of shit must bleed for this! This cannot stand! I will hurt them myself!"

Trudy stands up and turns to Petey, hands on her hips, eyes angry.

"You gonna take care of this problem, big man? I don't know everything about why this happened, but I do know it was one of yours that did this to my girl! She survived, but someone must pay for this!"

Then she turns to me and just as angrily spits, "You and I have worked together for a couple of years now. We work side by side. You're a great boss, best I've ever had, but you keep a distance between yourself and all others. I've respected that because I respect you. But that ends today. Like it or not, we're friends. We're best friends, and you're going to learn to like that we're boss and employee, but also friends. Got that, Chickie?"

Petey and I are both staring at her, mouths open, shocked to hell and back. I think we're both a little afraid of her too. But damn! I look over to Petey and see him with a little smirk on his face looking right back at me.

"I think you better agree and do it quick, Ava. She's a little scary and a whole lot of sexy and I, for one, like both."

I look back at Trudy and see her still standing, hands on hips, pissy look in her eyes.

"I think I'm kind of in love with you right now, Trudy. Yes, please. I got it, and I very much want you as my friend."

Instantly, her expression changes to the beautiful smile I'm so used to seeing.

"Yay! Okay then. I brought treats for everyone from the bakery. And I brought the makings for dinner. I'm cooking, you're relaxing, and Petey, you're staying for dinner," declares Trudy as she moves off to the kitchen.

"I like her," whispers Petey, smiling at me.

"Me too. But I like her for you too, Petey," I smile back, winking at him.

We had a wonderful evening, Gunner and me, Trudy and Petey. Dinner explained why Trudy works the front of the bakery and does not bake. And will never bake! We weren't sure what dinner was supposed to be, but we had a full night of laughing and hanging with good friends. And while dinner was a mystery, there were no visits to the E.R.

Weeks have passed, and things have gotten back to normal. I haven't stayed at my house since the attack, and Gunner constantly pushes me to just move in and give up my house. I might as well since almost everything I own is in his home anyway.

Gunner has adapted to having a woman and pets in his life remarkably well. I was worried that the pets might be too much for him, but he has gotten very attached, and Gee follows him around all the time. Gunner is great with all of them, but Gee treats Gunner like he's his hero. It's cute.

The Banditos have been M.I.A. since the attack. Their clubhouse is deserted, and Gunner and his club have been working hard trying to find the hidey-hole the Banditos have crawled into to regroup. The men are frustrated about this, but as long as I don't have to see a Bandito cut, I'm happy.

I don't know, and I don't want to know, what became of the two Banditos that Axel and Cash captured. I don't ask. That's the Devil's Angels business, and I know Gunner handled them as he saw fit. The ones I want to get my hands on are Fang and Katey. Neither has been sighted, and we have no idea where they are or what they're doing. But the club continues their efforts to locate them.

I'm leaving work for the day, and Trudy is leaving with me. We're on our way to a class together. Since her speech, we've become very close and spend a lot of time together, here at the bakery and at the club. Trudy and Petey have become close too, and I love it. He deserves a good woman, and he has that in her. Axel adores her and the other men have accepted her as family. With Petey's cast removed, him and Trudy ride with Gunner and me often. Stopping to eat and just enjoying the road, wind, and freedom.

Trudy and I arrive at Jax's Gym, the gym that Axel manages but the club owns, and walk inside. It smells like a man's gym. This is not a Planet Fitness type gym. This is a boxing, MMA, down and dirty, sweaty type gym. And I love it! Axel has accommodated the few women who come there and has available beginner through expert type classes for self-defense, boxing, and many of the martial arts.

I love that Trudy has decided to get some training in self-defense and MMA. I know how much they've helped me with my confidence, core strength, and endurance. I credit my training for my ability to stay calm, escape, and survive my abduction.

Trudy and I stow our purses in the locker room and then separate and go to our different areas to start our workouts. I had changed before leaving the bakery, so I was ready to stretch. I sit down on the mat and start stretching, looking around the gym.

The usual crowd is here, along with several of the club members, either standing around gossiping, helping customers, or working out. Cash approaches and stands on the edge of the mat I'm sitting upon. He's my striking trainer, and he's amazing to work with. He knows his stuff, he doesn't baby me because I'm a female, and I'm learning a lot of techniques from him.

Cash reaches down, I grab his hand, and he pulls me up to my feet. He looks over my shoulder toward the huge picture window at the front of the gym, and suddenly he grabs my arm, swings me around, and down to the mat, face first. Before I can ask what the hell he's doing, his big body comes crashing down on mine just as I hear a Pop, Pop, Pop and glass shattering.

Cash is off my body, I'm picked up, tossed over his shoulder, and he's running toward the office at lightning speed. I see Axel with Trudy, also tossed over his shoulder, heading the same way we are. We're both dropped onto our feet, ordered to stay put, the men are out the door, and they slam it behind them.

I look at Trudy and see her eyes are just as wide as mine feel. Holy shit balls!

The door's wrenched open and in comes Pooh, limping and holding his leg. I see the blood and immediately turn and grab a clean towel off the shelf behind the desk. Trudy helps Pooh to the couch, and he sits heavily. I wrap the towel around his leg and put pressure on the wound. Pooh groans but doesn't move.

Pooh's phone rings, and he digs it out of his jeans pocket, answers it, listens for a quick moment, and hands it to me. I take it, bewildered as to why he's giving me his phone, and put it to my ear.

"Yes?"

"You okay? You hurt? Why the hell aren't you answering your phone?" shouts Gunner.

"I'm okay. I'm not hurt. My phone's in the locker room, and I'm currently in the office holding a towel to Pooh's leg. Anything else you want to bark at me?" I answer him calmly.

"Jesus. Fuck, Ava. I get a call saying there was a drive-by shooting at the gym, and you're there. Of course, I'm barking. Fuck me!" Gunner responds, a few decibels lower than before.

"It's okay, baby. Trudy, Pooh, and I are hanging in the office while the rest of the guys are dealing with the shooting. Whoever it was drove on, and it's quiet here now," I tell him.

"Okay, Ava. Stay there until Axel tells you to leave. Someone will drive you women and Pooh to the clubhouse. Doc's on his way for Pooh. Be careful, stay alert. Yeah?"

"Yeah. See you in a while." I disconnect, hand Pooh his phone, and relay what Gunner told me.

I'm on my back in Gunner's bed, breathing hard and enjoying the little tingles still running through my body. Gunner's on his back next to me, doing the same, I'm guessing. Gunner was late in coming home due to the shooting and the aftermath. We ate dinner late and then Gunner started kissing my neck in the kitchen while I was cleaning up our plates. That led to an amazing make-out session on the kitchen counter, which now needs a thorough disinfecting, and then to the bedroom where he rocked my world. Twice.

I roll toward Gunner and swing my leg over his hips and sit up, planting my naked ass on his softening cock. I lean down and brush my lips over his. I raise my head a few inches, make eye contact, and surprise the hell out of myself when I blurt, "I love you."

His eyes widen for a split second before he grabs the sides of my face, pulls my mouth to his and devours me. After a hard and thorough kiss, he pulls away and, still holding my face, says quietly, "Love you too, Ava. So much."

My heart swells for this man. He's big, rough, and a biker through and through. But he's also tender, kind, and gentle. Best part, he's all mine.

Gunner does an ab curl, wraps his arms around me and stands. I lock my arms and legs around him and bite him gently on the neck. He growls as he walks us to the bathroom. Once inside, he sets me on my feet, turns to the shower, and turns it on. While it's heating up, Gunner reaches for me and crushes me against his body, wrapping me up tight in his arms. I relax against him and let my head rest on his chest. His chin rests on the top of my head when I hear him speaking.

"Never wanted to be tied down to one woman. Never wanted an Ol' Lady, a wife. Didn't want to wake up to the same face day after day. I liked my freedom."

I'm starting to get nervous hearing all the things he didn't want. Oh God, is he trying to let me down easy? Fuck, I thought he was as happy as I've been.

"But then I saw you, a couple of times, in your yard across from Petey's house. I couldn't get you out of my mind. Then your stupid neighbor gave me an opening to actually meet you. And I knew all the things I thought I never wanted were total bullshit. I want you in my life. I want you to be my Ol' Lady, and eventually, my wife. I want to wake up to your face every day. I want to be tied to you for the rest of my life because I can't imagine it without you in it. It would be empty and hollow. I love you, Ava. And I want you to be the mother to my kids. I want my children to have a mother like the one I know you will be. I want to come home each night to your laughter, our kids trashing the house, fur, feathers, and pig snorts."

I listen to him in awe. I look up at Gunner and smile huge.

"I want all of that too. With you. I need you in my life, forever. I want our kids to have your eyes and heart. I want them to be big and strong but kind and gentle. All the things that are you."

I stretch up as he leans down, and our mouths crash together. We kiss long and hot, sealing our words. He lifts me off my feet and walks us into the shower. Hands are everywhere—touching, soothing, stroking flesh.

I flick his nipple with my tongue, and his hand grips my ass cheek. I slowly kiss my way south and drop to my knees, looking up at Gunner.

"I have zero experience at this. I need you to guide me. I want you to feel as good as I do when you make me come with your mouth," I tell him quietly. "I'm sorry I don't have the experience you deserve, but I'm a quick learner," I smile.

"Fuck me, Ava. Christ. You've never sucked a guy off? You've no idea how happy it makes me that you have no experience at this. I want my cock to be the first one you've wanted enough to take into your mouth. Jesus. I won't last long knowing that," he growls low while placing his hand on my cheek.

"Put me in your mouth, baby. Let me watch you suck me off. I'll teach you what I like if you want, but just knowing you want me enough to do this is enough for me," he breathes out.

I grasp his cock with my hand and marvel at the velvety hardness. I've stroked him before, but I never tire of the feel of him. I carefully place my lips around the head and use my tongue to explore its texture. I find the small slit and use my tongue to slide back and forth across it. I hear Gunner release a low moan.

I roll my eyes upwards and find his pointed at the place we connect. His eyes are drooping slightly and incredibly sexy.

He likes what I'm doing, and that makes me bolder. I slide my tongue along the bottom of his head and feel the V shape there. I pump slowly with my hand as I take more of him into my mouth, sliding my tongue around and around. I take him almost to the back of my throat and slowly pull back with my lips tight around his length. At the same time, I reach with my other hand and gently grab his balls and roll them in my palm. I tug on them, and I hear and feel another moan, only this one is longer and lower.

I start sliding him in and out of my mouth at a steady pace, tightening my mouth on him as much as I can. I love his taste. I don't even notice the water spraying down on my back. I pull off his cock and bend lower to take a ball into my mouth and suck on it before switching to the other one.

Gunner's hand is resting on my head. It tightens and grips harder. He throws his head back and lets out the most pleasurable sound. I move my mouth back to his cock and slide it in as deep as it will go. I swirl my tongue and rub it up and down his length while sucking him. After another moment of this, Gunner suddenly bends over me, pulls me off his cock, and turns me toward the bench. He pushes my shoulders down until my hands meet the bench, and then his hands grip my waist and pull my ass higher until I'm bent in half.

His hand is in between my legs, rubbing my slit and then sliding a finger deep, pumping into me.

"Please tell me you're ready for me, baby," he says at the same time as his finger disappears, and his cock is pushed into me.

"So ready, Gunner! Harder, baby, please!" I moan as I push back against his hardness.

I brace against the bench and take all he has to give. His feet are planted outside of mine, and he's pounding into me. His hand reaches around my hip and hones in on my clit. He pinches it hard at the same time as his cock rubs against the exact place I need him to. I explode and start coming apart.

"Yeah, Ava, yeah! Just like that, baby. Don't stop! Fuck me!" Gunner shouts as he loses his rhythm, pounds hard into me a few more times before planting deep. We stay still for a moment, catching our breath, and then Gunner pulls out slowly and pulls me up to a standing position. My back is to his chest, and he wraps himself around me and rests his face on my shoulder.

I put my hands on his arms that are crossing my chest and savor the moment. It doesn't last long, though, because suddenly the water turns cold, and we both jump out of its spray. Gunner shuts it off, and we stand there laughing, dripping wet.

Trudy and I are at the shop, and we have a shadow again. In the form of an older, grumpy-looking biker. Petey's not happy that he's on guard duty when he'd rather be out looking for "the fucktards that want to die" (his words, not mine) instead. He's sitting out front in a booth, and not even great coffee, and all the sweets he wants is changing his mind or attitude. The only softening of his features is when Trudy or I are in his direct line of sight.

I've had to hire a few more employees and have spent the last few days training them. I've also spent hours with a contractor discussing the rest of the building and what I want to change it into.

Gunner and the men have been putting in long hours between the several businesses the club owns and searching for the Banditos. Gunner has had to make several trips out of town to the different support clubs explaining what's going on and asking for them to keep ears to the ground.

Surprisingly, a few of the Ol' Ladies have approached me recently and introduced themselves. At the cookout, they avoided me like the plague, but they have made the approach, so I'm making an effort to be friendly. Karen, Reno's woman, and Sissy, Reeves girlfriend, have come into the shop a few times and had coffee with Trudy and me. It's a start anyway.

Things with Gunner and I are great. We've slid right into a solid relationship, and I'm all but living with him. Things are easy with him. He has a temper and a mouth on him, but neither is ever directed at me. He endears himself to me every time I see how great he is with the pets. Gunner and Axel are even working on putting together a tiny little Harley for Gee to ride. I can't wait to see it when it's ready.

Vex has become a close friend. He does guard duty a lot, and while the man is smoking hot, he no longer flirts with me. But he does flirt with everything else that is even remotely female. He spends a lot of time at our dinner table along with Axel, Chubs, and Petey. I love that I have so many to feed now. And spoil with treats.

The one blip in our lives is the Banditos. And Rex has dug up some intel that has left chills running down my back. We now know for sure that the Banditos are working for Senator Carrington and his nephews. They benefit by having the powerful

Senator in their corner, and the Carrington's benefit by having their dirty work handled for them. And, scarily enough, I'm the dirty work the Carringtons want handled.

I don't know why they want their hands on me again. They did enough damage the first time. I don't know if they want their dirty money back or just a little revenge for the very small price Mark paid for their deeds. One thing I do know is that I'm terrified of them and what they would do to me again.

This time, I am not alone, though. I have people in my corner, and I'm better prepared to fight if I ever need to again. I didn't have any of that before, and they exploited that fact for their own twisted pleasure.

I have to trust in Gunner, the club, and my own abilities to keep me out of their hands. And Gunner is working hard to minimize anything the Senator can use against the club.

The Banditos have been sighted lately, so we know they haven't left the area. They're just hiding better than before. But there have been several incidents of vandalism at the various businesses the club owns, and the guys are all on high alert.

As I walk into the front of the shop, Petey waves me over.

"What's up, Pops?"

"Need to ask you a favor. Are you cooking dinner at Gunner's tonight?" he asks.

"Yeah, I am. He said he'd be home from the run today by 6:00 pm. Want to come for dinner?"

"Well, darlin', that's what the favor is about. I know you've worked all day, but would you be willing to cook dinner at the clubhouse instead and cook for about ten of the men, me, Trudy, Gunner, and you?" he smiles sheepishly.

"Do you know what you want for dinner?" I inquire.

"Anything you want to cook is fine with us. We love everything you put in front of us," he laughs.

I smile at him. How can you not love this guy?

"Be happy to, Petey. How about dinner at 7:00pm?"

"Perfect doll! Thanks," he says, giving me a one-armed hug.

The Devil's Angels MC

I'm busy in the kitchen at the clubhouse getting things ready for dinner. Trudy's hanging with me and helping with the chopping and cutting things up. That's as close to cooking as we allow her now. We're chatting, and Trudy is drinking a glass of wine.

Marti, the short, bad-dye-job blond, who was with Katey in Gunner's club room the day I walked in on them, strolls into the kitchen and slams to a stop when she sees Trudy and me. She just stands there with her mouth slightly open, wheels in her brain turning slowly. Very slowly.

"Marti. Need something?" I ask her.

"Uh. Um. No. I gotta jet," she mumbles as she turns to do just that.

"Wait!" I shout, stopping her in her tracks.

Marti freezes in place and then slowly turns around, big eyes looking my direction.

"What were you and Katey looking for in Gunner's room that day?" I question her.

Marti's eyes get even bigger, and she noticeably swallows.

No surprise there. That's kind of what she's known for. Ha ha.

"Are you going to use that on me?" she squeaks, pointing at me.

I look down and see my large chef's knife pointing at her. I didn't know I had waved it at her when I spoke. Oh, well. Go with what you have to work with, I always say.

"Not unless you don't start talking," I tell her.

I hear Trudy smother a choked laugh.

"I was cleaning Gunner's room. I clean some of the guy's rooms, and they pay me for doing it. Katey came in while I was cleaning and started going through his dresser. When I asked her what she was doing, she told me to shut up and help. or she'd snitch me out to Fang. She said Gunner had sent her to his room to get his spare set of keys for his house. I helped her look, and she found them just before you walked in the door. That's all, I swear," Marti rushes out almost all in one breath. Quite impressive really.

"Oh, wait! Um, well, she also poked holes in all the condoms in his nightstand. I didn't do that! She did," she spews out.

"Huh. Okay then. Thanks, Marti, appreciate the answer. You may leave, or you can stay and have a glass of wine with Trudy and me. Your choice," I tell her, placing the knife down on the counter.

She just stares at me for a moment and then says, "You'd be okay with me hanging with you two? I'm a club girl, and you two are not. You guys belong to someone. We don't normally hang with the Ol' Ladies."

"Neither of us are technically Ol' Ladies, and yet all of us are women. I don't see why we can't hang together. Why put labels on any of us if we can co-exist? I'll admit, I don't understand why any of the club girls would settle for that life, but it's not my place to judge you. I don't like some of the girls, obviously, Katey is one of them, but I have nothing against you in particular. Sit, have a drink, eat dinner with us if you want. You're invited and welcome, but it's your choice. I don't want you to stay if you're uncomfortable or if you don't want to. Not if it will cause you problems with the other girls. But I know I, for one, can always use another friend," I quietly and sincerely tell her.

"I would like that very much. And thank you, Ava," she replies, hefting up onto a stool near Trudy.

Trudy smiles at her and pours Marti a glass of wine.

I wasn't sure how many people would be there for dinner, so I made a ton of food. Petey had said us and about ten men, but around here, you can't count on there not being more hanging around. Especially if they know a meal is being cooked. And leftovers never go to waste here. Not with Chubs especially, but also because so many of the guys are single.

I've baked three hams, made two huge pans of scalloped potatoes, roasted mixed veggies with olive oil and fresh thyme, and a couple different kinds of salads. Add to that the desserts and home-baked bread and rolls I brought from the bakery, and dinner is ready.

Trudy, Marti, and I pile the food on the tables in the kitchen and lay out the plates and silverware. Buffet style. The men file through, filling their plates and then returning to the main room to sit at the tables and eat.

Chubs walks in, grabs two plates, and starts filling them while chanting, "Chubs loves Ava! Chubs loves Ava!"

He stops as he passes me, gives me a loud smacking kiss on the cheek, and continues on his way. I love that guy.

Gunner strolls in at the end of the line and comes directly to me, bends down, and lays a hot kiss on me. I lean into him, place my hand on his neck, and open my mouth for more. He obliges. I hear a few whistles and ignore them. I've missed Gunner lately. We go to bed together every night and wake up together every morning, but we've both been so busy lately, we haven't had time for much more than that. And some quickies in the shower. Okay, a lot of quickies that weren't always all that quick. Sue me.

We get our food and move to the main room to eat. There's a lot of laughing and joking around and the mood is lighthearted. After everyone is done eating and dessert has been demolished, Petey stands up and hollers for everyone to shut up. Yup, that's how he gets their attention.

"Shut up, assholes. I got something to say," he bellows to the room.

The room goes quiet, and every eye is on Petey. He pulls some papers out of his back pocket and smooths them out. He looks at me, and his face softens.

Petey turns to the room and starts speaking.

"As most of you know, Ava has no family. She was raised by the system, in and out of foster homes and orphanages. Why that happened is her story to tell, not mine. But Axel and I have talked about this for a while now, and we made a decision."

I feel my eyes widen, and I glance toward Axel to find his eyes on me, soft and full of love. I don't know what's happening here, but I know it's big. I feel Gunner pull his chair closer to mine, and he leans against me, arm over my shoulder, holding me tight. I look to his face, and I see a smile there. I look back to Petey when he continues talking.

"Ava has become an important part of mine and Axel's life, and we want her to know that she's family to us. And that she always will be, even if she gets smart and gets shot of Gunner."

The room roars with laughter before Petey turns back to look at me.

"Because you're not a minor anymore, we can't legally adopt you, Ava. If I had known you when you were, I would have brought you home and made you my daughter in a heartbeat. I would have been proud to be your dad, Axel your brother."

Oh God! I feel my throat closing up and tears hitting the back of my eyes. I put my hand over my mouth to keep from crying out loud.

"So, we did the best we could do to have you know how serious we are about you being our family. Me—your Pops, Axel—your brother. We went to an attorney, had him draw up adoption papers, like legit ones, and we've signed them. If you are okay with this, you can sign them too. You can also change your last name to ours—Taylor—and make it as official as it can get. Your choice, doll. But whether you do or not, Axel and I signed and are giving you the papers to keep and know that we claimed you as ours."

I'm shaking and full-on crying at this point but not making a sound. I can't. My throat is closed up tight, but tears are streaming down my face. I stand up on shaky legs, and walk to Petey, and look up into his eyes.

"You really want to have me as family? A crack baby that nobody wanted? Me, Petey? Scars and all?" I barely squeak out.

"Fuck yeah, we do," answers Axel, coming to stand next to his dad.

I throw myself into Petey's arms. He catches me and holds me tight. Then I pull back and do the same to Axel. He lifts me off my feet and squeezes tight. He sits me down, and Petey holds the papers out to me with a smile. Axel hands me a pen and turns his back to me so I can use it to sign my name. Ava Beaumont. Soon to be Ava Taylor.

When I'm done and still ugly crying, I tell them, "Love you, guys. Love you, Pops! Love you, big bro."

I hear clapping, laughing, and a few sniffles. I turn to look at Gunner and blurt loudly, "I have a real last name now! Ava Taylor! I'm not named after the street I was found on anymore! Yay me!"

Gunner laughs as he steps to me and drags me into his arms for a huge bear hug. As soon as he sets me down, I turn to Petey and snuggle under his arm and wrap mine around his waist.

I have a dad. A brother. It took twenty-seven years, but somebody took the chance on a crack baby. I'm smiling so big, my cheeks hurt.

Chapter 28

Gunner

It's been a few weeks since Petey and Axel adopted Ava. She hasn't stopped smiling yet. She immediately filed the papers for the name change, and it's official now. Ava Taylor.

Petey is now Pops, and Axel has earned all sorts of nicknames from Ava, not all of them nice since he's taken it upon himself to put her through all the brother/sister kinds of crap that they missed out on. She loves him to her bones, and it's returned by Axel, but he goes out of his way to annoy and torment her. His favorite method this week is teaching Mac to say things that Ava is not fond of.

I just finished up a ton of neglected paperwork and am sitting at the bar in the clubhouse enjoying a quiet moment and a beer. Mac's strolling up and down the bar, whistling different tunes, the current one being "Rebel Soul" by Kidd Rock.

Petey walks in, just having finished a shift at the custom bike shop, and plops down next to me. The prospect, Bozo, hands him a beer.

Mac walks down the bar and stops in front of Petey.

"Hi, Gramps!" says Mac along with his famous wing-wave.

"Gramps? What the fuck, Mac? I'm not your Gramps," laughs Petey.

"Are too!" insists Mac.

I've noticed that one of Mac's favorite past times is to argue. He loves the attention it brings him. And this is a prime example.

"Am not!"

"Gramps! Gramps! Gramps!" shouts Mac.

"Fuck me. I'm arguing with a bird." Petey shakes his head at himself.

I have to laugh at this because Mac has gotten all of us, at one time or another, to argue with him.

"So, what's new on the Banditos?" Petey asks.

"A couple of them were sighted and scooped up by Reeves and Cash. They're on their way here with them now. Should be here soon. I'm hoping we can get some information out of these two. Those last two didn't give up much."

"Axel's at the bakery with the women." Petey starts laughing, hard. I look at him with an eyebrow quirked.

"Ava texted me and asked why she couldn't have been an only child. Axel's on her last nerve, she said. Trudy called, laughing her ass off, and said that Ava was putting icing on a cake, and Axel came up behind her, pushed her face into the cake, and then ran into the front of the bakery thinking Ava couldn't do anything with the customers there." Petey has to take a moment to quit laughing before telling me the rest of the story.

"Ava, cake on her face and in her hair, not caring that the customers saw her, grabbed two heaping handfuls of pink frosting, took off running, sliding sideways into the front, and slammed her hands on Axel's face. Covered his whole face and head. Stepped back, put her hands on her hips, and shouted to the room, 'And that, ladies and gents, is what a pain in the ass brother gets when he messes with his sister!' Then she stomped into the back, leaving Axel covered in frosting in a room full of shocked, laughing, and clapping customers."

Petey and I are laughing, picturing Axel in pink frosting, when the door crashes open, and in comes Cash and Reeves, each manhandling a Bandito. All laughter ends. But the fun is about to begin.

Petey and I help the guys get the scum to the basement room. After chaining them both to the wall, we step back and look them over. They didn't give up easily if the injuries to their faces and bodies are any sign.

Cash had stripped them of their cuts before we chained them to the wall, and he now tosses them to the floor and grinds them under his heel. The guys start cussing him out and making useless threats.

"I want first shot at that one," Reeves growls, pointing to the guy on the left. "Fucker bit me. Like a damn dog."

"Do your damage," I tell Reeves.

And he does. After a few minutes of working the man over, the guy on the right shouts, "Okay! Okay! Stop! We'll tell you what you want to know. Just stop for fuck sake!"

There's a coward in every group, and we just found the Banditos' one.

"Start at the top, and don't stop until we know everything. If you do, my woman, the one you kidnapped, is going to come in and demonstrate her knife skills on your balls. Got it?" I snarl at them.

"Javier wants to end your club. We want your territory, and we don't want the hassles your club hands out over dealing on your turf. He took a liking to your woman and knew taking her would damage you. He also recognized her and knew he could bargain her for favors from a Senator. Having a Senator on our side would make it much easier to take over any turf we wanted. Your rat, Fang, gave Javier the info he needed to get to Ava. Was easy with him being her guard of the day."

The asshole smirks at me. He loses the smirk when Cash plants his fist in his stomach. After a few coughs and gasps for air, the smartass starts talking again.

"Not sure why the Senator wants your woman so bad, but I know his nephews are hot to get their hands on her."

"What does Javier have on Fang to get him to turn?" barks Petey.

"Fang's been hooking up with Javier's favorite whore, Maria. Got her pregnant. Guess it wasn't just a fuck for Fang, and he fell for her. Wants her and the kid. Javier leveraged her safety for Fang's cooperation."

"Where's your club hiding?" questions Cash.

The dumbass that bit Reeves spits at Cash. He pays for it immediately by way of Reeves' fists.

"In a cabin near where the bitch escaped. The Senator has a friend who owns it, and it's on loan to us to lay low," the talkative one continues.

"Shut the fuck up, Carl!" bellows fuckface number one.

"Javier hung us out to dry, and you're still loyal to him? No, just no. Fuck him and the rest of them. And fuck you!"

"See if you can get any more intel from them on anything planned for the future. Feed, give water to, and play nice with Carl. Do as you wish to the biter," I say as I turn and walk out.

Church is over, plans have been made, and several of the guys are getting our shit together to carry them out. I haven't told Ava everything I know yet about the motives behind the Banditos' moves against us. I don't even want the name Carrington to cross her mind. They can't have her. She's mine. It's that simple.

Axel and I have taken Ava shooting a few times now. She wants to learn, and she's trying hard. But I can't understand how someone with such good eye and hand coordination to make the cakes that she does can't hit the broad side of a barn. She really sucks at shooting. Axel is determined, though, and so is Ava.

While her shooting abilities suck, her martial arts classes over the years have paid off. Cash is impressed with her take-downs, strikes, and submission holds, and he doesn't get impressed easily. She works hard at it and is determined to continue improving. And, lucky me, she feels the same way about blow jobs. Life is good outside of the Bandito problem.

Ava has convinced the club to quit breeding dogs and to rescue them from shelters and train them for more than just protection services. Reno's on board with this wholeheartedly, and him and Ava have gone together and adopted several. We have two already sold when their training is complete. They also have a few of those dogs in training to be service dogs that will be donated to vets with disabilities.

The other change that Ava instituted was on Sundays, she either cooks a huge meal at the clubhouse for anyone that wants to come or if there is a big game or UFC fight being televised, she makes game-day snacks instead. And she makes a lot of them. The guys are in love with this change, and Sundays have become a "lie around the clubhouse and eat day." Ava loves this and spoils them terribly. And me too, of course. She's even gotten interested in brewing beer, and the men are always happy to test out a new recipe she's come up with.

The pets have become accepted by everyone as honorary club members and are treated like royalty. Even Duffy has a favorite person now. It's Vex and Vex isn't sure how he feels about it when Duffy decides his lap is the only place to take a nap. When a cat that size decides he wants to take a nap somewhere, he does, and not many of us are brave enough to try to move him to some other place. More than a couple of the club sluts are now sporting scars from trying to take Duffy's place on

Vex's lap. Ava was right—he does hold a mean grudge.

Even ornery old Trigger has softened up some. He spends a lot of time with Mac on his shoulder sharing cashews. And Trigger never leaves the clubhouse without finding Ava and giving her a kiss on the temple. The old bastard actually has a heart after all.

It's been a long day, and I'm getting home later than usual. As I walk in the door, I see Chubs sitting on the couch with a huge bowl of Ava's homemade salted caramel ice cream in one hand and the TV remote in the other. He looks up and grins. I just shake my head. He's here as much as I am, it seems.

I hear laughter from the master bedroom, and I walk that direction. Upon hitting the door, I lean against the jamb and sigh at the sight before me.

Loki and Gee are crashed in their beds along the wall, Mac is on his perch near the window, whistling "Another One Bites The Dust," and Ava is sitting cross-legged in bed, painting her toenails. None of that is what I sigh at. It's the big, bald bastard flat on his back watching my TV, in my bed, next to my woman. Axel.

"Do you even know where your home is, Ax?" I ask.

"Yup. With my sister. I think I'm going to sell my place and move in here. Then she can take care of me 24/7," he smirks up at me.

"The fuck you are. We have enough animals living in this house. You're not going to be one of them. Get out of my bed, asshole."

Ava's smiling like a loon. Not having family her whole life, she soaks this shit up with Axel and the other men.

"Don't want to. Ava's doing my toenails next, so I need to stay put."

"Wait. What? You're getting a pedicure?" I question, more than a little surprised.

"Well, yeah, Gunner. I already trimmed my pubes. I can't go out in public only half-assed groomed!"

"Oh, fuck me. You better have trimmed them at your own damn house," I mutter.

"Oh! Speaking of going out in public, you're coming with us tomorrow night, aren't ya?" Axel asks, smirking at me.

I shoot him a death glare. He knows I don't want to tell Ava where the guys and I will be tomorrow night. We have several new hires at the strip club, and we have always gone as a group to watch their first night. It's tradition. But not something I'm eager to tell Ava.

"Where you going tomorrow night?" asks Ava, looking between the two of us.

Fuck! I'm tired and just want a shower, bed, and Ava cuddled close, but I might as well get this conversation and the oncoming fight out of the way. Thanks, Axel, you fucker!

"The strip club has a bunch of new girls, and tomorrow's their first night to dance. It's kind of a club tradition that all the men show up for their first night. Kind of like moral support." I wait for the argument. So does Axel, if the look of happy anticipation on his face means anything.

"Oh, okay. Do you want dinner before you leave, or will you get something to eat with the guys?" she asks, after staring quietly at me for a moment.

"Uh, we usually eat at the club," I say, dumbfounded that she hasn't exploded on me yet.

"Okay, cool. Maybe the girls will want to have a girls' night then if you men are all going to be gone for the evening. I'll check in with them tomorrow and see."

Axel's mouth is hanging open, and I'm guessing mine probably is too. But I'm smart enough not to poke the bear, so I'm going to let it drop here.

Axel, the fucker, is not, though.

"Ava, honey, you really okay with your man going to a strip club to watch the dancers?"

"I trust Gunner. If this is something the club does together, I don't want to interfere," she responds calmly while going back to painting her toenails.

"But there will be a lot of T&A on display, Ava. No man can resist that!" adds Axel.

"Better I find out now if he can or not than later down the road when maybe a kid would be involved," she replies evenly.

"Lap dances, Ava! Are you okay with lap dances? Some skank grinding her bits on your man?"

"Jesus fuck, Axel! Knock it off! Quit trying to stir the pot. It's strictly a 'lookie, no touchie' night for me. Ava knows how I feel about her, and she knows she can trust me. Right, Ava?"

"Of course, honey. Axel's just worried where his loyalty would lie if you did do something that would cause us problems. Does he have his brother's back and stay silent, or would he tell his sister so she can dump your ass? That would be a bad position for Axel," she says gravely. After thinking for a moment, she turns to Axel and asks, "Which side would you be on, Ax? Mine or his? Hmmmm?"

Axel looks horrified at the thought. He scrambles up out of the bed and tosses a "fuck you both" over his shoulder as he leaves the room and then the house, slamming the front door.

Ava giggles. Fuck my life.

I'm at the strip club with the men. It's loud and raucous tonight with all of us plus the regular customers. I could care less about the dancers, but the guys are having fun, and it's nice to see after so many weeks of stress with the Banditos.

Ava didn't act any different today, and she didn't bring up the strip club. She only said that a few of the girls and her were going to see a show tonight in Denver. I told her that Bozo would be tagging along, and she said that was fine. When I was leaving tonight, she had just gotten out of the shower and was drying her hair. It was difficult to leave a naked Ava at home to go watch a bunch of strippers, who didn't interest me any, but I couldn't let the guys think I was so pussy whipped that I couldn't come tonight.

So here I am, sitting next to Petey, who looks as thrilled to be here as I am. I asked him how Trudy took the news, and he said she didn't say a word. She picked up her phone, texted Ava for a few minutes, put her phone down, and smiled at him. Said her and Ava had plans too. Both women took the news very well, and because of that, I have a bad feeling it's going to bite me and bite hard.

I pull my phone out of my pocket when I feel it vibrating. It's a text from Bozo. That feeling just got worse.

It's a picture. It's of Ava, and my eyes about fall out of my head. She's standing next to Trudy, Marti, and Karen, and she's wearing a little black dress. And it's stunning on her. Her hair is down, the golden and almost white locks are curled in sexy fucking waves. They hang well past her shoulder blades. I've never seen Ava dressed up before. It's always work clothes or jeans and t-shirts. My woman cleans up nice.

Her shoulders are bare except for small straps. The front of the dress is square cut but low enough to show a little cleavage. My girls are beautiful and perky! The dress nips in at her tiny waist and hugs her rounded hips and ass. The dress ends mid-thigh. I can't see her shoes, but I just know they are fuck-me heels. Ava is not looking at the camera because she is laughing with her head tossed back a little, and I see a few men in the background looking her direction. Fuck me!

While I'm still memorizing the image, another text comes through. This one has words.

Bozo: WTF? Thunder Down Under? I'm not sure I want my patch enough to stay here for this shit!

Me: You are not to leave their side!

"What's going on?" asks Petey.

I turn my phone his direction, and his eyes pop out too. I guess Trudy is probably dressed similar to Ava, but I never noticed.

"What the fuck is Thunder Down Under?" he asks me.

"No clue. Whatever it is, the prospect's not happy."

"Vex! Hey! What's Thunder Down Under?" Petey shouts to him over all the noise.

Vex's eyebrows shoot to his hairline. Oh shit.

"Why're you asking?" Vex asks carefully.

Our shouted conversation with Vex has caught Axel's ear. He tunes in, unfortunately.

"Thunder Down Under? It's an Australian male stripper show. Why?"

"Oh, fuck no!" shouts Petey.

And just like that—Bam!—I know why Ava was so calm about me being in a strip club. And I don't care. She's not going to watch a bunch of pansy-ass male strippers strut their stuff!

"Holy fuck! Is that where the women went tonight? Is that the show they were going to see?" shouts Axel, already dissolving into roaring laughter.

Some of the other men have cottoned onto what's happening, and there are a lot of smiles, smirks, and laughter around our table. Except Reno. He's not smiling at all. His Ol' Lady, Karen, is with Ava and Trudy.

Vex holds his cell phone up for us to see, and it's a YouTube video of a Thunder Down Under performance.

Oiled, muscular, male bodies gyrating to music. Pumping their asses, shaking their dicks. What the fuck! Of course, being a guy, it completely escapes my mind that I'm sitting in a strip joint watching the same damn thing only with tits and ass instead of cocks. Doesn't matter, though. Ava's watching a male stripper group, and that's just wrong! What if one of those douchebags touch her? Is she putting money into their G-strings? Oh, hell to the no!

Axel is howling and holding onto his stomach. There're tears in more than one set of eyes from the laughter around the table. I notice Petey is texting furiously on his phone. I bring up Ava's contact and text:

Me: WTF Ava? Where are you at?

A few minutes go by before she replies.

Ava: At the show with the girls. After it, we were invited to go backstage. Have drinks. Then will probably be home.

Me: Fuck no you won't go backstage! Get your ass home now!

An even longer few minutes pass before she replies.

Ava: Excuse me? You must be drunk because I thought you just gave me an order. And you'd know better than to do that if you were sober.

Me: U R at a stripper show!

Ava: So are U

Me: Is that what this is about?

Ava: What's good for the goose is good for the gander.

Me: I didn't want to come here tonight. It's a thing we do. I explained that.

Ava: And this is a thing we women do too. New tradition.

Me: U want to see a cock, I have 1 for you

Ava: You want to see tits, I have 2. Lookie, no touchie. Same rules for me as you. I'm a fair person. Even if you're being a hypocrite!

Okay, fuck, this isn't getting me anywhere. And she's kind of funny. That damn woman has turned my life upside down, and I now want things I never thought I wanted. The weird thing about that is I like it. A lot.

Me: I'm leaving for home now. I want you, not this shit.

Ava: Love you

Me: U coming home now too?

Ava: Um, not just yet. Next set is supposed to have the guy with the monster cock in it and I don't want to miss the chance to see a monster cock. Be home after though. (eggplant emoji)

Me: Get your ass home and you can see MY monster cock!

Ava: I need to see this guy's first so I have comparison material.

Me: Will it get you home any faster if I say I'm sorry and that I get what an ass I was for thinking you should be ok with this?

Ava: Yeah, maybe, but new rule: If you do something that hurts me, I will return the favor. Got it biker boy?

Me: Got it. In spades. Please come home.

"Any luck with Trudy?" I say to Petey.

"Jesus, no. Just some nonsense about a monster cock, and then she turned off her phone," he moans.

"You have been schooled by women! Hahahahaaa! I'm never getting chained down to one bitch. Suckers," chortles Axel.

Petey rises from his chair, smacks Axel in the back of the head, and I follow him out the door to the sound of roaring laughter. But I do notice Reno right behind me.

Chapter 29

Ava

Well, that was fun. Us women high-five each other and decide to stop for something to eat on the way home to let the men stew a little longer in their juices. We're all dressed to the nines and looking pretty damn hot, if I do say so myself. We draw a lot of eyes our way when we make our way through the restaurant we've chosen. Maybe four women, dressed to kill, being followed by a young, tall, reed-thin, bushy-haired ginger in a cut is a sight to see in this part of town.

We order, eat, and laugh. It was a good night, and I am thrilled to have girlfriends. The club has been good to me. I have a man, family, and friends, mostly because of the club. I guess it's time to give in to Gunner about letting my house go. Other than getting clothes and kitchen things from it, I haven't been there in months. Even Petey is talking about moving to a house at the club. That would be awesome! Petey and Trudy are all but living together now too, and that would put both of them closer to me.

I walk into Gunner's house, and it's dark except for a light coming from the master bedroom. I walk in and see Gunner leaning against the headboard, shirtless, reading. On the bed is Duffy on my side, sprawled out on his back. Gunner's eyes rise to mine.

"Hey," I say, leaning against the door jamb.

"Hey."

I stand up from the doorway and start into the bedroom to get undressed when Gunner speaks.

"I'm fucking you in those shoes with that dress pulled up over your ass. And you will be getting a spanking."

"Okay, babe."

"And make no mistake about it—it's you I'll be seeing and thinking about while doing the fucking.

Not going to be fucking you and picturing any other body I saw tonight. Nothing at the strip club is better than what I have here with me now. You understand that, Ava?" he quietly says.

"I think so."

"I get why you did what you did. I don't like it, but I get it. I had it coming. It's disrespectful for me to hang out watching strippers but expecting you to be sitting home waiting for me. I can't guarantee that we won't run into these types of things again with me being the Prez of the club. And we'll deal with them as they happen. But it will always be you I come home to, and it will always be your body I want beneath me when my dick is getting wet. I know how you must have felt those times when the girls were rubbing on me because all I could think of tonight was some guy with his hands touching you. I was angry, but I was also hurt thinking you might like some other guy touching you instead of me. It was torture knowing what you were seeing and wondering if you liked it better than what you have in me here."

"While you're fucking me, I'll only be seeing you, your face, your body. Nothing at that show tonight compares with you. You ready to fuck your woman in her shoes and dress, biker boy?"

Gunner sits quietly and stares at me for a long moment. Then he lunges suddenly across the space between us and grabs my wrist. Rising to his feet, he uses my arm to turn my back to him and runs his other hand over my hip, then my ass. He moves it north and pinches my nipple lightly. I feel his breath on my neck, and I arch it to the side, hoping he'll take the hint.

His mouth hits my neck, and it's wet, warm, and nipping at my skin. He breathes into my ear as he grinds his cock into my ass.

"You're smart, beautiful as all fuck, talented, and evil as shit, woman. I have to up my game if you're going to keep me around," he whispers into my ear.

"I'm keeping you," I reply quietly.

"You're going to be my Ol' Lady and my wife," he states.

"Is that a proposal?"

"It's an order," he chuckles softly.

"Are you going to give me babies?"

"Naturally, adopted and/or fostered. Don't care how many. Just need you, baby. Need you now."

Gunner says those beautiful words and then pushes my front half down on the bed as he pulls my dress up over my ass. I rest my face sideways on the comforter with my arms above my head.

I feel his hands rubbing my ass and pulling my thong down, and then hear it snap as he breaks it and tosses it aside. My man. Such a Neanderthal. I feel his mouth on my ass as he lightly nips. I groan and widen my legs a little.

Whack! A stinging slap lands on my unsuspecting ass, and I arch my back upwards before Gunner's hand pushes me back down to the bed. He chuckles while rubbing the sting off my skin.

"Told you there would be spanking involved."

When his hand slides in between my legs, I relax again.

That is, until Mac screeches loudly, "Spank that ass!"

Gunner is across the room and picking up Mac in a second. Out the door they go with Mac squawking, "Mom! Help! Mooooommmmm!"

Gunner returns to the bedroom, sans Mac, and calls the rest of the pets out the door. Even Duffy got up, stretched, and left. The door gets shut, and

Gunner is back behind me on his knees, hands back on my ass.

"We're moving the rest of your stuff in this week, and the pets are getting their own bedroom," says Gunner.

I nod my head in total agreement. I'm already envisioning Mac strutting around the clubhouse yelling, "Spank that ass!"

"You're wet. So fucking wet," groans Gunner while sliding his talented fingers through that wetness.

"Please, Gunner. I need you now too," I beg.

I feel his hands leave me, and I know he's dropping his boxer briefs. I love those briefs. They cup him so nicely!

"Spread your legs more, baby," he says while running the tip of his cock along my slit.

Instead, I pull my knees up under me on the edge of the bed and raise my ass higher. His hands on my hips help me move into a better position considering his height. He groans when I push back to make contact with his cock.

"Fuck. I love seeing you opened up to me like this, baby. So wet. So mine."

Gunner slides a finger into me and pumps a few times before pulling it out and pushing his cock in hard. I feel him bottom out and pull back before plunging in again and again. I'm meeting him stroke for stroke and getting close when he suddenly pulls out all the way, grabs my hips, and flips me onto my back.

He places my heels and my ass at the very edge of the bed and drops to his knees. His mouth hits my pussy, and his tongue starts swirling around my clit. It feels glorious! I reach down and put one hand in his hair as his tongue plunges inside of me.

I'm barely breathing; it feels so good. He has an energetic and talented mouth, and he's not stingy with it. I look down toward him just as his eyes rise to mine. He lifts his mouth, and I almost slam his head back down, but I refrain.

"Pull your dress up, Ava. Let me see your tits. Play with your nipples for me."

His head disappears back where I need it most, and his hands are parting the way for him. I feel him teasing me with both fingers and mouth, and I'm back to being so close. I reach down, yank up my dress, pull down my bra, and pinch a nipple. It zings straight to my pussy right at the same time that Gunner nips my clit, and I go over the edge. I'm writhing around, grinding myself on Gunner's face and hands, and moaning uncontrollably.

Gunner is back up on his feet before I even come all the way down. He's yanking my dress off and then my bra goes flying. He pulls my body to the headboard and braces my back against it. He puts my feet flat on the bed and pushes my knees wide. He then climbs onto the bed, onto his knees between mine. His hand is on his cock, and he's stroking languidly while looking at my pussy.

"Touch yourself, Ava. I want to see that hand touching that pussy. Now."

"I've never done that in front of someone, I…" I start to say when Gunner speaks over me, looking me in the eye now.

"It's just us here, baby. Nothing is wrong between us if we both enjoy it. I won't ever make you do something you don't want to, but I would love to see you try it before you say no," he rumbles.

I slide my hand down and slowly stroke my clit. It feels good, and I love the look in Gunner's eyes as he sits back on his heels and continues stroking his cock. He's mesmerized, and that's a huge turn-on for me. I carefully dip a finger into my wet opening and drag the juices over my clit.

"Hold yourself open with one hand. Please. And let me watch."

I place my other hand so that the fingers on it can spread open my pussy and allow Gunner to see everything while I continue stroking and dipping, stroking and dipping. Knowing he is looking so intently at my pussy while stroking his cock is very arousing.

I feel the tingling start. I rub harder and dip further inside of me. Gunner catches his breath, and I find myself pulled down the bed so I'm flat. Then Gunner turns me on my side and pushes my top leg toward my chest. In a short second, he's planted himself deep inside of me. He has one hand on my calf holding my top leg in place and the other on my hip while he pushes in and pulls out of me. I turn my head so I can see his face and find his eyes are locked on where our bodies connect. He thrusts hard and holds my body still at the same time. After several hard thrusts, his hand slides over to my breast, and he covers it with his palm.

"Gunner, baby, I'm close. I'm going to come," I gasp out. "Harder, please, God, harder!"

Gunner instantly slams into me hard, and I'm grinding myself on him when his hand leaves my breasts and pushes in between my legs, and finds my clit. I come and I come hard. Gunner groans long and loud, slams a few more times into me, and then stops, planted deep. For a moment, neither of us move, catching our breath. It was quick, intense, and so good. A quick fuck with Gunner is better than a long one from anyone else.

Then Gunner removes his hand and does a few slow glides in and out of me before pulling out the rest of the way, pushing me onto my back and leaning on his forearms over me until our mouths meet. He kisses me long and hard, pulls back a bit, and says, "Stay here. I'll be right back."

I'm a melted pile of goo, sprawled out in the bed, bones non-existent. Gunner returns with a warm, wet washcloth and runs it between my legs. Gah! That feels so good! He returns it to the bathroom and then slides in bed beside me, pulls me into his arms, and pulls the comforter and sheets over us.

I relax against him, head on his chest. It's quiet for a few moments, then Gunner pulls me tighter and up a little, so his nose is close to mine.

"When things are done with the Banditos, I'm buying you a ring, and we're having a short engagement. Short, as in about two months. Yeah?" he says quietly.

"Yeah," I smile at him. "But I'm not wearing one of those 'Property Of' vests. Not happening."

"No vest. I'll just buy you a larger ring, so no one can miss that you're taken. Deal?" Gunner laughs.

"You're wearing a ring too. And a tat on your forehead that reads, 'Ava's Property. Touch and die!'"

"Fuck! Axel would love to see that happen," he laughs even harder, knowing the shit Axel would dish over that tat.

I yawn big and tell Gunner, "Love you, baby."

He gives me a little shake and replies, "Don't even think about going to sleep. We're not close to being finished yet."

And we weren't.

Lola Wright

Chapter 30

Gunner

The men and I've been busy cleaning out the clubhouse and garages of anything illegal. We've moved our gun inventory to a warehouse under a shell company name that Rex assures us can't be tracked back to the Devil's Angels. We've been relying more and more the last few years on our legal businesses and less on the ones that could put us behind bars or in the ground. Today every business we own outright has no illegal activity or merchandise held within or around it.

We're getting our ducks in a row because we're planning a move on the Banditos. We want to be prepared if the Senator uses his clout or Stanaway to try to bring heat to the club. This was a unanimous vote. I'm impressed that a few of the hotter-headed members agreed, but they saw the wisdom in securing our properties.

Carl, the Bandito we scooped up, has given us a wealth of intel on his club. He has no loyalty to anyone but himself, and that has worked to our advantage. We've had a few minor things happen that his club has instigated, but nothing serious. We've been biding our time, letting them believe we're in turmoil and still trying to locate them.

Nobody has been asking about the four of their club members that we've acquired, so maybe Carl was right, and Javier doesn't care about his men. Makes no difference to me.

At Church this week, we finalized our plans for our attack on the Banditos. Another unanimous vote. Rex has gone way above and beyond getting us the information we need and also doing his thing on the dark web. He's spent some long hours following the money trails and doing some creative "bookkeeping" for the Banditos and the Carringtons. There will be some unhappy, and broke, people soon.

It's evening, just past dark, and the men and I are kicked back in the clubhouse having a beer after we completed all our tasks today. Feels good knowing that everything's done and ready for us to carry out the rest of our plan.

I hear screeching tires and a loud crashing sound just as my phone rings. I answer it as I aim myself toward the main door to see what's going on outside.

"Prez! You need to come to the gate," pants Bozo.

"What's up?" I bark.

"Banditos! Crashed the gate. Shoved a body out of their van and reversed out of here," Bozo answers.

"Fuck!" I disconnect. Me and several of the guys jog to the main gate as I fill them in on what happened.

When we come into view of the gate and gatehouse, we see a body on the ground and Bozo standing over it. The gate is hanging at an angle from its hinges on one side. As I approach the body, I can't tell if it is a male or female through all the facial swelling and the copious amounts of blood covering it from head to toe. I don't even know if it's breathing yet or not.

Axel arrives at the body the same time I do. He takes his foot and rolls it to its back.

"Holy fuck! It's Fang!" Axel shouts.

He's almost unrecognizable, but I can see his club tattoo on his bicep, so I know it is Fang. He turned on his brothers and then didn't deliver to our enemy. He ends up in our lap, beat to shit. And his bad times are not over yet. He'll now have to answer to his club brothers for being a traitor and to me for taking my woman.

"Take him to the basement. Let him hang with our other guests for now. Toss some water on him. Don't want him missing out on any of the pain. Since most everyone's here right now, let's have Church in twenty minutes," I tell the guys.

While Axel and Rex grab Fang by the arms and start dragging him up the driveway, I pull my phone out of my pocket and text Ava.

Me: Sorry. Going to be a late night.

Ava: ok honey. I'm going to bed then. Love you

Me: Love you

I pocket my phone and head for Church.

Chapter 31

Ava

I'm in the clubhouse kitchen cooking again. Trudy, Marti, and Karen are hanging with me, but it's a tense room. Not much is being said. The other women are drinking beer and wine, and I'm working my nervous energy off by cooking and baking.

Pooh and Bozo are here also, but Bozo is at the main gate, and Pooh's sitting in a recliner in the main room drinking a beer. He limps into the kitchen and checks on us periodically, and then limps back out to his chair. He's irritable, and I'm guessing it's because he didn't want to be the one left behind. But with him being shot in the leg a few weeks ago, it only makes sense.

The guys all left together a couple of hours ago in vans, trucks, and a few bikes. They were all armed, including the ones left behind. None of us women know where they're going or what their end goal is, but we all know it concerns the Banditos and that one of our guys could be hurt.

Before leaving, Gunner held me close, gave me a hard kiss, told me he loved me, and then ordered me to stay in the clubhouse close to Pooh and Loki. I noticed Reno and Petey were speaking quietly with their women also. After Gunner walked off, Axel approached and gave me a long, hard hug. He kissed the top of my head and pulled something out of the back of his jeans. He slid a handgun, a Colt Defender, into my hand. It's the handgun I've been practicing with when Axel and Gunner took me to the club's range.

"Keep that within reach, Ava. Everything should be fine, but I want you to have that in case shit goes sideways. Keep your phone on you at all times. Be safe, sis. Love you."

"Love you too, Ax. Be careful."

Another kiss to the forehead, and Axel followed the rest of the guys out the door.

The Devil's Angels MC

Trudy and Marti have moved to the main room to watch TV with Pooh. Karen's staring out the back door with her arms crossed, shoulders tense. I'm beating the hell out of bread dough. No way can this be called kneading.

Suddenly, I hear a loud explosion just as the building shakes. I'm startled and frozen in place. Karen lets out a scream and runs to the main room. I become unstuck and bolt in that direction also.

Pooh's up and on the move, handgun in hand. He hollers to us women to get to the basement and to lock the door behind us. Karen, Marti, and Trudy are heading that way, taking Gee, Duffy, and Mac with them, when a few gunshots ring out.

I'm closest to the basement door, so I jerk it open and wave the women and pets through. When the last one clears the door, I slam it shut, leaving me in the main room with Pooh and Loki.

I dive behind a couch, Loki coming with me, and see Pooh taking cover behind the bar. He sees me and waves his hand toward the basement door, but I shake my head no. I'm not leaving him alone facing down however many assholes come through the door.

I carefully peek out far enough to see three men come slowly through the main door with guns drawn. They're scanning the room, and one man signals for them to fan out. When the one doing the signaling turns his head my way, my blood runs cold.

It's Mitch Carrington. The sheriff, Mark's brother. But he's not in uniform, and those are not deputies with him. And I know why he's here at this moment. For me.

Pooh must see a panicked look on my face because when I focus back on him, he's signaling for me to stay down.

Loki's as still as death next to me, but I can feel his energy. He's ready for whatever needs to be done, and I'm so grateful he's with me and yet scared that he's in this mess too.

I no more than think that thought, and I hear a voice I haven't heard in years. The voice from my nightmares. The last time I heard that voice, I'd been beaten, raped, and left for dead. I feel a shiver run down my spine.

"Nobody home?" asks Mark.

He must've just walked into the building.

"Haven't cleared it yet, but I'm guessing she's here or at that fucker's house. We'll get your Ava, and she's going to pay for the trouble she's caused us and Uncle Ray. We're not going to be as easy on her as last time," says the voice that I know is Mitch's.

Mark chuckles. The fucker actually chuckles!

"This time, we'll have all the time in the world. No rushing. We can take turns fucking every hole she has and making new ones when we get bored. Fucking cunt!" spits Mark.

"You two, start clearing the outbuildings. Don't leave survivors. Men, women, or kids, don't matter. End them. Fucking Banditos will get the blame for it anyway. We'll clear the clubhouse. You find Ava, no fucking her until we do first. Got it?" Mitch tells the other men with them.

"Got it, boss," says a voice, and then I can hear feet leaving the building.

I finally raise my eyes to Pooh, and I see a myriad of emotions there. Hate, anger, compassion. I raise my chin a bit higher and take a few deep breaths. And I wait for my chance to make these two spoiled, entitled, raping fuckfaces to give me some payback of my own.

I hear footsteps coming my direction, and I pull my head back behind the couch. I place my hand on Loki's head and give him a rub. He's almost vibrating.

Everything happens at one time, suddenly and violently.

The basement door slams open with Trudy in the lead. Pooh and I both come up to our feet, swinging our guns toward Mark (me) and Mitch (Pooh).

Mitch brings his gun up and points it at Pooh at the same time, Pooh's gun barks, and Mitch spins sideways and stumbles. Mitch shoots as he's going down, but it goes skyward and buries into the ceiling. Pooh's on him instantly, landing a hard pistol whip across Mitch's head. Without wasting a moment, Pooh has Mitch's hands behind his back, gun tossed away.

Mark swings his gun toward Trudy. I pull the trigger and shoot at Mark. I miss him, but the distraction is enough time for Loki to lunge over the couch and take Mark down hard before I can even pull my trigger again.

I glance at Trudy and see she's holding a shotgun. She looks like she knows what she's doing with it too.

I'm still pointing my gun at Mark, who's now on the floor being mauled by Loki. I dash over and start landing kicks to Mark wherever I can get one to land. Mark's screaming, and it's a sound I've never heard before. It's almost inhuman. And, sadly, it gives me a warm little fuzzy feeling knowing he's getting some back.

I finally realize that Pooh is barking orders, and Karen and Marti are currently dragging an unconscious Mitch down the stairs. His head is bouncing off of every step. Pooh grabs my arm and kicks Mark's gun away from him. Pooh's speaking to me, but it takes a moment for my mind to clear enough to hear what he's saying.

"We don't know how many others there are, Ava. Get to the basement. Now!"

"Fuck no, Pooh. We're in this together, and I'm not leaving you!" I spit back at him.

I see movement over his shoulder, and one of the men from before is coming in from the kitchen door. I point my gun at him and pull the trigger. I keep pulling it as I see Trudy whirl around and unload her shotgun his direction also. He's down, and I don't think he's ever getting back up again. Trudy's a badass.

"Call Loki off, Ava! We have to lock him up with his brother and get ready for more men to come through those doors!" Pooh hollers at me.

But I'm staring down at Mark being drug around by Loki, and I don't make a move. I hear Pooh, but his words aren't getting through to my consciousness.

"Your men are going to kill me if either of you gets so much as a hangnail! Fuck! Just go downstairs and lock the door. Anyone comes through it, shoot," yells Pooh.

Just as Pooh's trying to herd us to the basement, we hear engines coming our way.

"It's our guys! They're back!" Trudy shouts and Pooh hurries to the main door. Trudy scoots over to my side and places a hand on my arm, but I'm stuck staring down at Mark, and it's like I'm in a trance that I can't pull out of.

Memories are flashing through my mind unbidden. I can't get them to stop. Memories of being held down by one as the other violates me viciously. No compassion, only glee in their eyes. Taking turns hurting me. The pain and the blood. It's all flashing through my mind. I can even hear the sounds again and the taste of blood in my mouth.

"Loki, come," I say softly as I point my gun toward Mark's face as he lies there bleeding and mauled. He's staring back at me, and he's got a sneer on his face. His right ear is hanging by a thread, his face bloody. Numerous wounds are showing on his arms and legs.

Gunner, Petey, and Axel bust through the door, nearly running Pooh over, and all three have guns in their hands, eyes searching the room. They pull to a stop when they see Trudy and I standing together, armed and unhurt, and me holding Mark at gunpoint.

"I'm getting too fucking old for this shit," Petey wheezes.

I don't notice them or the other club members that charge into the building. I hear a roaring sound in my ears and my vision is getting dimmer, but all I see is Mark and that sneer. The same one I saw just before everything went black on me four years ago.

"Ava? Honey, put the gun down. We got this now, baby," Gunner says quietly as he slowly approaches me.

My hands are trembling, but I keep my aim straight on Mark's face. I can't stop the memories. I can't stop hearing their laughter as they took everything from me. I want them dead. I want them to feel even a small bit of the fear and pain that I felt. I want them to know what it's like to be afraid of going to bed at night, wondering if someone will break in while I'm sleeping and attack me again. I want them to know the fear that's so strong you can taste it. The feeling of being helpless and unable to defend yourself. Of sleeping in the corner of my closet for months with a knife in my hand. Of moving several times to new houses or apartments because I didn't feel safe enough in the ones I lived in. Of the hours I spent in rehab and training, so I'd be healthy again and able to defend myself.

I have no idea how long I stand there with those memories or how many times Gunner spoke to me, trying to bring me back to him. But those memories shatter and only white-hot anger remains when Mark opens his mouth and speaks.

"You're not going to shoot me, Ava. You're not that brave. You'll crumble and cry just like you did when I shoved my cock into that tight, sweet pussy. You don't dare shoot me because you know Uncle Ray will rain hell down on you and these miserable fucks you've taken up with. How many of them have you fucked, Ava? How many since Mitch and I broke you in? You know you loved it when we fucked you! You might have cried and begged and said no a thousand times, but you wanted it! You wanted it even after you said you didn't want to see me again. You don't get to decide that, bitch! I say jump, you jump. That's how it works! You played hard to get, but you weren't. We got you! Poor little Ava! Fucking shoot me, I don't care because I know in the end, I'll win because you'll all rot in hell by the time Uncle Ray's done with you. And if you don't, I'll never stop. I'll ruin you!"

Mark's eyes are wild, and he's spewing spittle with every word he speaks. I can see his madness and his truth. He won't ever stop.

"Ava, baby. Look at me," Gunner pleads.

I slowly raise my eyes to Gunner and hand him my handgun. He sighs with relief and pulls me into him, and holds me tight.

"He's not worth the bullet, baby," Gunner whispers into my ear. "But the reason I don't want you to shoot him is because Rex has this room covered in cameras. Everything that piece of shit just said is caught on video. He's going down, along with his brother, uncle, and the Banditos. And you won't have to live with the thought that you sunk to his level."

I pull away and look up to Gunner.

"That's good. I'm glad they'll finally pay for what they've done to me and to the club, but I still need him to hurt. More than what Loki has done. I need it, Gunner," I plead, hoping he understands why.

I know he does when he gives me another squeeze, kisses me on the forehead, and steps back.

"Do what you have to do. I love you no matter what, and me and the club will be at your back," Gunner replies.

He then sends a look toward Rex, who instantly starts fiddling with his phone. He gives Gunner a nod, and Gunner then turns to me and gives me a nod. I get it. The cameras are now off.

For the first time, I notice that nearly the entire club is standing in the room, quietly watching me. I see looks of pride, some of compassion and understanding, and a whole lot of anger. They all know what happened to me years ago now that they heard Mark run his mouth, and somehow it no longer bothers me that people know the truth. I know they won't judge me, and I know they'll always be the support I need.

"Get to your feet, you piece of shit," orders Gunner to Mark.

Mark, slowly and painfully, gets to his feet and smiles huge at me.

"Knew you'd see the sense of not shooting me. Better for your little biker scum this way."

As the last word leaves his mouth, I strike hard and fast, just like all my training has taught me. Ironic that it was because of him that I took all those classes to begin with. I land a hard blow to the side of his jaw, and his head snaps sideways. A tooth goes flying across the room.

Before Mark even registers that I've hit him, I land a knee hard in the balls. As he bends over to grab his little boy parts, I do a swinging back kick and land my foot against the side of his head, and he goes down in a heap. He's out cold.

I land a few hard kicks to his ribs anyway. They had no mercy on me; I have none for him. After the last kick, I stomp on his groin with everything I have. That brings him around, and he's moaning and crying out. I drop to the floor next to him, grab his arm and put it in an arm bar, but I don't stop at that. I pull until I feel his elbow pop out of joint. I drop his arm, get to my feet and step back.

"Who's crying now, bitch?" I snarl at him.

Axel charges up and lands a hard kick to Mark's back, and I know how bad that shot feels to the body. I had taken several from Mark and Mitch that night.

Gunner bends down and hefts Mark to his feet, but he's barely conscious. He lands a hard right hook to Mark's face and lets him drop back to the ground.

Axel rushes to me, picks me up in a bear hug, and lands a wet sloppy kiss to my cheek.

"Proud of you, Ava. Love you, girl!"

I lean my head against his shoulder and whisper back, "Love you too, Ax."

Axel transfers me to Gunner's arms, and I wrap myself around him. He holds on tight.

Rex does his magic, and the videos of the Carringtons and Bandito members storming the club compound make their way to the state police headquarters, bypassing our local departments. The fallout is immediate. It was only a short time before two FBI agents are at the clubhouse wanting to know everything. They'd been working an investigation against Senator Carrington and his nephews for some time now. The video and my statements of the original attack and then the kidnapping helped tie up a lot of loose ends for them.

They take Mark, Mitch, and a Bandito into custody and leave the crime scene techs finishing up and having the dead removed. The clubhouse falls silent. I'm exhausted and I think everyone else is too. Gunner's been busy making calls and arrangements for Bozo, and the rest of us have just been sitting quietly.

I'm sitting on a couch with my head resting back and trying to sort through my thoughts and emotions when I feel the couch depress next to me. I roll my head to the left and see Pooh sitting there.

He places his hand on my knee and gives it a slight squeeze. I place mine on top of his, and we just sit that way for a while. Then he turns to me and says, "Proud of you, Ava. I would've pulled that trigger and ended his miserable existence, but you did the right thing. Prison time will not be good for him, for either of them."

"I would probably have missed his head anyway," I snort.

Pooh's lips twitch a bit when he says, "Yeah, probably."

"I'm surprised Trudy didn't blast his ass when she heard what he was saying," I mutter.

"She was out of ammo. She was pulling the trigger for all she was worth, though."

"She's badass, and I'm a little afraid of her now," I tell him.

"You both are. It was kind of hot watching you two mete out some damage," he chuckles. "You have any other friends that I can meet? The idea of being tied down doesn't seem so horrible now that I've watched you and Trudy in action."

Before I can answer, Reno approaches us with Karen attached to his side.

"We need to talk about getting one litter out of Loki. Half the clubhouse wants a pup out of him after seeing what he's capable of today. It'll take a lot of stitches to sew up that piece of shit," Reno states with a small smile.

"You pick the perfect female for him, and I'll agree to one litter. He's earned some vacation time, and who doesn't want to get laid on vacation?" I smirk at Reno.

"Fucking Amen to that sister," mutters Karen.

Chubs walks up, grabs Pooh by the arms, and heaves him up and off the couch. Then Chubs plops down next to me and rests his curly-haired head on my shoulder.

"Ava loves Chubs," I say as I pat his head.

"Good, because Chubs wants one of those pups," he smiles up at me.

Lola Wright

Epilogue

Five years later...

Gunner

"Your son wants you," Ava says in a sleepy tone.

I try to ignore her, but it never works. After not answering her, I get an elbow to the ribs. Shit, that hurt!

"Gunner, your son wants you," she repeats with a yawn.

"Which one?" I ask, stalling and hoping she'll just get up and take care of things so I can go back to sleep.

"Gunner, do you like sex?" she asks sweetly.

I'm up and out of the bed in a second flat. I know where this is going, and it's going nowhere if I don't get a move on and take care of our son.

I stumble out of our bedroom with blurry eyes. I walk to the kitchen, warm up a bottle, and walk into the next bedroom past ours down the hall. Flipping on the light, I see the pets all crashed in their beds or perch, except for one little piggy who's grunting and snorting and basically chewing me out for taking so long to get his food.

"Hi, Dad," says Mac from his perch.

"Hey, Mac," I reply quietly.

I snatch Little Ax up, wrap him in his baby blanket, and take a seat in the rocking chair. He latches onto the bottle's nipple and slurps away happily while I let my mind wander to the last five years. The best five years of my life to date.

I had held true to my word, and Ava became my Ol' Lady and my wife within a few months after the blowout at the clubhouse. It was a simple affair, and it was exactly how Ava wanted. Axel was my best man, and Petey walked Ava down the aisle. There were a lot of tears shed on that walk. Most were Petey's. Trudy was the maid of honor, though Chubs put up a good fight for that position. Loki was the ring bearer, and Mac was the usher. We decided he would do best at that since he loves telling people where to go.

Within a year of saying "I do," Ava gave birth to our gorgeous identical twin daughters, Mia and Zoe. They have my dark hair and her green eyes. They're stunning. They are also the club's princesses, spoiled by one and all. Petey was instantly in love, and he dotes on them. Loki seldom lets them out of his sight, and you can usually find him next to their beds at night. Ava showers her love on them, all the love she never received. Just last year, we adopted a son, Luke. He's six years old now and thriving, but he is all about Team Axel.

Once the girls were old enough to start talking, Mac quit accepting cashews for swear words and charged cold hard cash that he would walk to the twin's piggy bank and drop the money inside. Mac has taken on a big brother role and loves the attention from the girls.

When Ava came home with a tiny abandoned piglet, I took one look and fell in love. Little Ax (usually called Little A) is now another member of our wild and crazy family, and Gee has been mentoring him from day one.

We're a family of one more dog also. We couldn't let all of Loki's pups go to the club members, and luckily, his woman gave birth to twelve adorable pups. Loki is the best dad possible and looks out for his brood, even to this day. Cain's now three years old and takes after his father in looks and temperament.

Ava and my anniversary's coming up soon, and I know what the guys have planned. Ava doesn't, but she's going to love it. The guys and I are going to put up a fence and a barn so Ava can finally have her goats, mini donkey, and a horse or two. Her and our kids will be thrilled, and I can't wait to see her face when it's all done.

After it was all said and done, the Carrington brothers were charged with numerous crimes, including stalking, rape, and attempted murder. The Senator is no longer a senator but now an inmate in a federal prison for his various crimes of corruption, murder, and mayhem. All the dirty money they'd made over the years has somehow found its way to various charities for abused women and kids, animals, and veterans.

Javier and the Banditos are no more. Several members, including Javier, were rounded up and prosecuted. Others fled the area and are lying low somewhere far from Denver. Fang recovered, had his club tattoo burned off, took a serious beat down by several club members, myself included, and we cut him loose. He may have been a rat to our club, but we handle that stuff within, so he wasn't turned over to the cops. Katey has never been seen or heard from again. Officer Stanaway was fired and has disappeared off the map.

I was incredibly proud of Ava during all the trials. She sat tall and straight and told her story of her attack and rape and then the kidnapping. Ava never wavered. She held her head high and spoke about the atrocities they put her through. She didn't shy away from looking directly at her attackers. Her strength amazes me. I could see the looks in the jurors' eyes and knew the brothers were going to get hammered. Every single club member sat in the courtroom through all the trials in support of Ava.

Ava no longer has nightmares. The girls, Luke, me, and the club members give her all the love she's always deserved. And her dream of catering came true. We expanded her shop, and she's busier than ever but loving every moment of it. Chubs is still Ava's best buddy, and he actually babysits for us quite often. The kids all love him and the feeling is mutual.

Axel is at our home more than he's at his own. He and Ava spend a lot of time together, alone and with the kids, and Axel is greatly loved by all of them. He's been known to be found curled up on our couch sleeping while the girls paint his toenails, fingernails, and smear makeup on his face. They think he hung the moon, and I pity any guy that thinks he's going to date either of them because they will have to get through Uncle Ax first.

Petey and Trudy were married a few months after Ava and me and live two doors down from us. They're Papa and Tru Tru to the kids and Ava's biggest fans.

I look down and notice that Little Ax is done eating and back to sleep. I carefully place him back in his bed next to Gee and slip out the door and down the hallway. I peek into our daughters' door and see my little angels asleep and peaceful in their beds guarded by Loki.

I then peek into the room across from the girls and see Luke, asleep with Cain lying nearby. He no longer has nightmares either from the situation we adopted him out of and is a well-adjusted kid. Lots of love and support from his mom, me, his little sisters, and the club has healed him. He fits into our world perfectly and is as much ours as the girls. If you see Axel, you'll find Luke not far behind.

I move on to our bedroom door, open it, and walk to the bed. I slide in behind Ava, put my arms around her seven-month pregnant belly and pull her to my chest and bury my face in her neck. She automatically pushes back into me and relaxes in my arms. I close my eyes and drift off to sleep, knowing I'm exactly where I always want to be.

Life is good.

The End

Lola Wright

About the Author

Lola Wright currently lives in the great state of Michigan with her husband. She has enjoyed living in several different areas of her home state and the USA, but Michigan is home. Her kids are grown now, and between them, her grandchildren, and numerous furry family members, Lola keeps busy. When Lola has free time, she will most likely be found outside riding her horses or being entertained by her rescued minis, her dogs, and cats. Lola has a passion for feeding the wildlife and enjoys watching them come and go on her property. If indoors, Lola is usually cooking up new recipes, reading, or is in front of her computer dreaming up who she hopes is the perfect couple.

Amazon
In the Kindle Store on the Amazon site, search for "Lola Wright"

Facebook
On Facebook search for "Lola Wright, Author" to find *Lola's Profile, The Devil's Angels Page, Lola's Angels Group Page,* and the *Angels Spoilers Group Page.*

Twitter
@LolaWri47124635

Join Lola Wright's Mailing List for the latest news on her books! Go to the **Lola's Home page**—https://www.lolawright.store—and scroll to the bottom of the page.

Also by Lola Wright

The Devil's Angels MC Series

The Devil's Angels MC: Book 1 - Gunner

Ava

Left to die as an infant, Ava Beaumont has not had an easy life. Being raised by the system has taught her to be independent, hardworking, and cautious. When Ava becomes a victim, she uses her inner strength to put it behind her and move forward. Now she lives a good life with the family she's created through adopting pets that were also throwaways, including a smart-mouthed parrot and a skateboarding pig. When Ava meets Gunner, she realizes what her life is lacking but does she have the courage to trust a big, rough biker enough to let him into her safe little life?

Gunner

Being the President of The Devil's Angels MC was not something Gunner asked to become, but through the loss of his dad, the job was thrust upon him. While he loves his club and club brothers wholeheartedly, Gunner wants his club to move in a better direction. And when Gunner spots bakery owner, Ava, he realizes that's not the only change he wants to make in his life.

Nothing worth having is easy to acquire.

This is an MC story with a heart. Come meet the crazy pets and even crazier club members of The Devil's Angels MC.

The Devil's Angels MC: Book 2 - Axel

Bailey

I'm the sensible, independent, quiet, and hardworking accountant girl next door. My life is safe, sane, predictable, and boring. My biggest concern is dealing with my free-spirited, wild-child parent.

Until it's not.

The day I see something I shouldn't have and crash into the crazy lives of The Devil's Angels MC is the day my life changes forever. That's the day I looked into the bluest eyes I have ever seen and knew nothing would ever be the same.

Axel

My life is perfect. I'm the Vice President of my club, The Devil's Angels MC, and we've moved the club in the right direction. I manage the club's gym, own my own home, and have women around that are always up for a night of fun. I have my club brothers, the world's best dad and a new sister. Family is everything in my world, and I have a great one. What more could a guy want or need?

That question is answered when a tiny, little woman slams her way into my life. I never saw her coming, but I'm not letting her leave.

The Devil's Angels MC: Book 3 - Pooh

Pippa

Owning and operating a home for victims of domestic violence doesn't leave a woman wanting a man in her life. Not a permanent one anyway. Having been a victim myself, I chose to open this refuge to help others that are in a similar situation that I had been. I was one of the lucky ones because my foster mom was always my rock, my safe haven. It was never me alone against the world. We decided, together, that we wanted to be just that for others. New Horizons is born, and we are on a mission to save all that we can.

Pooh

I'm restless, bored, and I want more. I want what some of my club brothers have found. I want that one woman that is meant to be mine.

The problem is I don't know any women that qualify. Being in a motorcycle club brings women around in flocks, but they're not meant to be mine when they're clearly everyone's girls.

Then I meet her. The One.

Now the problem is that she is not interested in me or a relationship and not a big fan of men in general. She's a strong, independent woman, and a little spitfire when it comes to protecting those she's sworn to keep safe.

She will be mine, and I'll prove to her that men like me and my club brothers from The Devil's Angels MC are nothing like the men she's known before.

The Devil's Angels MC: Book 4 - Vex

Vex

I've lived my life free and easy. No attachments, no entanglements. I easily move on after an evening with a woman. For a night, they get all I have to give. After that, it's time to go. They're warned ahead of time, so tears and ploys have no effect on me. I love my MC family, The Devil's Angels, and my bikes. Not much else. Certainly, none of the various women I've known.

Then I meet someone who changes all my rules, thoughts, and beliefs. But as luck would have it, she's the unattainable one. She seems immune to my charm, and that tweaks my ego. After being warned away from her, I try to push her to the back of my mind. She doesn't stay there for long, though. Now I'm determined to have my night with her, consequences be damned.

Taja

Trying to raise my sister, working any job I can while fighting to keep a roof over our heads, I don't live the life of a normal woman my age. I don't have time for dating, sex, or men. Especially a member of an MC. My father's an MC President, and I want nothing to do with that lifestyle. Not even for the gorgeous biker whose nearly golden eyes follow my every move. Common sense tells me he's in it for a night, and that's not my style. Best to keep my head on straight and ignore what my body's craving.

Actions have consequences, and fate has a way of messing up the best-laid plans.

The Devil's Angels MC: Book 5 - Cash

Livi

Being a female in a male-dominated career can be daunting, but I refuse to allow others' attitudes to deter me. I always try to be professional, compassionate, and non-judgmental. Through hard work, I have earned respect within my department. Wearing a badge and uniform, I've seen the best and worst of humanity. Heartbreaking, dangerous, hectic, or hilarious, I approach each shift and person with an open mind.

As all cops know, the partner you're teamed up with makes all the difference in the world, and I struck gold. Work partners and best friends, James and I have a tight, unshakable bond. We're each other's support system when things get rough and defend each other's right to wear the uniform against anyone who believes otherwise.

Cash

Muscled, tall, tatted, and The Devil's Angels MC Sergeant at Arms, some see me as an intimidating man. Others see me as quiet, thoughtful, and dedicated to my blood and MC families. I'm the first call everyone makes when things are going sideways. Whether it's bullets or fists flying, I'm the man you want at your back. Highly respected within my club, I live by a strict biker code.

When a life-altering event occurs in my life, I will not waver in doing what's right. With the love and support of my two families, I'll face my new circumstances with determination.

The Devil's Angels MC

More books to follow in this series!

Printed in Great Britain
by Amazon